## USA Today Bestselling Author
# KRISTEN PAINTER

A MIDLIFE FAIRY TALE

# THE SUMMER PALACE

**THE SUMMER PALACE**
**A Paranormal Women's Fiction Novel**
MidLife Fairy Tales Book 2

Copyright © 2023 Kristen Painter

All rights reserved. No part of this book may be reproduced in any form or by any electronic or mechanical means, including information storage and retrieval systems—except in the case of brief quotations embodied in critical articles or reviews—without permission in writing from the author.

This book is a work of fiction. The characters, events, and places portrayed in this book are products of the author's imagination and are either fictitious or are used fictitiously. Any similarity to real person, living or dead, is purely coincidental and not intended by the author.

Published in the United States of America

Newly crowned queen of the Radiant fae, Sparrow "Ro" Meadowcroft has two goals. First, to show her fae subjects that despite growing up in the mortal realm, she plans to honor the customs and practices of her new world. Second, to reunite the Radiant fae with the Grym fae. Or at least broker peace between the two estranged kingdoms.

How? By returning to the Summer Palace, an old tradition that once brought both kingdoms and their rulers together for a time of relaxation and fellowship. She's invited the ruler of the Grym, too: Queen Anyka

Ro hopes the neutral ground of Willow Hall will provide a fresh start and a chance at diplomacy, but the old palace holds dark secrets that could mean the end of the Radiant fae. Or a new day for the Grym.

Can Ro win Anyka over or has too much blood already been spilled? And why does Willow Hall seem like the start of more trouble? All Ro knows for sure is that magic abounds in the Summer Palace. And not all of it's good.

*For all the readers who make it possible for my cats to live the life they believe they deserve.*

# Chapter One

The clang of metal striking metal rang out through the practice room as Queen Sparrow Meadowcroft defended herself against the charge from her personal security guard and sword skills teacher, Gabriel Nightborne.

He was attempting to teach her some skills, not actually attacking her, thankfully. Otherwise, she'd have been done for almost instantly. He was very good. The best, really. Which was why he was head of palace security *and* her personal guard.

His handsome face and nicely muscled body were just…perks.

With a loud exhale, she stepped back and dropped the blade to her side. She shook her head. "I can't do any more today." She was sweaty and tired and her shoulders ached. "I'm worn out."

Gabriel nodded, letting his sword drift to his side as well. "You managed more practice than I expected, my lady. You did well." He held out his hand. "Blade."

"Thanks." Ro gave him her weapon, even though it wasn't much of one. The sword's edges were dull and the tip blunted so there was little chance either of them would be hurt during the session. The practice weapons were still a step up from the wooden sticks they'd used for the first two days. "I'm not sure I'm ever going to get any better at this."

He frowned. "You've already gotten better."

"You think so?"

He nodded as they walked across the room to the benches along the wall. "I know so. We'll keep up the practice at Willow Hall, too. If you want."

"Probably not a bad idea." Tomorrow, they traveled to the Summer Palace. All to celebrate the long-lost tradition of spending the warmer months in the mountains at Willow Hall. Besides Ro, her son JT, her aunt Violet, quite a few of the professors and council members, a good number of royal guards, Gabriel and his daughter, Raphaela, there would be a hundred citizens joining them.

Those citizens had been chosen through a lottery system and they'd be replaced every week by a new one hundred, meaning that in the course of the three months Willow Hall was open, twelve hundred citizens would be able to join them.

Ro had been pretty excited to find that out. Not only would she get to meet and interact with many of her citizens, but they, in turn, would hopefully get to know her a little and accept her as one of their own.

She understood that for some of them, having a queen who was not only a crossover from the mortal world, but who came with a son who looked more Grym fae than Radiant, wasn't the easiest thing to accept.

But holding that lottery was only one of the many things that had been accomplished so far this week. Something she'd done almost immediately was to replace a few of the council members. Those who'd been less than active in their positions or, in some cases, blatantly shirking their responsibilities had been replaced by new leadership, all of whom had pledged to support the new queen's rule.

Ro had spent one of her days listening to the petitions of the people. Aunt Violet and JT had sat with her, offering their support. She imagined it had been a learning experience for JT, as well.

The council members had been there, as well. All of whom seemed plenty eager to tackle any problems that arose. Ro was happy about that. Replacing council members had been hard, but obviously the right thing to do.

She'd met with the royal seamstress, Luena, several times for fittings, as an entire wardrobe was being created for her. JT, too, but he had his own tailor, Henry, Luena's father. Violet had a seamstress as well, as she was having a few things made at Ro's request. Wouldn't do for the queen's aunt to be underdressed. Today, their things were being packed for tomorrow's trip.

And while Ro was looking forward to spending time at Willow Hall, she had some reservations about the adventure that lay before her. She went to the bench against the wall and sat to remove the protective leather gear Gabriel had insisted she wear.

Her reservations seemed reasonable to her. After all, it would be the first time the Radiant fae and the Grym fae had come together in many, *many* years. Meeting

Queen Anyka, who'd responded to the invite by only saying that she'd consider it, filled Ro with all kinds of trepidation.

It was no secret that there was animosity between the two kingdoms. Ro hoped inviting Queen Anyka and her entourage would help change that, but she was filled with doubt about how successful this trip would be.

Gabriel put the practice swords away, then came to join her, stripping off the thick leather vest he wore. His shirt was damp underneath. "Are you excited about tomorrow, my lady?"

She nodded. "I am. I can't wait to see the place. One question, though. Why are we traveling by carriages instead of by portal? I'm looking forward to seeing more of the country, don't get me wrong. Just curious."

"Because it's tradition. Also because there are so many of us and there is so much baggage to be transported."

"Ah. Well, tradition is important. And while I'm eager, I'm also a little concerned. Do you think Queen Anyka will show up?"

"I do. It would be an interesting choice to turn down your invitation. Something like that could work against her if it got out that you'd extended such an offer and she'd declined."

"Who would know?" Ro asked.

"I'm sure she has council members and people close to her, just like you do. And then there's her daughter, Princess Beatryce."

"True," Ro said.

"Anyway, I don't think the citizens would like it if you

reached out to their queen and she refused the offer. Unless she's poisoned them against you already."

"Let's hope not," Ro said with a roll of her eyes.

"That reminds me, your highness," he added. "What did Uldamar say about the gifts that Anyka and Beatryce sent? The book and the mirror?"

Ro laced her fingers together. "Both of them had what he called residual magic. Traces of spells. He couldn't determine exactly what the spells were, but he used magic of his own to decontaminate them. All the same, I boxed them back up and sent them to the vault. I didn't feel comfortable keeping them around."

"A wise decision," Gabriel said.

"Thanks." She set her gear aside, then pushed to her feet. "I have to go to the stables so I can meet my new horse and take her out for a short ride."

He put both sets of protective gear onto one of the nearby shelves. "I'd be happy to escort you, my lady. If you plan on leaving the palace grounds, you should have someone with you."

"You don't mind?" She'd thought he'd want to go get cleaned up. Not that she minded him a little sweaty.

He shook his head. "It's my job to be at your side."

"All right. Also, I have no clue where the stables are."

He smiled. "Follow me."

He led her from the sparring room down a long hall. They were on the first floor of the palace in a wing that was much more utilitarian than the rest. The armory was here, as well as some workshops and craftsmen's rooms. She'd just been on the first floor and in this particular wing for her practice sessions, and she was still learning her way around. She tried to pay attention to where they were going, but the palace was enormous, and she knew she'd have a lot left to explore when they returned from Willow Hall.

They went all the way through the western wing of the palace and finally exited onto a large grassy area surrounding a dirt exercise yard, fenced with wood and iron. On the other side of the yard was the royal stables.

"There must be a lot of horses." Ro had never seen such an expansive stable. It looked L-shaped and had a second floor.

"There are," Gabriel said. "But the building also houses many of the grooms and a large number of the mounted royal guard. Obviously, the stablemaster, too."

"How many guards are coming with us to Willow Hall?"

"Twelve, along with myself, Raphaela, and a lieutenant by the name of Vincent, who I'm assigning to guard your aunt."

"That seems like a lot for a trip that's supposed to be a vacation."

He stopped at the edge of the exercise yard. "I understand, your highness, but if Anyka shows up, she'll have her own contingent of staff and guards. Did you say anything to her about bringing citizens with her?"

Ro shook her head. "I didn't say anything about that, just invited her and Beatryce. Should I have? Can Willow Hall hold that many people?"

"It can. It's far bigger than Castle Clarion and was

designed for that purpose, but I don't think you needed to mention anything about her bringing citizens." He nodded, looking very much like he was thinking that over. "Although she might assume that. That's how it always used to be done."

Ro sighed. "It would be really nice if she actually replied with a definitive answer."

"Agreed."

"It briefly occurred to me to send it again, but only briefly." Ro shook her head. "I won't, because I don't want to seem desperate. Which I'm not. I've extended the olive branch. Up to her to take it or leave it. That was my policy at the museum, too. Unless we needed an exhibit more than the current exhibitor, I made it a point not to push too hard. Some people will see that as a weakness and use it to their advantage."

He smiled. "Wise. Would you like to meet your stablemaster?

"I would."

"Follow me."

They walked around the exercise yard and through the wide opening in the side of the stables.

"Gabriel Nightborne."

Gabriel turned, smiling. "Stoddard. How are you?"

An older man approached them, his face lined by days in the sun. "Good, good." His gaze shifted to Ro and he bowed.

Gabriel held his hand out. "Queen Sparrow, this is Kent Stoddard, Castle Clarion's stablemaster."

The man returned to his full height.

Ro smiled. "Pleasure to meet you, Mr. Stoddard."

"The pleasure is all mine, your highness. I have your horse ready for you."

"Very good. I can't wait to meet him or her."

"Her," Stoddard said. He turned and called out over his shoulder. "Bring the Queen's horse."

A young woman in royal livery brought a horse out from one of the stalls. "She's ready to ride, sir."

"Thank you." Stoddard smiled proudly. "May I present Featherstone's Silver Lady Indira. Around here, we call her Indi."

"She's gorgeous," Ro breathed out. The horse was a deep silvery gray, a color Ro suspected would look more lavender in the sun, with a gorgeous white mane and white tail. The horse was outfitted with deep purple tack and a saddle, ready to ride.

Ro stroked the horse's velvet-soft muzzle. "Hello, beautiful."

The horse nickered and Ro smiled. She looked at Stoddard. "Thank you. She's amazing."

He was still grinning. "Pleased you're pleased, ma'am. Would you like to take her out?"

Ro nodded. "I would very much. Gabriel is going to ride with me."

Stoddard nodded. "I figured as much. I've got Storm ready to go." He took Indi's reins and nodded to the young woman. "Bring Storm out."

"Yes, sir."

Stoddard tipped his head toward the exercise yard. "Let's get you seated, my lady."

They all walked outside, with Stoddard leading Indi. He stopped them at the front of the exercise track. There was a step nearby.

"I don't need that," Ro said. "I can mount a horse."

"As you wish." Stoddard held onto the reins.

Ro was thankful she was still in her sparring outfit of loose pants tucked into soft boots, a tunic top and vest. She took hold of the saddle, got her foot in the stirrup, and lifted herself up, swinging her leg over.

Stoddard nodded in appreciation. "Nicely done, my lady. It does my heart good to know our new queen is not unfamiliar with horses."

"Been riding since I was a child, thanks to my aunt."

Just then, the young woman returned with Gabriel's horse. The enormous creature was a mottled black and charcoal gray with a black mane and tail. As horses went, it looked more like a storm cloud.

Gabriel followed her line of sight and turned. "Orion's Dark Storm Rising," he said softly.

Ro shook her head. She'd never seen a horse like that, with the darkest colors concentrated around its legs. "That's some animal."

Gabriel went over and took the reins. "A Grym horse for a Grym rider."

"That's a Grym horse?"

"Partially," Stoddard answered. "Gabriel was instrumental in the breeding program that led to us having these fine animals. Say what you will about the Grym, but they produce the best warhorses anywhere in the kingdoms. We

Radiant are better known for breeding exceptionally beautiful animals."

Ro could see that. The horse under her was about the prettiest one she'd ever seen. She nodded at Gabriel's. "So that's a warhorse?"

"He could be," Gabriel answered. "He's never seen battle, though."

Ro took a breath. "Let's hope it stays that way."

# Chapter Two

"*An invitation.*" Queen Anyka Blackbryar shook the paper in her hand as she strode across the receiving room. She'd been stewing about this for days. The very nerve of that *woman*. It was unfathomable. Galwyn, her raven, shifted on his perch, tipping his head to see her better with his bright black eyes.

Her uncle, Ishmyel, just sat back, lips pursed, arms folded. "I don't see what the problem is. Isn't it the opening you've been looking for?"

She spun around to face him, glad they were in her royal apartment and that Trog, her personal guard, was at the door. It would make throwing her uncle out so much easier. "What right does she have to invite *me* to the Summer Palace? Grym have been going there as long as the Radiant fae have been. If you think about it that way, I have more right to do the inviting. Not to mention *half* of it sits within the Malveaux borders!"

He sighed. "Anyka—"

"No. Do not try to change my mind. And do not try to tell me that we are somehow the ones who need to be invited. The Radiant fae killed my parents. Your brother. They admitted to it. By all rights, the Summer Palace ought to be mine. The Radiant should have stopped going there. Not us."

"I understand what you're saying, but your parents were killed in retaliation for the deaths of the Radiant queen and her two children."

She glared at him. "Are you really telling me I should attend this nonsense because we are to blame for starting the trouble in the first place?"

"Well, we did." He frowned. "And it's not nonsense. Time at the Summer Palace was once how the best young people met their spouses, new deals were made, alliances brokered, advantageous friendships kindled, trades bartered. It was never just a time of leisure for those with a modicum of power."

She remained unmoved.

He sighed. "There's not a day that goes by that I don't miss my brother or wonder where we might be now as a kingdom if he'd lived. I am as eternally heartbroken as you are. I pledge that truth to you."

She shut her eyes for a moment, the memory of that awful, wretched day filtering through the shutters of time she'd bolted against it. Part of her understood what her uncle was saying. And part of her wanted to burn Summerton to the ground. She touched the tip of one ear, rubbing it a little.

She opened her eyes and looked at him. "What would you have me do?"

"Tell Queen Sparrow you are coming. And then go. You and Beatryce. I will go, too. Perhaps some of your selected ministers. A good contingent of guards, no doubt.

It could be the beginning of a new era for all of us. Wouldn't you like to open trade with Summerton again? Think of how happy that would make the people."

She stared out the rain-streaked window, thinking about more than that. Beatryce would enjoy it. That much Anyka knew. Her daughter had been pushing to go to Willow Hall since before the Radiant queen had arrived.

"It might even lead to the lifting of the curse."

She snorted with derisive laughter as she looked at him again. "The curse will never be lifted."

He shook his head. "There is no proof it must remain." He went silent for a few moments. "Are you not at all in some small part interested to see this new queen? I am. A crossover from the mortal world who's pulled *Merediem* from its stone?" He laughed. "I very much want to get a look at her."

Anyka sank into the closest chair, the invitation still clutched in her hand. "I am curious. But I don't trust her. I trust no one. Not after what was done to my family."

"At some point, you'll have to trust *someone*. How else will we put the past behind us? How else will you move Malveaux forward? Would you have us stay in this wretched limbo?" His eyes narrowed. "I thought you wanted to leave something more for Beatryce."

Anyka sighed. As much as her uncle irritated her, he was occasionally right. Which was equally irritating.

He leaned forward. "My darling niece. You are a stunning woman with a dressing room full of exquisite gowns and vaults stuffed with gems and jewelry that would make a dragon's hoard seem miniscule. When's the last time you were able to enjoy any of those things? The last time you saw an envious gaze cast your way because of some priceless bauble on your person or you were wearing a gown no other woman could hope to show off so beautifully? Don't you deserve to be seen just as much as Summerton's new monarch?"

Anyka laughed. "You have a way with words, Uncle."

He smiled. "This can be very good for us." He steepled his fingers. "For you as queen, obviously, but for Malveaux as a kingdom, as well."

"Perhaps." Anyka wasn't so convinced. "It will be a lot of work. And what of the citizens who think they should be allowed to come?"

"Send out a decree. That you are going to test the waters on behalf of your people and that perhaps next year, the lottery might begin again."

"I suppose that would suffice." She stood. "There is so much to do. So much to pack. Guards to make ready. But I am not telling Queen Sparrow anything further. She doesn't need to know."

"Your decision." He got to his feet a moment after she did. "I can handle the guards. Your maids can deal with the packing, as can Beatryce's handle hers. Wyett can handle the rest."

Wyett, her valet, had been absent from this meeting because her uncle had wanted to talk to her alone. In hindsight, Anyka saw nothing in their discussion that had necessitated that. "Trog, bring Wyett in again."

Trog nodded, opened the door, and grunted.

Wyett entered the room and stood waiting.

She looked at him. "How long will it take to get us ready to go to Willow Hall?"

To his credit, Wyett's brows barely lifted in surprise. "We can be ready in whatever time frame you need, my lady."

"See?" Ishmyel said.

Anyka sighed and nodded, her gaze on Wyett. "Get the preparations underway. We depart in two days' time."

Wyett nodded. "Yes, my lady."

"Dismissed." But Wyett remained. "What is it?"

"The troll delegation is scheduled to arrive here later this month."

She sighed and rolled her eyes, grateful for the reminder all the same. "I'll draft a letter to them this evening. If they can come here, they can journey slightly farther to Willow Hall. I'll meet with them there. I'm not about to leave in the midst of things to deal with them."

"Very good, my lady." Another bow and he was gone.

As Wyett took his leave, Anyka pointed at Ishmyel. "And you—not a word to Beatryce. I'll tell her myself."

"Of course. I'll just go see General Wolfsbane about those troops, shall I?"

"Yes. Very good."

"Which ministers will you be taking?"

She frowned as she thought about that. There were a number who probably wouldn't want to come and a number who would fully believe she was out to ruin them if they weren't included. "I don't know yet. I'll have a list made up this evening and notes sent around. I don't want to take all of them."

"Agreed. You can't make it seem like you've brought every single advisor you have. You must look as powerful and independent as possible, albeit with a good number of dutiful subordinates at your beck and call."

He wasn't wrong. "I am out of practice at this kind of thing." She threw her hands up. "I've also never been to Willow Hall. Maybe this is a bad idea."

"Queen Sparrow has never been, either."

She sighed, unconvinced.

He lowered his head to stare directly at her. "My dear Anyka, you are perfect in everything you do. This trip will be no different. You have been queen all of your life. She has been queen for, what, a spark of time? She will look to you for an example. You will set the tone and pace of this event." He held a finger up. "Mark my words."

All truth, but Anyka wasn't so sure this woman would care how Anyka did things. Even so, Anyka did want to impress her and inspire in her a certain healthy sense of fear and respect. Those were goals Anyka could work toward. "Go see General Wolfsbane. I'm off to let Beatryce know."

He bowed as she left the room. Trog followed her.

Anyka walked until she reached the music room. Beatryce and her new lady-in-waiting, Iysette, were practicing a piece, Bea on her harp, Iysette on the lyre. Anyka opened the doors, smiling broadly. "You sound wonderful, Beatryce. How lovely."

Beatryce looked up as she stopped playing. "Thank you, Mother."

Anyka walked to the center of the room. "I have some

news I think you might like very much, but before I tell you what it is, you must promise that whatever happens, you will do as I tell you."

Beatryce's brow furrowed. "I don't even know what we're talking about."

"I understand that. We're talking about taking a trip. And while we're there—"

Beatryce shook her head. "I do not wish to return to the mortal realm."

"I know, my darling. We aren't going there. I promise." Anyka clasped her hands before her. "Instead, we are going to Willow Hall. In two days."

Bea's fingers fell away from her harp. "You're jesting."

Anyka shook her head. "No, I am not. If you want to go, I suggest you get to work. Call your maids to help you pack. Organize whatever gowns you might think you'll need. Shoes, jewelry, the whole lot. I'm sure there will be evening meals to dress for along with other events."

Beatryce stared at her mother, her mouth hanging open in a very un-princess-like fashion, then she jumped up. "You are serious. Please tell me you're serious."

"I swear to you that I mean every word I've spoken."

Beatryce snapped her eyes at Iysette. "Get up. We have work to do." She grinned at her mother. "Willow Hall? I can't believe it."

Anyka nodded. "Bear in mind, we go to meet the new queen of Summerton. It won't just be us there." She lifted her chin imperiously. "You must be every inch the princess of Malveaux."

Beatryce nodded enthusiastically. "I will, I promise. Thank you so much. I can't wait."

Then she and Iysette sped from the room.

Anyka turned to watch them go, her smile fading as they left. She spoke to Trog without looking at him. "I already hate this."

Trog grunted.

"Come along. She's not the only one who has work to do." Anyka would pull everything she wanted packed and let the maids handle it from there, but her jewels she would take care of herself. Or Wyett could deal with them.

But there was more than just herself and her daughter to worry about. She'd need someone to do her hair. She'd need a seamstress in case there were any repairs or alterations to make. Trog would remain as her personal guard, but Beatryce would need a guard, too. And they'd need transportation.

She hoped Ishmyel was taking all of that into consideration. She wanted to arrive in the grand carriage. It was the most impressive. Ishmyel would want to ride with them, she supposed. She might have to let him.

He'd complain if he, as a member of the royal family, was made to ride with one of the ministers.

Which reminded her she still had to sort out which of them were going.

She heaved out a sigh. Well, she knew one thing for certain. She wasn't taking a single one of them who'd given her a modicum of trouble over the last couple of decades. This was her trip and she would have the last word about who went to Willow Hall and who remained at Castle Hayze.

It would serve some of them right to stay behind. Perhaps help them to better remember their place. There was never a bad time to strengthen your own position of power, especially with those who worked under you.

Her smile returned ever so slightly. Maybe this trip wasn't such a bad idea after all.

# Chapter Three

The ride was everything Ro could have hoped for. Calm and peaceful and the incredible scenery of the world she was just getting to know. Sunlight dappled the ground as it filtered through the trees and the breeze carried the smell of fresh green things and blooming flowers. Jewel-colored insects flitted past and birdsong filled the air.

Ro moved as one with the horse beneath her. She patted Indi's side, marveling at the horse's glossy coat and placid demeanor. "This forest is beautiful. The trees are enormous. Must be very old growth."

Gabriel was a few paces away. He just nodded and his head went back to the constant swivel he'd been doing for much of the ride, scanning the forest for whatever he was scanning the forest for.

Large, dangerous animals? Or large, dangerous people? She had no idea. She knew he was always working, though, and ever diligent when it came to her safety. But she also got the sense that he wasn't really paying attention to her so much as everything around them. "Maybe we can find some frogs to eat."

"Mm-hmm."

"Or is it better just to lick them? I never know when it comes to frogs."

His head whipped around, his brow furrowed. "What did you say?"

"Nothing." She laughed to herself. "Just seeing if you were paying attention. If you don't think it's safe out here, we can go back. I'm obviously well-suited to Indi." She patted the horse's side. "You're a marvelous horse, aren't you, Indi?"

The horse shook its head as if answering her.

"No, it's fine," Gabriel said. "I'm sorry. I have too much on my mind and that is no state for your personal security to be in. Forgive me, my lady."

If there was anything she disliked about being queen, it was the formality that had come between her and Gabriel. The man who'd kissed her in the garden after dinner, when they'd both thought she was turning down the crown? That man was gone.

Instead, this new Gabriel had taken his place. One who abided by royal protocol and did his job as though his life depended on it.

She appreciated and admired his dedication to that role. But she missed the man who'd kissed her. She was starting to think that was something that would never happen again. She hoped she was wrong. "There's nothing to forgive. You're only human." She chuckled. "Sorry. That turn of phrase no longer works in this realm. Listen, it's fine. There's a lot ahead of us with this trip tomorrow. Why don't we turn back? I'm ready."

"All right."

They wheeled their horses around. He rode a little closer to her this time. Slightly behind her, but not so far they couldn't talk.

Which was good, because she had questions. "What is Willow Hall like?"

"Big," he answered. "Bigger than anything else I've ever seen."

"So you've been to Willow Hall?"

"I have. I go once a year to do a security check on the Summerton side. It falls under my purview, since I am head of palace security, and it becomes the palace when you're in residence."

"I see. I've been told it's perfectly divided between Summerton and Malveaux."

"It is. You'll see when we get there. Even the sky above it is visibly different. One side overcast, one side sunny. Of course, there are days when it's overcast on both sides."

"I'm glad you've been there. Somehow that makes me feel better. That you know your way around a little."

"I do. I've never seen it full of people, though. Or even partially full. That will be something."

"Are you looking forward to it?"

After a moment, he said, "Yes. I am. It will be a new adventure. And the grounds are beautiful. Very different from Castle Clarion."

"How so?"

"Willow Hall straddles the river that fills Celestial Lake. That river divides Summerton from Malveaux. But because of the falls, the river, and the lake, nearly every room has a water view of some kind. You can hear the water from most rooms, too. More so at the rear of the property than in the front, but it makes for very peaceful sleeping."

"You've stayed there, then?"

"I have. When I make my trip up there, I usually stay overnight and leave the following day."

"It sounds nice. So, is there a staff that lives there year-round and takes care of the place?"

"There is. Everything is maintained, from the grounds to the stables to the interior. I am sure those halls must be filled with excitement now that they will once again have visitors."

Ro nodded. "Imagine keeping things in order for so long but not having anyone to share it all with. Kind of sad, isn't it?"

"It is."

"Makes me extra glad we're going now." She glanced over her shoulder.

He smiled at her. "I have no doubt the staff of Willow Hall will be thrilled with your arrival, my lady."

"And what about Queen Anyka? If she comes."

"They'll be ready for her, too. Up until the good relations between the kingdoms were destroyed, Willow Hall was always occupied by both Radiant and Grym. It was built to accommodate two monarchs. There won't be an issue. She'll have her half and you'll have yours."

The stables were just in sight. "Good to know," Ro said. "What are you doing for the rest of the evening?"

He urged Storm forward and came up alongside her. "Whatever you require of me."

"I don't need anything this evening. I'll be packing and probably relaxing with JT and Violet before the big trip tomorrow. I was just making conversation." They were nearly back to the stables.

"Oh." He nodded. "I'll probably doing much the same with Raphaela. As well as going over a few things with the guards who'll be accompanying us. In fact, unless you want me to escort you back to your quarters, I might do that now, since I'm here."

A pair of grooms came out of the stables to take their horses.

"No, I can find my way back. Thanks for the sword lesson. And for coming with me on the ride. I guess I'll see you in the morning." She dismounted, her legs a little wobbly from not having ridden in a while.

He slid off his horse. "In the morning then, my lady." He cut a quick bow, as did the grooms.

She nodded at all of them, then started back into the palace. She was reasonably sure if she just walked toward the middle, she'd find the grand staircase that led up to the second floor. From there, she could probably find the staircase that went to the royal chambers. If not, she could find a guard or a member of staff who could direct her.

Once she was in her rooms, she was going to take a long, hot soak in the huge pool that was her bathtub. After sparring with Gabriel and riding, she had no fantasies about what she must smell like.

Not very queenly, that was for sure.

It took her a good twenty minutes to locate her rooms. JT and Aunt Violet were in their rooms. Both of them seemed to be going through what had been packed for them, probably to make sure everything they wanted was in their trunks. "I'm home," she called out.

JT stuck his head through the adjoining door that connected their apartments. "Hey, Mom. How was your day?"

"Good. I met my horse, Indi. She's beautiful. You have to learn to ride. Maybe you can start while we're at Willow Hall. They have a stable."

He nodded. "I'm game. I'm not sure what else I'm going to be doing."

"I think you'll be busier than you realize. Have you seen Mrs. Wigglesworth, by the way?" Mrs. Edna Wigglesworth was Ro's former cat who'd been turned fae, thanks to the transformative powers of the portal crossing.

He laughed. "She's in here. Sleeping on the bed in the room I'm not using. I'm pretty sure she thinks it's hers now."

"That doesn't surprise me." Ro shook her head. "Just making sure I knew where she was. I don't want to leave her behind tomorrow." They were taking Benny, too, Ro's other cat. Ro had no idea how long they'd actually be at Willow Hall, but if it really was going to be three months, there was no way she was leaving Wiggy or Benny behind.

Aunt Violet came out of her apartment. "I'm so excited about the trip tomorrow and seeing the famed Willow Hall. I can't believe I'm going. And I get to bring a friend with me. Posey is *so* thrilled." She pressed her hands together in front of her, the anticipation on her face undeniable.

"I'm excited, too," Ro said. "Seems a little unfair that I've just become queen and now I'm off on a three-month vacation, but if that's what's done, who am I to stand in the way of tradition?"

They all laughed.

She gestured over her shoulder to the depths of her quarters. "I'm going to take a long soak, then I was thinking we could just have some dinner brought up. If that's all right with you? If you already have plans…"

JT shook his head. "I'm fine to stay in."

"So am I," Violet said. "I think tonight will be an early night for me."

"That will be our plan then." Ro went off to her bathing room, stripped off her sweaty clothes, and deposited them in the hamper. She made sure there were towels on the bench beside the pool, which there always were, then went down the steps into the blissfully hot, steaming water.

She sighed and closed her eyes as she settled onto one of the stone benches against the pool wall. She did nothing but sit for a few minutes, letting the water soak the day out of her.

A little meow caused her to open her eyes, and she looked up into Benny's face. "Hello there, sweet boy. How was your day?"

He flopped down on the pool's edge and rolled a bit.

"Don't fall in, you silly thing. I'm pretty sure you would not like that."

He stretched a paw out toward her.

She smiled and touched his foot with her wet finger,

which caused him to flick his foot to get the offending droplet off. "You know, Benny, you're a little bit of a diva. But I love you anyway. I hope you do all right on the trip tomorrow."

Thankfully, she had his carrier, so he'd be riding in that inside the carriage with her, JT, and Mrs. Wigglesworth. Violet would be riding in a second carriage with the friend she was bringing, Posey Wildacre.

Ro had thought it only fair that Violet be allowed to bring a friend. There was no telling how much royal business Ro would be required to do. JT, as well, for that matter. She didn't want her aunt to feel like she'd been abandoned, so having a friend along would help.

Not only that, but Aunt Violet was now Madam Meadowcroft, the queen's aunt, and her royal privilege meant she absolutely could bring someone with her. So why not?

On a more selfish note, Ro was glad her aunt having a friend along would mean Violet would be less likely to be by herself at any time. Gabriel was assigning a guard to her, which pleased Ro. But ever since Ro had been told that Queen Anyka might use Ro's son or aunt to get possession of *Merediem*, a new fear had been born in her. One she'd never experienced before in her life.

It was one thing to worry about those you loved. Another thing to believe they might be used by an enemy to coerce you into doing something against your will.

She stared into the steam, once again questioning her decision to invite Anyka to the Summer Palace. Deep in her gut, Ro knew this wasn't going to be a vacation.

She slipped beneath the water, completely submerging

herself, then came back up to get the shampoo. The next three months at Willow Hall, if they actually stayed that long, were going to test her.

She could feel it in her bones.

Thankfully, she'd have Gabriel and Uldamar and most of the other professors to help guide her through whatever sticky wickets presented themselves.

She massaged the shampoo into her hair, rinsed, added conditioner, then used soap and a washcloth to get the rest of herself clean. She loved the smell of all of them, sweet and floral, but fresh, too. What she loved even more was that by the time she returned from the Summer Palace, there would be a shower room in her bathing area here.

She was looking forward to that. She'd been informed that they already existed at Willow Hall, but there hadn't been one here because the former king and queen had been traditionalists.

Did that mean she wasn't a traditionalist? Having not grown up in the fae realm, she supposed there was no way she could be. She was only just learning the traditions.

That was one of the reasons some of her citizens were hesitant to fully accept her as queen.

Hopefully, the reopening of Willow Hall and the return to the tradition of spending the summer there would sway more of them. Show them that she meant to embrace as many of the old ways as she could.

If that didn't work, she could only pray that they'd see, over time, she wanted all the best for Summerton and the people who called it home.

Which now included her and her son.

She dipped under to rinse again, then reluctantly climbed out of the pool and wrapped herself in one of the luxurious towels from the bench. She wound her hair up next. She was going to wear one of her new lounging gowns of light green trimmed in white and silver.

As she headed for the dressing room, Benny swirled around her ankles, meowing, and nearly making her stumble.

"Careful there, little man. Are you hungry?" One of the palace staff had taken a trip to the mortal world to stock up on Benny's favorite foods, both canned and dry, so maybe he just needed a new bowl. She walked out into the dining lounge where his food bowls were kept to check. His kibble was nearly empty.

"All right, I'm getting it." She laughed as she bent to pour some more into his dish. She'd fed cats as an assistant curator; now, she was feeding them as queen. Apparently, some things never changed, no matter how high up you got promoted.

# Chapter Four

Dinner was a simple meal of meat pie with vegetables and a side of mashed potatoes with butter and gravy. The pie reminded Ro of chicken pot pie, but with red meat and bigger pieces of veggies. It was very good. She'd yet to eat anything from the royal kitchen that wasn't. They clearly knew what they were doing in there.

JT sat back. "I'm stuffed. I think I ate too much, actually, which isn't something I usually say."

Aunt Violet's brows lifted. "You ate your weight in mashed potatoes. How did you think you were going to feel?"

He laughed. "Fair point. But they were so good."

Ro nodded. "They were. It all was. And I happen to know they'll be bringing dessert up soon."

JT groaned. "How can I eat dessert after that? Tell them no."

Ro smiled. "I can't. We're about to be gone for three months. They want to be sure we remember how good the food is here so that we come back."

Violet wiped at her mouth with her napkin. "Also, those of us who didn't eat like little piglets might have room for a bite or two of something sweet."

Ro could only shake her head and chuckle. "I have missed this so much."

JT nodded. "It's kind of hard to believe we're all back together, isn't it?"

"It is," Violet said. "I wake up every morning hoping it wasn't just a dream. Then I see these beautiful rooms and remember it's my real life now."

Ro tapped a finger on the table. "Something just reminded me—Aunt Vi, you're getting a personal guard. A man named Vincent. Gabriel hand-selected him."

"Oh, pish. I don't need a guard." She waved her napkin at Ro. "Save the crown some money."

"No," Ro said with a little more firmness than she'd meant to. "We are going to be around Grym for the first time. Real Grym from Malveaux. Not to mention Queen Anyka and her retinue. I'm not taking any chances. None of us should."

She looked at JT. "How's Raphaela working out?"

His brows went up as he nodded. "She's amazing. And a little scary. I wouldn't want to cross her, I'll tell you that."

"How's the training coming?"

"All right, I guess. It's unlike anything I've done before. And she mentioned wanting to start teaching me evasive maneuvers on horseback while we're at Willow Hall."

"That sounds pretty worthwhile. And interesting." Ro hoped Gabriel didn't have anything like that planned for her. It sounded like something that would lead to a lot of bruises and she was already anticipating being sore tomorrow from today's ride.

Violet shook her head. "I'm not doing any of that, in

case either of you were wondering. I will compromise with the guard. But that's it."

A smirk crossed JT's mouth. "You took that dagger from the royal armory without any complaint."

She cut her eyes at him. "Everyone in Summerton carries a blade of some kind. It's what the fae do. Comes in very handy in everyday life."

"Or for defending yourself," JT said.

Ro held her hands up. "Which she won't need to do now that she's going to have a guard."

Aunt Violet sighed. "I still don't think I need one."

"Maybe you don't. But I'd rather err on the side of caution. Besides, how would it look to have your niece as queen and me not providing you with some kind of security detail?" Ro shook her head. "It wouldn't look like I cared very much, that's how."

"I suppose that's true," Violet said.

The door chime sounded.

"Come in," Ro called out.

She expected to see footmen come to clear the dinner things and bring in a dessert tray. Instead, she saw Uldamar walking toward her.

He tipped his head. "Your highnesses."

Ro stood. "Is something wrong?"

"No, nothing. I did not mean to alarm you, but we were supposed to speak this evening before you retired and as it was getting later, I thought I should come by. I see I was too early."

Ro sighed. She'd completely forgotten. She smiled, despite her memory lapse. "Actually, you're just in time to join us for dessert in the sitting room. It should be here at any moment. Let's go through, shall we?"

"How kind of you to include me. Thank you."

As they moved to sit down, the door chimes sounded again. This time it *was* the footmen. The two with dessert came in first and set everything up in the sitting room. One large tray of assorted cakes and sweets, another with coffee, spiced cocoa, assorted teas, and a decanter of blackberry brandy.

The other two went to work clearing the dinner dishes.

JT and Violet joined Ro and Uldamar in the sitting room.

Violet smiled at Uldamar as she took a seat in her usual spot. "How are you, sir? All ready for the big trip tomorrow?"

He nodded. "I am. Are you looking forward to it?"

"Very much," Violet answered. She studied the desserts. "These all look lovely, don't they? I think I might try a slice of that dragonfly cake." She glanced up at Uldamar. "Just to see how it compares to mine."

One of the footmen who'd stayed behind came forward and got Violet her cake.

The other two footmen appeared with the trays of dinner dishes that they'd gathered from the table.

"You may all go," Ro said to the staff. "We can help ourselves."

She didn't know just what Uldamar wanted to discuss but she didn't love talking in front of the staff as if they weren't there. Seemed rude to her, although she supposed she'd have to get used to it at some point.

JT leaned forward and took a dish of something that looked like chocolate pudding with whipped cream.

Ro wanted to ask how he'd suddenly found room for that but held her tongue. She poured herself a cup of coffee with sugar and cream, added two cookies to the edge of her saucer, then settled in her chair. "Please, Uldamar, help yourself."

"Thank you, your highness." He poured a cup of tea but took nothing else. "I won't stay long, but there was something I wanted to discuss with you before we left."

She sipped her coffee. It was very good, now that she was getting used to the slight difference in flavor. "Go on. You have my attention."

"Thank you. The gifts that Queen Anyka and Princess Beatryce sent, I was wondering... Did you want to take them with you?"

Ro blinked. "Why? You said yourself they were tainted with residual magic."

"I did, you are correct, but the more I've thought about it, the more I realize that the magic could be nothing unusual. Books in our world are very often touched with magic. You'll see that for yourself at Willow Hall."

She had no idea what he meant by that. "Okay, but the mirror?"

He smiled. "I know the old story of Snow White exists in the mortal realm. Mirrors have been touched with magic since time immemorial. It may just be that the mirror held a slight spell so that the viewer might appear more beautiful than they truly are."

"Oh." She hadn't thought about that.

"I might have overacted, weighing more heavily the origin of the gifts as opposed to the sentiment behind them. Taking the gifts to Willow Hall with you, especially when I know you are hoping to create some kind of common ground between you and Queen Anyka, might go a long way toward softening her attitude."

Ro dipped one of her cookies into her coffee and ate it while she thought. She glanced at Uldamar. "And you're sure they're safe?"

"As sure as I can be." He swallowed half the contents of his teacup. "I would be happy to encase them in a separate enchantment, one of my own making that would nullify any other magic applied to them."

She nodded. "Do that, and they can go. But at the same time, let's keep them packed up and out of sight. Unless there's a reason for me to put them out, like Anyka's coming over for tea, I'd rather them be a safe distance from me and my family."

"That is a perfect solution, your highness. I'll take care of it immediately." He finished his tea and set the cup aside before rising to his feet. "Now I will leave you to your rest. Morning will be here soon enough."

"Good night, Uldamar," Ro said.

He bowed. "Your highness." Then he left.

JT pointed at her with his spoon. His dessert was nearly gone. "It's actually not a bad idea. Having the evil queen's gifts around for her to see."

"JT, you can't call her the evil queen. For all we know she's as nice as anyone else."

"Sure," JT said. He snorted. "Raphaela's been telling me some stories about Malveaux. That place is crazy."

"To the best of my knowledge," Ro started. "Raphaela has never lived in Malveaux, so anything she might tell you is secondhand."

He shrugged as he returned his empty dish to the tray and picked up a triangle of something that looked like it might be a cookie or a very thick slice of torte. He bit the end off. "Are we having breakfast up here tomorrow? Might be a little busy to go down to the dining room."

"Mercy," Violet said. "How can you even be thinking about your next meal? You haven't stopped eating the last one."

"Exactly what I was thinking," Ro said. "We'll eat up here. I already sent instructions to the kitchen. We won't eat again until we reach Willow Hall. They're supposed to have lunch ready for us."

"Sounds good." Aunt Violet yawned. "I'm done. I need to go to bed. And I know we have to look nice tomorrow, since we're representing the royal house of Meadowcroft and all that, but I'm traveling in my most comfortable gown and slippers. I promise to put on some nice jewelry, though."

Ro laughed. "No one will judge you for wanting to be comfortable. Luena made me a traveling outfit. No idea how comfortable it is, but I guess I'll find out tomorrow." She returned her cup to the tray before getting to her feet. "I'm going to bed, too. Are you staying up, JT?"

"No. I'll go in, too." He stood, offering Aunt Violet a hand up. "Night, Aunt Vi." He kissed her on the cheek.

"Good night, sweet boy."

"Night, Aunt Violet. Night, JT." Ro went over and pulled the rope near the door so that the staff would come clear the remaining food and drinks away, then she kissed him on the cheek.

"Night, Mom."

Violet stood by her door. "See you kids in the morning."

Ro smiled. "Tomorrow will be quite an adventure, I'm sure. Sleep well, both of you."

She went off to bed. Benny was curled up on one of the pillows. Not the one she intended to use, thankfully. She climbed into bed and whispered, "Light," at the oil lamp on the side table. It flickered to life. She was tired, for sure, but not quite ready to sleep just yet.

She had the oddest sensation of forgetting something. Of course, she couldn't remember what that thing might be. And she generally felt that way before a trip.

She consoled herself with the knowledge that Willow Hall would be as well provisioned as Castle Clarion and if she needed something, she was sure it could be procured.

If not, Summerton was just a two-and-a-half-hour ride back. A guard or messenger could always fetch whatever was needed.

She picked up the book she'd been reading, a history of Summerton's kings and queens. All those who'd gone before her. It was interesting enough and something she fully believed she ought to read, even if only for the sake of the people she was now ruling, but her mind wasn't on it.

Maybe she'd try again tomorrow during the carriage

ride. She set the book down, said, "Lights off," and settled in to sleep.

Before sleep came, she did a little thinking about Gabriel and wondering if he would ever treat her like a normal woman again.

Maybe that would change at Willow Hall.

# Chapter Five

Anyka looked through the gowns in her dressing room. She had new ones made every year, but she wasn't sure why. The only time she wore them was when she met with the various delegations that came to reaffirm their treaties.

And those louts wouldn't care if she was wearing an old coarsecloth sack that had once held kurra nuts.

All the same, she liked to project a certain image. She was queen, after all, and needed to look regal. Powerful. A little fearsome never hurt, either.

Her clothing, gowns, capes, accessories, and jewelry were almost all designed with that image in mind.

However, as she surveyed her choices, she worried that it might be a bit much for Willow Hall. Could one wear dragon hide during the summer anyway? Perhaps that cloak should stay behind.

She exhaled, already exhausted by the fuss of it all. But she'd told Beatryce they were going, and the entire staff of Castle Hayze was now working toward that purpose.

Bother.

Maybe she was overthinking it. She probably was and she abhorred that. She was not an overthinker. She was a woman who made up her mind then charged forward.

Queen Sparrow had ruined everything.

Anyka pulled a dress out and examined it more closely. A sleek gown of the deepest blue-green silk beaded in an iridescent scale pattern from bodice to hem, it had a simple drape of whisper-thin marula wool that cascaded from the shoulders. That would work for dinner.

But if she dressed in that fashion every day, the Radiant would think she was arrogant and too good for them. And while she was definitely too good for them, that wasn't something to put on display.

She frowned at the clothes before her and yelled out, "Wyett!"

The soft clearing of a throat turned her head. He was right beside her. "Yes, my lady?"

"Nothing I have is right."

"Might I make some suggestions?"

"Yes." Huffing out a breath, she retreated to the large padded chair in the center of her dressing room to watch what exactly he thought he could come up with.

He went farther down the rack, divided the clothing, and pulled an outfit of mossy green silk. A tunic with a low vee neck, split at the sides and meant to be worn with the slim matching pants that hung with it. Flat, burnished bronze and amber beads trimmed the neck in a geometric pattern that seemed to lift the eye toward the face.

She stared at it. Where had that even come from? It would certainly work. She just didn't know how it had gotten into her dressing room. "I've never seen that before in my life. I'm not even sure it's mine."

"It is," he assured her. "I had a few pieces made for you

several summers ago, when Zephynia predicted a heat wave unlike anything we'd ever seen."

Anyka snorted. "That never happened."

"No, it did not. But the clothing did. This is one of those pieces."

She smiled. "That looks very Willow Hall. Show me the rest."

He pulled five more outfits, two of them with pants like the first and the last three gowns, much more summery and lighter than anything else she owned.

"You did well, Wyett." She leaned back. "Now what am I going to do for the rest of the time I'm there?"

He proceeded to work his way through her entire dressing room, showing her pieces that seemed utterly brand new and somehow also perfect.

As he continued, she started to wonder if he was actually using magic to produce these gowns, outfits, robes, tunics, and pants. It was that impressive. He even suggested shoes and other accessories for some of them, all of which she approved.

When he was done, she had more than enough clothing for a month's stay, and she doubted she'd be there that long. She shook her head. "How did you do that?"

He smiled. "My lady, you tend to choose your wardrobe from only the first section or two of this vast closet. Half the things that are made for you each year go unworn and unnoticed. I merely brought some of them to your attention."

"Perhaps. Or perhaps you have skills I've not yet realized. Thank you."

He bowed. "As you command, I do."

She got to her feet and watched as several housemaids began taking the selections off to pack in trunks. "Could you check in with Beatryce? Find out how she's doing?"

"Of course, my lady."

"I'm off to the carriage house to make sure the grand carriage is ready."

"I'd be happy to do that for you, if you like."

She shook her head. "I believe they'd find a personal visit much more inspiring."

"As you wish."

He left and she took one more look around the dressing room. Amazing, what he'd pulled from the racks. She walked over to a random spot and parted the clothing, moving through the pieces one by one to see if she could find anything new and interesting herself.

She did. A gown of ice blue that deepened to darkest sea blue at the bottom and was covered in crystals that swirled like waves. She added the dress to the rest to be packed.

Then she put on her cape and headed to the carriage house via the kitchen so that she could acquire a bunch of carrots.

The facility that stored the royal carriages wasn't far from the stables and she intended to visit Nymbus, her personal mount.

She went to see him first. He neighed as she entered, the sound of his throaty welcome recognizable to her even though she hadn't seen him in a few days. She smiled up at the gorgeous creature. His coat, mane, and tail were charcoal but from his hooves to his knees he was a fiery russet, giving him a fierce look she loved beyond measure. Almost as though he'd stood in blood. As warhorses went, he was one of the most superior examples she'd ever seen. "Hello, my darling Nym."

She fed him the carrots one by one. "I'm going away for a bit. I won't be able to take you, I'm sorry. I know we haven't ridden much lately. I'll do better when I return, I promise."

The clink of metal on stone caused her to look down the row of stalls. At the far end, the stablemaster was bringing in another of the horses. Probably from the exercise yard. "Mucklow," she called out.

The man straightened, realized who she was, and bowed. "My lady," came his firm but distant response. "Do you wish me to saddle Nymbus for you?"

She patted the horse's nose as Mucklow came closer. "No, I just came to see him. I want you to take special care of him while I'm away."

"Absolutely, my lady. Will you be gone long?"

"I'm not sure yet." She gave him a tight smile. She'd always liked Mucklow. He was an excellent trainer and very good with the horses. And she'd known him for as long as she could remember. "We're off to Willow Hall. It's being reopened and I'll be meeting the Radiant queen."

His brows lifted. "Willow Hall. My word. Isn't that something." He grinned, his eyes taking on a faraway look. Then he seemed to remember himself and regained his composure. "You be safe, my lady."

"Thank you, Mucklow." She stroked Nymbus's neck. "I wish I could take Nym with me."

"So why doncha? They do a fair bit of riding up there, from what I understand. They have stables and everything. And not just for carriage horses. They do rides through the hillsides and such."

She looked at Mucklow again. "They do?"

He nodded. "Sure. My father told me about it."

Mucklow's father had been the stablemaster before him. "I wonder if I should bring Beatryce's mount, too. I'd hate to get up there and have to rely on unfamiliar horses."

"I can have Nymbus and Plum ready to travel pretty quickly. When would you need them?"

"Not until the morning after tomorrow." She nodded, her decision made. "We won't ride them. We're going in the grand carriage, but we will take them. Make sure daily tack and ceremonial tack is sent with them."

He nodded. "I will, my lady. The morning of travel, shall I dress them in their blankets with the royal crest?"

"Yes, that will be perfect." She gave him a genuine smile, something few in her employ ever earned. "I'm so glad I came to see Nymbus. Well done, Mucklow."

"You flatter me, my lady. Glad to see you looking so well."

She started to go, then hesitated, turning back to look at him once again. "Your assistant stablemaster—he's doing well?"

Mucklow faced her. "Yes, my lady. Very well. Very competent and loves the animals just as I do."

"Good. Leave him in charge. I'd like you to accompany

us to Willow Hall so that I don't have to worry about my horses being taken care of properly."

He blinked a few times, one side of his mouth curving up in a slow smile. "I'd be honored, my lady."

Anyka nodded. "Bring your wife if you like." What was one more?

His mouth opened. "She'll be pleased as punch." He shook his head as he breathed out the words, "Willow Hall. Thank you, my lady."

"Day after tomorrow. First thing in the morning. If you're late, you'll be left behind. Oh, and send a horse and rider up to the castle. I'll have a message to send shortly."

"Right away, my lady."

Anyka headed for the carriage house.

There was no reason she couldn't bring people if she wanted to. Willow Hall could house plenty. And the Grym had as much right to be there as anyone did. In fact, *she* could have reopened the Summer Palace, if she'd so desired.

She just never had.

That line of thinking reaffirmed her belief that she didn't need to tell Queen Sparrow that she was coming. Anyka owed that woman nothing. But she would inform the staff at Willow Hall so they could properly prepare for her and her guests.

And the more she thought about it, the more names she came up with of citizens she wanted to bring along. People who might be useful for a variety of reasons.

If precious Queen Sparrow had a problem with

Anyka's guests, well, that would say a lot about the new queen's real intentions, wouldn't it?

Only someone with nefarious purposes would want Anyka to come alone. To feel isolated and separated from her court and citizens.

Anyka had been in power far too long to be a pawn in that game. She smiled. What sort of a name was Sparrow anyway?

Anyka laughed. The poor little bird was going to wish she'd never flown her nest.

# Chapter Six

Morning came early, but Ro didn't mind. She stayed in bed, staring out the windows. There was something so peaceful about waking up to the sight of the gorgeous sunrises here. It was enough to make her realize how easy it might be to become a morning person.

Something she should probably work on. Queens were undoubtedly early risers.

She got out of bed and pulled on her robe, then put on her slippers. Benny didn't move from the center of the bed where he was curled into a ball. Now that was the life.

Being an early riser would probably be easier if she didn't have to wait for coffee. Maybe there was something that could be done about that. She pulled the rope to let the staff know she was up. No sign of JT or Violet yet, but she was sure the aromas of breakfast would bring them around.

She opened the door to the balcony and stepped outside. It was a beautiful day, as always. She imagined that at some point there would be a less than pleasant day. Some rain maybe. Or snow, eventually. But when there were so many days of sun stacked end to end, days like that would probably seem novel and exciting.

In the city, days like that were just big, fat inconveniences. She went to the railing and leaned against it, looking out over her kingdom. She didn't miss the city. She'd thought she might. And maybe she would, but not so far.

"Ma'am?"

She turned to see two footmen and two housemaids. The footmen each had a tray loaded with dishes of covered food. One housemaid had the tray of the coffee service with cream and sugar and Ro's now standard pot of spiced cocoa; the other had a tray with pots of jam, butter, and things like that.

"In the dining room," Ro said.

"Very good, my lady," one of the footmen said. They all disappeared to set breakfast up.

That hadn't taken long at all. Maybe they'd been anticipating her early rise, since today was a travel day.

She looked forward to getting to see more of the kingdom but for now she figured she'd better wake JT and Aunt Violet.

But Violet was already coming through the door when Ro went to knock. "Morning, sweetheart."

"Morning, Aunt Vi. Breakfast is getting set up. I'm just going to wake JT."

"I'll see you in there."

Ro knocked on his door. "JT. Breakfast."

He answered a moment later, looking sleepy, but in his robe. "Hey."

Mrs. Wigglesworth pushed through the door and

zipped past them both on her way toward the food. "I smell sausages."

JT sighed. "I never realized how much she snores. I can hear her through the walls. I really need some coffee."

Ro suppressed a laugh. "There's plenty. Maybe we can find her a room of her own a little farther away from yours at Willow Hall."

He shrugged, smiling a little. "She's all right." He yawned as they started toward the dining room together. "I might take a nap in the carriage today. If that's all right."

"Do whatever you like. I'm bringing a book, so if you want to sleep, go right ahead."

"Okay, cool." When they reached the table, he took a seat across from Aunt Violet.

Ro sat at the head of the table, which had become her default spot. As soon as she was in her chair, the footmen stepped forward and removed the metal covers from the plates in front of them, as well as those on the other dishes.

"Now this is what I'm talking about," JT said.

The plates held a layer of crispy fried shredded potatoes and carrots, on top of which were two poached eggs, and then all of that had been covered with a golden sauce that looked like Hollandaise. She nodded. "Eggs benedict. Or something similar."

The other dishes on the table held bacon and sausages, slices of toast, and pastries.

"I won't eat lunch after this," Aunt Violet said.

Ro helped herself to what was either blackberry jam or blueberry preserves for a slice of toast. "That's probably the point. I think lunch today will be later than usual, since we won't be eating until we arrive at Willow Hall and get settled in."

Despite that, she only ate about half of her breakfast. She didn't want to be uncomfortable on the ride. With that meal behind them, they all went their separate ways again to finish up whatever last-minute things needed doing so they could leave.

The footmen cleared the meal, then returned to carry any items that would be going to Willow Hall. A trunk had been packed for Benny with food, toys and whatever else he might need. Ro had been assured that a litter box and litter would be supplied to the royal quarters there and needn't be transported.

Somehow, an hour or so later, they were all downstairs, under the portico, and getting into their carriages.

Aunt Violet and her friend Posey were in the carriage behind the one Ro, JT, Benny, and Wiggy would be in. Ro prayed Wiggy slept and didn't do something crazy like try to jump out the window because she saw a rabbit. Or take Benny out of his carrier.

For the day of travel and to meet the staff at Willow Hall, Ro was wearing the gown Luena had made for that purpose. It was sturdy iridescent green silk embroidered with vines and, thankfully, fit a little loosely. The gown had a few sparkling crystals around the neckline but no beading or crystals anywhere else. The fabric's sheen and the pretty embroidery kept it from being too plain.

She would have been fine with plain, but there was

very little in her wardrobe these days that fit that description.

Her slippers were soft leather in deep green, also embroidered with gold dragonflies. The circlet of green gold and diamonds on her head was new, but from now on whenever she acted as queen, it was expected that she wear some kind of crown. The slim band was as light a crown as she could get away with.

Her hair had been pulled back at the sides in a few braids, the style she favored the most. It kept her hair out of her eyes, honored the fae tradition of braids, and depending on how tight Helana did them, they gave her face a bit of a lift. Never a bad thing.

Helana and Luena were both accompanying Ro to Willow Hall. They'd been deemed absolutely necessary. Diselle and Pearlina, her jeweler and cobbler, had previously provided her with all the accessories she might need, so they'd be staying behind. Neither of them had minded, as they had active businesses in the village to look after.

Gabriel and Raphaela arrived, both dressed in the royal guards' uniform of dark leather breeches tucked into leather boots and a leather vest over a dark, trim-fitting shirt. All of the guards, Gabriel and Raphaela included, wore pointed hats that dipped over their eyes. Additionally, they all had swords at their hips and at least one dagger on their person.

But then, so did every fae here. Ro's was attached to a chain that draped her hips. She'd worn it so much she'd become accustomed to the reassuring weight of it.

As always, Gabriel looked better than he had a right to.

He tipped his hat to her. "Morning, my lady. You look beautiful. A perfect representation of Summerton."

"Good morning, Gabriel. Thank you. Will you be escorting my carriage today?"

He nodded. "I'll be on one side, Raphaela on the other. Vincent will be with your aunt's carriage. The rest of the guards will be scattered along the convoy and there will be another guard escorting your horse. Just so you know, I've increased the number of guards coming with us from twelve to twenty."

"That's a pretty big jump. Any particular reason?"

His eyes narrowed slightly. "Anyka has let it be known that she is definitely going to Willow Hall."

"She didn't tell me. All I got in response to that invite was that she'd think about it."

"I received a messenger pigeon today from Willow Hall. She let them know she was coming and not alone."

"Beatryce, right?"

"More than just her daughter. She's bringing staff, ministers, and other guests."

"Other guests?"

Gabriel glanced beyond Ro as if watching something else for a moment. "I can only assume she's bringing anyone with her that might feel indebted by being included on such a significant occasion as the reopening of Willow Hall. It's a political move."

"Makes sense. I need to start thinking more like a politician and less like a museum curator, I suppose."

"If I might be so bold," Gabriel said. "The way you think currently seems far superior."

Ro frowned. "This is turning into a whole thing, isn't it?"

"A whole thing?"

"You know. A big to-do. An event. I was thinking it was just going to be a nice getaway with a chance for the citizens to get to know me and an opportunity for Anyka and me to meet and talk. Now it feels very different than all of that."

He nodded. "I understand. I'm sorry. Perhaps there will still be a way for you to talk with Queen Anyka. Although I don't suggest you spend much time alone with her. Or any, really."

Skeptical, Ro slanted her eyes at Gabriel. "You don't actually think it's going to be like that, do you?"

"It's my job to think it's going to be like that and to safeguard against it, my lady. While keeping you safe, as well."

"I appreciate that. But I can't think like that. Not when I'm trying to befriend the woman and ease tensions between our two kingdoms. If I go in defensive, she'll pick up on it."

"It's all right not to have a defensive attitude, so long as you're still on the defensive. Letting your guard down, even for a moment around a woman like that, could give her an opportunity you don't want."

She touched his arm. "Gabriel. Have you met Anyka? Has anyone here?"

He sighed. "No. And I understand what you're saying, but we are not without sources of information. Things get back to us. Her feelings about Summerton. Her desires for

Malveaux. It's easy enough to put two and two together." His jaw tightened for a second. "And I do not want to see you hurt."

"Thank you. I promise I'll be cautious. But I am going to do my best to make her see that I'm a woman just like she is, who wants the best for her citizens, and that there must be a way we can work together."

"I wish you luck," Gabriel said. He glanced toward the main carriage. "I believe they're waiting on you, my lady."

"I'm sure they are." Lined up behind her carriage were all the other smaller carriages and many more people on horseback along with the carts of the citizens. People milled about, most of them chatting while also watching her. She raised her hand in greeting. "Safe travels, everyone."

Lots of waves and cheers were returned to her as she climbed into the carriage. It was a large conveyance, pulled by a team of four. The interior was upholstered in deep purple leather with gold trim. Two seats faced each other with storage boxes underneath. Ro figured the book she'd sent ahead must be in one of them. The seats themselves were wide enough to hold three people easily.

Which was good, because Wiggy was currently laying on one, holding a ball of yarn in her paws. *Hands*, Ro corrected her thoughts. Benny's carrier was at the very end of the seat. Wiggy's feet were flat against it.

"Wiggy, feet off your brother's carrier right this instance."

Wiggy muttered something too soft for Ro to hear but

put her feet down. Her attention remained on the ball of yarn.

Ro settled in next to JT and tipped her chin at Wiggy. "How long has this been going on?"

"Since we got here," he said, smirking. "Not entirely sure where she got the ball of yarn, but there's a very good chance she stole it from one of the villagers' carts when I wasn't watching her."

Ro shook her head. "Wiggy. We don't steal."

"Not stealing," Wiggy said. "Borrowing."

Ro looked at her son. "We need to find out who it belonged to and compensate them for it. I'm making that your first official project as prince."

JT snorted. "Not exactly setting the fae world on fire with that one."

"We all start somewhere."

Gabriel, now atop Storm, came alongside the carriage. "My lady?"

Ro looked out and melted a little at the sight of him. How could any one person be that good-looking? All the time? "Yes?"

"We're just waiting on your word to begin."

"Really? Sorry. Yes, we can go."

Gabriel knocked on the side of the carriage, then raised his hand into the air with a swirling motion. "Forward."

Tibly, the carriage driver, clucked his tongue twice and the horses started moving. The carriage rolled forward.

Gabriel kept pace on one side of them, with Raphaela on the other. Inside his carrier, Benny tucked his front feet under him and closed his eyes. Wiggy fell asleep shortly after, the ball of yarn forgotten to roll around the floor of the carriage.

Ro picked it up and pulled out one of the storage boxes to keep it contained, but the box already had a few things in it, all wrapped in brown paper or waxed linen. There were two corked jugs as well.

"Snacks," JT said. "One of the housemaids brought them. Cookies, cheese and meat sandwiches, fruit, water, and wine. Aunt Violet's carriage was stocked up, too."

"Good to know none of us will go hungry." She pulled out the next box and found her book. She took it out and stuck the yarn in.

She held the book on her lap but didn't open it. Instead, she watched the countryside go by. It was mostly farmland and very beautiful.

Here and there, workers in the fields would stop and wave. Ro and JT waved back.

JT seemed content to watch the scenery, too.

"This trip might not be exactly what I had hoped it would be," Ro confessed.

JT looked over. "You mean because it's gotten a lot bigger and more complicated?"

She nodded, more than a little pleased at how astute her son was. "Yes."

He reached over and squeezed her hand. "Don't worry, Mom. Whatever happens, you're not alone."

# Chapter Seven

Anyka read through the list of names of the people she'd invited to join her at Willow Hall. All of them had accepted, as was to be expected.

Preparations were well underway. She was nearly packed, but still wanted to check in with Beatryce to see how things were coming along there.

Chyles, Anyka's young scribe, had gone off to pack, although she couldn't imagine that would take him very long. He would ride in the small carriage with Wyett and Anyka's seamstress. Anyka thought about putting Zephynia in there, too, but Zephynia would fuss. As the Royal Seer, it was her place to be seated with some of the council ministers.

Wyett didn't deserve to be trapped with that shrill old harpy, either.

Actually, maybe Anyka would keep Zephynia here. She was an old woman. Travel wouldn't be good for her. Anyka nodded. That was a far better plan.

Other than for a few people, Anyka didn't really care who rode where or how they got to Willow Hall. Her responsibility had ended once she'd extended the invitation. And if those who were coming hadn't figured out their transportation by tomorrow morning, then that wasn't Anyka's problem.

She was already providing every available carriage in the royal carriage house.

She'd be in the grand carriage, along with Beatryce, Ishmyel, and her beloved Galwyn. There was no way she could leave her raven behind. He'd miss her terribly and she didn't trust anyone to take care of him properly.

Trog would accompany her carriage on the back of Mol, his enormous horse. Troll-bred horses made Grym warhorses look small, and they were not. And Mol, according to Trog, wasn't even the largest of his kind.

Legend said Grym horses bore some troll horse blood, which was where their size came from, but Anyka doubted it. Troll horses weren't even built the same. They had hooves like anvils and bones laced with iron. Some of them could supposedly breathe fire, too. The last bit was unproven, but true according to tales she'd heard.

Mucklow would take care of getting Nymbus and Plum there, something that gave her comfort. She praised her own quick thinking in inviting the stablemaster. There was no better way to be sure their horses were well looked after.

He and his wife were in a small open carriage with a leather rain bonnet.

The various council ministers could fight amongst themselves as to who sat in what carriage. She didn't care. Nazyr Marwood, her Minister of Magic, would undoubtedly ride his own horse, a ghostly white stallion known as

Phantom. Perhaps he'd use a mule to carry his belongings. Then again, he had his own carriage. He might very well take that and tether Phantom behind it.

She shook her head. Again, she didn't care. Although it would be entertaining to see just how things sorted out in the morning.

She looked at the time. In just a few minutes, dinner would be served in the dining room this evening so that she, Beatryce, and Ishmyel could discuss the upcoming trip.

She took her time changing into a long-sleeved gown of black silk, the bodice and hem beaded with garnets and black pearls. When she was dressed, she set a narrow circlet of black diamonds on her head, then changed into embroidered silk slippers.

She looked at herself in the full-length mirror in her dressing room. It was only dinner with her uncle and daughter, but it would behoove them both to remember she was the one in charge during this trip. Not Queen Sparrow.

Which was one of the reasons she planned to arrive for dinner a few minutes late. Waiting on her would be the perfect reminder that she was more than just their niece and mother. She was their queen.

It wouldn't do to have her authority undermined in any way. She would not look weak in front of the Summerton queen. It fell to Beatryce and Ishmyel to set that standard for the rest of the Malveauxians who would be accompanying them.

She walked back to the sitting room and stretched out her arm. "Come."

Galwyn left his perch to alight on her shoulder. Then she headed for the door. Trog opened it for her.

"Dinner."

He grunted and followed behind.

Footmen opened the dining room doors as she approached. She could hear chairs beginning pushed back as Beatryce and Ishmyel got to their feet.

Anyka walked in, smiling benevolently. "Hello, Uncle. My darling Bea. I'm so glad you joined me for dinner."

Trog took his place against the wall while she took her seat at the head of the table. Galwyn hopped from her shoulder to the back of the chair. "Sit, please," she said even as they were in the process of taking their seats.

A footman came forward to pour a little wine in her glass. She glanced over her shoulder. Trog nodded, indicating he'd already tried it. So she tasted it, then gave her approval. Her glass was filled the rest of the way, then Beatryce's, then Ishmyel's.

Anyka sipped a little more of the wine. It was very good. She wondered what the wine would be like at Willow Hall. She hoped they had blackberry brandy. She did so love a glass of that in the evenings.

She nodded to no one in particular. "You may serve."

The footmen departed to bring the first course in.

"How was your day, Beatryce? Did you get yourself packed?"

"I did. I'm afraid I'm bringing too much."

"I'm sure whatever you have is fine. Even if you don't wear it all. Better to be prepared, I think."

Beatryce nodded. "I agree."

Anyka looked at Ishmyel. "And you, Uncle? Are you ready?"

"I am. Very much looking forward to it, also. I understand the libraries at Willow Hall defy imagination."

She wasn't going there to read, even if that was the primary goal of most attendees. "I'm sure they'll be something to see."

The footmen returned with bowls. "Mushroom and onion soup, my lady."

Once the bowls were placed in front of them, Beatryce picked up her spoon. "There will be more to do there than read, won't there?"

Anyka nodded. "I'm sure."

"Yes," Ishmyel said with unexpected authority. "If things proceed at Willow Hall as they did in the old days, there will be all kinds of things to do if you don't want to just read. Riding, archery, fencing, painting classes, music and skits in the evening, boating on the lake, bathing in the communal baths, walks in the hills or gardens, birdwatching, stargazing, and, of course, ongoing discussions about the books that have been read. Really, more things than I can tell you about."

Anyka tried the soup. It was good enough, but she hoped there was a joint of meat for the main. Otherwise, she might order some fish for Galwyn. "You seem awfully knowledgeable about what happens at Willow Hall."

Ishmyel smiled. "I've been reading some historical

accounts. Trying to gain a little insight into what we might expect."

"Very smart, Uncle Ishmyel," Beatryce said. "I'm so excited, I can barely stand it. Although, I've never really known any Radiant fae. What will they be like, do you think?"

Ishmyel kept his mouth shut this time, looking at Anyka to let her answer.

"I hope," Anyka said. "That they will be kind and respectful and utterly mindful that you are the heir to Malveaux's throne. Just as I hope they are mindful that I am its queen."

She shook her head. "I don't know who ever decided the mingling with commoners was a good idea for the royalty of either kingdom, but there will be commoners there." She glanced at her daughter. "You should have a guard with you at all times, Beatryce."

"Mother, you're scaring me. I thought Willow Hall would be a safe place. A place where I could be myself and it would be understood that I was to be treated according to my place."

"Beatryce, none of us has even been before. How can any of us imagine what it will be like?" Anyka smiled at her daughter. "Forgive me if I hope for the best even while planning for the worst."

"Your mother's right," Ishmyel said, surprising Anyka for the second time that evening. "You are dear to this kingdom. You must be protected like a priceless jewel."

"Thank you," Anyka said. "See? Even your uncle agrees with me."

Ishmyel leaned toward Anyka. "I can go see Wolfsbane after dinner, get him to assign a guard to Bea. Maybe even a pair of them."

Anyka nodded. "That would be greatly appreciated."

"Of course. You and Beatryce are all I have left. I would defend you with my own life, should the need arise."

Anyka felt a warmth toward Ishmyel she hadn't before. "That is very kind of you, Uncle. And something I hope never happens." She smiled at him. "We've had too much loss in this family already."

"We have." He nodded and lifted his glass. "To those who've gone before us."

Anyka raised her glass, her mind on her parents, her emotions unexpectedly churned up.

They all drank and, thankfully, the footmen swooped in to take their bowls and bring in the next course, which was a cold dressed salad of greens, dried apple, roasted nuts, beetroot, and marula's milk cheese.

Anyka gave Galwyn a piece of dried apple, which he gobbled down. She picked at the salad herself. "While we are there, we must be careful what we say when we can be overheard. We must also listen very carefully."

Beatryce seemed more interested in the salad. "It's supposed to be a vacation, Mother."

"I know that, but no royal is ever truly on vacation when surrounded by subordinates. We will be watched the entire time we are there. And if you think the Summerton queen has nothing but goodness in her heart toward us, I would tell you that you are very much mistaken."

"Do you know that for certain?" Ishmyel asked. "I

know you have sources I'm not privy to, as you should, but do you have real information confirming that she's a threat to either of you?"

In light of what he'd just said about giving his life for them, Anyka chose her words carefully. "Nothing...actionable. But I'm sure her head has been filled with all the evils of Malveaux this past week while they've educated her on the history of the kingdoms. It seems to me a foregone conclusion that she would see us as the enemy. As do all Radiant."

He nodded thoughtfully. "Are you going to try to change her mind? To find some common ground? It would be a real boon to have trade open again. The people of this kingdom have made do with too little for too long."

"I have done my best," Anyka snapped.

Ishmyel nodded, brows bent in concern. "I know you have. And you've done an incredible job against insurmountable odds."

She exhaled, aware she'd overreacted when perhaps he hadn't been suggesting she was to blame after all.

He cleared his throat softly. "I was only asking about your objectives in meeting the new queen."

Anyka stabbed a piece of roasted beetroot, causing red liquid to ooze from it. "I can't really say until I meet her and see if she's open to such conversations."

He nodded. "Of course. Very wise to suss her out first."

Beatryce's salad was nearly gone. "So if she wants to open trade, does that mean we will?"

"Maybe," Anyka said. "It means there will be many more discussions. It isn't as simple as just reopening relations between us. There are terms and conditions that must be met. Tariffs to be agreed upon. Rules to be followed."

"I know," Beatryce said. "But if all of that works out, then we'd have trade with Summerton again. Even travel between the two kingdoms?"

There it was, Anyka thought. Her daughter's dissatisfaction with Malveaux rearing its ugly head again. She had to find a way to distract Beatryce from wanting to leave. She just didn't know how to do that yet. Maybe this trip to Willow Hall would do the trick, but she'd thought the same thing about their recent trip to the mortal realm.

All that had done was scare Beatryce away from the mortal realm. A valuable result, but Bea still wasn't content being here, it seemed.

Anyka laid her fork across her plate, signaling she was done with the salad. A footman removed her dish as well as Ishmyel's and Beatryce's. She sat back. "I just want you both to be aware of who is around you while we're there. Anything you hear or see that might be useful to me, I'd very much like for you to pass on."

"Of course," Ishmyel said.

"I am there," Anyka continued. "To forge a way toward better things for Malveaux and all of us who live here. In whatever way that manifests." She made herself smile at Beatryce. "Which I hope brings about a better life for the next head to wear the crown."

Beatryce smiled back. "I hope for that, too."

Anyka wasn't so sure. There were times she thought, if

given the choice, Beatryce would run from the crown and all of its responsibilities.

For that, Anyka couldn't blame her. It was a thankless, lonely job.

One that no trip, not to Willow Hall or anywhere else, could make any better.

# Chapter Eight

Ro read off and on, but then got engrossed in a chapter. When she finished it, she put the book down and looked up to see where they were. The scenery had changed somewhat as they'd climbed in elevation. There were mountains visible now. Some with snow on them. "How pretty," she said softly.

Wiggy was still asleep, and JT had drifted off, his head against the side of the carriage.

The trees looked different. They were taller and thinner, but full and deeply green. They didn't look like pines, but it was hard to tell.

The air, which had been sweet and floral at the castle, had a crisper edge to it. She leaned toward the window.

Gabriel was slightly ahead so that he was in line with the horses closest to the carriage. He looked from side to side, scanning the way ahead.

She smiled. He was always on the job. She wished she was riding beside him. Maybe tomorrow, they could do that. Ride together into the hills and have a look around for themselves. Wouldn't that be nice? Although Gabriel would probably insist on at least one additional guard, so they wouldn't really be alone.

She'd lost track of time, so she had no idea how much further they had to go.

Gabriel glanced back and caught her watching him. He slowed and brought Storm closer to the carriage. "I thought you'd be asleep."

"No, I was reading. It's really beautiful here."

He nodded. "The Serpentines. Named so because the ancients thought the mountains looked like an enormous snake curled along the horizon." He smiled. "Some say the Serpentines are the home to the last remaining dragons in the fae realm."

She blinked at him, her mouth coming open. "There are dragons?"

He shook his head. "There were. Now, just rumors of them. There's been no proof that any remain in a very long time."

"I guess that's good. Are we close?"

"Half an hour or so now."

"Okay, thanks." Ro heard a yawn and looked over as JT came awake. "Enjoy your nap?"

"I did, actually. I had the weirdest dream. I was walking in the forest and there was this scary-looking wolf keeping pace with me. I tried to get away from it but there was no shaking it. Then this bear came after me and the wolf scared it away. After that, we were friends. Me and the wolf, I mean."

Ro smiled. "So you dreamed about Raphaela?"

"What?" He shook his head. "I don't think that was about...I guess I can sort of see that." He reached for the storage box under the seat that had the food in it and pulled out a couple of things. "You want something?"

"No, I'm good. Gabriel said we're only about half an hour away." She couldn't wait to get there and see the place, meet the staff, and settle in.

"This is just a little snack before lunch." He unwrapped a sandwich and took a bite of one half. "After I figure out who Wiggy stole that yarn from, what do you want me to do? I mean in general during this trip."

"Well, you know my goal is to foster better relations with the Grym queen, so obviously be your most charming self around her. But I'd like you to get to know the Radiant citizens that are here with us, too."

He nodded, chewing the bite he'd just taken. "So that they can see I'm not a bad guy just because I look Grym."

"Yes. I'm sorry that's even something that needs to be done."

"Hey, it's not a big deal. You didn't know. Do you think...I'll ever get to meet my dad?"

They'd talked about this a few times in his life, but certainly not since the revelation that JT's father had actually been Grym fae. "I don't know. Do you want to meet him?"

"Part of me would like to." JT took another bite, chewed, and swallowed before speaking again. "It's probably not the best reasoning, but I'd love to ask him why he abandoned you like that."

She reached over and touched his arm. "You know it wasn't because of you. He never knew about you."

"Yeah, because he disappeared on you, and you weren't

able to tell him." JT frowned. "Probably wouldn't have made a difference but I can't get past that he did that to you. What kind of a man just abandons a woman?"

Ro spoke softly and with kindness in her voice. She cherished JT's protectiveness toward her. "I don't think it had anything to do with the quality of man he was so much as that he thought what we had was strictly a temporary thing. He had no reason to keep in touch. He didn't owe me anything."

JT shrugged, his cranky expression a clear sign he wasn't giving in.

"And now that we know he was Grym, it all makes so much sense. He was obviously just in the mortal world for a short time, then went back to Malveaux."

"Or Summerton," JT said. "We don't know he was from Malveaux. Gabriel and Raphaela are proof that's not always where Grym are from."

"True. Do you want me to see if he can be found? I could certainly have it looked into."

JT unwrapped another package. This one held cookies, small squares that looked like shortbread. "No. Not yet anyway. I'd think if he were around, he would have spoken up by now. I guess that means he's from Malveaux after all."

She picked up a little disappointment in his tone. "It could also mean that he's gone back to the mortal world."

JT exhaled, turning one of the cookies over in his fingers. "Right. Or that he's dead."

Could Rhys, or whatever his name really was, have passed away? Ro had no way of knowing, obviously, but it wasn't something she'd considered until now. "Even if he is, he could probably still be found. At least a record of him. If you want."

JT nodded and put the cookie in his mouth. He stared out the window, chewing. "I don't want. But maybe I'll change my mind. Someday."

"You just let me know."

"I will."

Wiggy finally stirred from her nap, sitting up and peering through partially closed eyes. Her nose wrinkled as she looked at the brown paper on JT's lap. "Food?"

"Are you hungry, Wiggy?" he asked. "You can have half of a meat and cheese sandwich."

Wiggy, now fully awake, nodded with enthusiasm. She stuck out her hands. "Yes. Give."

Laughing, JT shook his head. "All right, have patience."

"I know," Ro said. "Becoming fae hasn't changed her a bit. I'll take that water."

"Okay." He handed her the corked jug as he handed over the other half of the sandwich to Wiggy.

Ro took a sip and went back to looking out the window. Rhys was on her mind, of course, but she didn't think of him often and couldn't really see his face clearly in her mind. She hadn't been able to for quite a few years now.

She knew JT must resemble him in some way, but her memory couldn't make the connection. All fine with her. JT was the only person in that relationship who mattered.

She was good with him not wanting to look for Rhys,

too. Tracking that man down, which Ro had no doubt was possible, could open a can of worms.

One she'd deal with if and when JT made that decision, but it certainly raised a lot of questions. How would Rhys react to the news that his son was now the prince of Summerton? And Ro its queen?

Maybe he wouldn't care, but she found that very hard to believe. There weren't many people in the world, fae or otherwise, who didn't find the allure of power seductive. She doubted Rhys would be any different.

Who could be that close to so much power and not want to utilize it in some way?

She exhaled and took another sip. The water had stayed remarkably cold in the earthenware jug. For now, it was better that Rhys remained lost in time.

They had too much ahead of them to focus on something else. Her energies had to be fixed on getting to know Queen Anyka and doing whatever she could to patch things up between the two kingdoms.

And if Ro couldn't patch things up, then she would do her best to be sure war wasn't on the horizon.

The very thought sent a cold shiver through her. That was the last thing she wanted. What kind of a queen would she be if she took the throne only to send her people into battle months later?

No, peace of some kind was the goal of this trip.

She felt pretty confident she'd be able to make that happen. People weren't so hard to figure out, no matter where they were from.

Everyone wanted something. In order to get what you

wanted from them, you first had to figure out what they wanted.

She'd done it numerous times as assistant curator. Loaning two pieces to get one. Shortening the span of an exhibition. Or lengthening it. Adding someone's name to the signage. Giving them a fictious title that was vague but still sounded important. Promising to lend pieces the museum had yet to receive.

There were all sorts of ways to make things happen. Ro would just have to figure out which way would work best with Anyka.

# Chapter Nine

Gabriel rode closer to the carriage again. "Your highness, if you look out Prince James's side, you'll see the Moonfire Waterfall. It's that streak of white on the face of the Serpentines."

Ro leaned down to see through JT's window, easily spotting the vertical stripe of white. She wasn't sure she'd have realized it was water if Gabriel hadn't pointed it out. "I see it." She could also see the distinct line of clouds in the sky that delineated the Malveaux border.

"Wow," JT said. "That's a long waterfall."

"It feeds the river that Willow Hall was built across, which in turn is what supplies the Celestial Lake."

Ro smiled and looked at him. "So we're close then?"

He nodded. "Very close. Within ten minutes or so."

"Thanks for the heads up."

He squinted his eyes at her phrasing but nodded. "Of course, my lady."

In her small bag, Ro had a little folding mirror and a comb. She checked herself over in the mirror, happy to see things hadn't gone amiss during the ride. She touched the circlet serving as her crown to be sure it was secure. It was. She smiled, as full of excitement as a kid about to ride a roller coaster and she couldn't pinpoint why.

"Holy cow," JT said. "Mom, look, you can see it." He pointed out the window. "That has to be Willow Hall."

She slid closer to him and stared in the direction he was pointing. At first she saw nothing but trees, the waterfall, and the mountain range.

Then a roofline came into view. The rest of the palace followed.

Her jaw dropped open. "It's enormous. I've seen some large palaces in my time. Versailles. Hofburg. But that's got to be the biggest I've ever seen."

The closer they got, the bigger it seemed to get, too. Built of white stone with a blue-gray slate roof and trims of copper long ago patinaed to verdant green, Willow Hall stretched across a river in both directions, two thick stone supports making four arches over the water. She couldn't guess how long the building was. It didn't seem to end.

In height, it looked to be five or six stories. One side was under shadow, one side under sun. Not hard to tell which piece of ground belonged to Summerton.

A long, wide portico allowed the carriage to come to a stop under cover. There was a duplicate portico far across the river on the Malveaux side, along with another set of double doors. At least it looked like a duplicate. Ro couldn't be sure at this distance.

Staff fanned out on either side of the massive double doors, currently flung open. The staff were all dressed in pale gray and white and standing at attention.

Gabriel brought Storm to a stop, holding his hand up. Behind them, the rest of the convoy halted as well. Then he came down off his horse, keeping the reins in his hand. He nodded to someone on top of the carriage.

A footman, Ro soon learned, because he descended from the back of the carriage and opened Ro's door. Then he faced Willow Hall and loudly proclaimed, "Queen Sparrow Meadowcroft of Summerton."

Ro came down the single step and smiled at all of those waiting as she walked toward them. "I'm so pleased to be here at Willow Hall."

The staff all bowed. As they straightened, an older man stepped forward. "It's a privilege to have you here, your majesty. I'm Trence Underwood, Master of the House. Anything you need, anything at all, I will see that you get it. You have only to ask."

"Thank you, Trence."

Gabriel was now at Ro's side, but his gaze was sweeping the staff and surrounding area.

There was a little noise behind her and the footman made another proclamation. "Prince James Thoreau Meadowcroft of Summerton."

Ro gestured to JT. "This is my son, JT." Although she imagined none of them would dare call him that.

Trence bowed again. "Prince James, welcome to Willow Hall."

"Thanks," JT said. "This place is amazing. Very happy to be here."

Raphaela took her place slightly behind him. Wiggy then nearly fell out of the carriage. JT grabbed her hand. "Stay with me, Edna."

Thankfully, Mrs. Wigglesworth seemed momentarily subdued by all the goings on.

Ro gestured to the carriage parked behind theirs. "My aunt is here as well, Violet Meadowcroft. She has a friend with her, too, so we'll need an extra room."

Trence nodded. "The royal suite has five bedrooms, but there are several additional guest suites in the royal wing. We can accommodate you in any way you're most comfortable."

"A guest suite would work just fine for my aunt's friend." Nothing against Posey, but Ro didn't want to be discussing state business with an audience.

"I'd be happy to escort you to the royal suite now if you'd like."

Ro looked at Gabriel. "I'm sure you'd like to look at that."

He nodded. "I would."

Ro looked at her aunt's carriage again, this time waving for the older woman to join them.

"Coming," Violet called out. Another footman came down to open Violet's door, then Vincent, her new personal guard, walked with her to meet Ro. "It's so pretty," Violet said. "I can't believe we're here. Should I get Posey, too?"

"Sure," Ro said. "This is Mr. Trence Underwood, head of the household staff. He's going to take us up to the royal suite. Posey's rooms will be close by there."

Trence bowed. "Please call me Trence."

"Wonderful," Violet said. She looked back at the carriage. "Posey, come on."

While that was happening, Trence turned to the row of footmen to his left. "Fetch their majesties' things."

The footmen swarmed to the carriages as they'd been bidden. Trence smiled. "Right this way, my lady."

"Just a moment." Ro reached back into the carriage and grabbed Benny in his carrier. She wasn't about to leave him behind.

Trence led them inside, where the floors were made of more white stone, all polished and gleaming. The walls were also white with accents of bright blue, yellow, and brass. The Summer Palace did seem pretty summery, living up to its name. Lots of tall windows let in plenty of natural light.

Directly in front of them was a wide, sweeping staircase. Trence paused there. "Living quarters start on the second floor, which is where the Royal Summerton suite is. The common areas are all on the first floor. Libraries, meeting rooms, reading rooms, dining rooms, recreational areas, bathing rooms, direct access to the lake, the galleries, the solarium, the gardens, anything else you might need are all here."

Ro nodded. "Thank you."

"The third and fourth floors are more guest accommodations, and the fifth floor is entirely for staff."

Ro frowned. "You mean you have to climb all those flights of steps every day just to do your job? That doesn't seem very fair."

Trence smiled. "Your concern is touching, my lady. I assure you, we use a system of portals to move about Willow Hall."

"Oh." Ro laughed. "That makes so much sense."

"I would be happy to show you to the main guest portal now, if you'd like."

"Yes, thank you." Couldn't hurt to at least learn how to use it and know where it was. Ro wasn't too bothered by the steps, but Aunt Violet might be.

"Very good. Right this way." He led them to a set of double doors near the steps. Ro would have guessed they led into a room, but when he slid them open, what lay beyond looked very much like a large elevator car.

Trence went inside and stood in the immediate front corner while the rest of them walked in. Before him was a metal panel set into the wall. Set into that panel was a dial with a single yellow gemstone on it. The circle around the dial had five gemstones at one-inch intervals. He put his hand on the dial. "All you have to do is select which floor you'd like to go to, one through five, then line the sunstone up with that gem. The entire room acts as the portal."

"It really is like an elevator," Ro said.

"The fae version," JT agreed.

"Floor two," Trence said. He closed the doors, then turned the dial so that the sunstone was paired with the amethyst.

There was a wobble of air and space. Trence slid the doors open and they were in a new place, a large sitting room that had a hall straight ahead. "Right this way to the royal suite, my lady."

The color and décor weren't much different, although there was carpeting here. Thick, stuff that Ro's slippered feet sank into. She wondered if the carpet was to help keep the noise down. If Willow Hall was near capacity, that would be a lot of people.

She followed Trence.

He led them down the hall and to a small alcove that had a tall set of gilded doors with a bell set into the wall beside them. "The Royal Summerton suite."

He gestured across the hall where there was a short, open hall with four more doors. "Adjacent guest rooms for anyone you'd like near you."

Posey put her hand on Violet's arm. "That'll be me, Vi. You go on with your family now."

A footman who seemed to appear out of thin air stepped up to escort Posey to her room.

Trence opened the doors into the suites, then stepped out of the way. "I hope your highnesses find everything to your liking."

Ro and JT walked through a small foyer and into a large formal sitting room. There was a decent-sized fireplace, but Ro didn't imagine it got used often in a summer palace. There was enough seating for twenty people, maybe more, but the room was large enough to allow plenty of open space as well. Perhaps this was where past rulers had done most of their entertaining.

Over the fireplace was a painting of Castle Clarion awash in sun.

"Pretty fancy," JT said. He led Mrs. Wigglesworth over to the couch and told her to sit. She did and immediately became fascinated by the fringe on one of the pillows.

Ro nodded. It was very fancy. "It's beautiful." She meant it, too. The suite was nothing like their rooms at

Castle Clarion, but that was all right. The white, yellow, and blue color scheme was bright and airy and happy.

Marble-tiled floors were overlaid with plush rugs and everything was clearly of the finest quality.

There was a hall off the sitting room. Trence motioned toward it. "Three of the bedrooms, the private dining room, and the smaller sitting room or lounge are through there. The other two bedrooms are off the door near the fireplace. I'll leave you to inspect things at your leisure, unless you have further need of me."

Ro glanced at JT, then Violet. Both shook their heads. "I think we're fine to look around on our own. Thank you."

"Should you need anything, you have only to pull one of the bell ropes. The footmen will be up shortly with your luggage. Preparations for lunch are underway and service should begin in about an hour, if that suits you."

"That suits us just fine." Ro smiled at the man. "Thank you again, Trence."

He bowed. "My pleasure, my lady. I speak for all of us here at Willow Hall when I say we were so very glad to hear about your ascendance to the Radiant throne."

With that, he left.

Gabriel cleared his throat. "Before anyone settles in, I'd like us to have a look through the suite. Make sure everything is as it should be."

Ro knew he meant "us" as in himself, Raphaela, and Vincent. "Go right ahead," she said.

Gabriel, his daughter, and Vincent went down the hall.

JT took a seat in a large winged chair. "You want Aunt

Vi and I in the main part there with you or do you want your own space, Mom?"

Ro came around and sat as Aunt Vi moved to do the same thing. Ro set Benny in his carrier on the cushion next to her. "I'd like to have you there with me, unless you'd rather have some space."

"Better we stick together," Aunt Vi said.

Ro nodded. "Then it's settled. We'll take the three bedrooms down at the end of the hall with the lounge and dining room."

She was happy about that. For reasons she couldn't name, being at Willow Hall, this enormous, sprawling palace that was about to be filled with a whole lot of people, made her want her family close.

# Chapter Ten

Gabriel, Raphaela, and Vincent came back from their inspection looking happy enough.

Gabriel spoke first. "Everything looks fine. If you're all going to stay at that end of the suite, it'll make you easier to guard. We'll take the remaining guest suites across the hall for our personal use, if that's all right."

"Of course you can have the guest suites," Ro said.

"There will be a guard standing outside the suite door here at all times, night and day."

Ro stood. "I hate that a twenty-four-hour guard is necessary. This is supposed to be friendly territory. Isn't it?"

"It is," Gabriel answered. "But it's still our job to protect you regardless of the circumstances."

Raphaela nodded. "Also, there will be more citizens than you realize thinking they can just stop by to visit. We need to make it clear that's not allowed."

Ro glanced at her aunt and son. "I hadn't thought about that. Which is why I'm not in charge of security."

Gabriel smiled. "There will be guards on walking patrols throughout the palace, as well. Willow Hall has its own guards; ours will be supplementing them."

Ro hadn't had any idea he was setting up that kind of

security. It made her wonder if she was in more danger than he'd made her aware of.

Aunt Violet pursed her lips. "Well, I want Posey to be able to visit me whenever she wants. I invited her so we could spend time together."

Vincent nodded, looking slightly amused. "I promise, Madam Meadowcroft, we won't turn away anyone you say is all right."

"Good." She got to her feet. "Let's go see those bedrooms."

Gabriel took a step toward Ro. "We'll stay here and supervise any footmen that bring luggage up. Also, there's something I need to show you in your quarters later. Assuming you take the largest of the three bedrooms, my lady."

"All right." She couldn't imagine what that might be. "Do you think everyone else is getting settled now? All the professors and citizens and so on?"

"I'm sure of it."

She sighed. "I should have asked Trence about putting Luena and Helana near me."

"I have a feeling he's already thought that far ahead, but I can go find him and make sure of it, if you'd like."

She shook her head. "You're the head of security, not an errand boy. Just find a footman and send him."

Gabriel smiled. "I'll do that."

"Thank you." She smiled to herself, mostly at how eager he was to be helpful. But she didn't really want or need him to do such little things for her. Even if he was okay with it, she wasn't.

She went down the hall to find the smaller lounge, which had a beautiful view of Celestial Lake and the valley below it. There was a nice big balcony with a seating area off of the lounge, then further back was the dining area and the bedrooms.

All three doors were open already. JT came out of the middle room and pointed to the door to the left of him. "That's the biggest room. We thought you should have it."

"All right. Thank you." She headed in to inspect it.

The room was done in the same shades as the rest of the suite, but here they were softer. The walls had panels of pale blue silk that matched the drapes. The bedding had the same soft blue in a delicate pattern against white with accents of creamy yellow.

Mother of pearl, crystal, and brass oil lamps sat on the bedside tables. The room was large enough for a seating area near the fireplace, where a brass and crystal screen patterned like dragonfly wings blocked the way of escaping embers. On a table near one of the chairs was a low vase of fragrant white and yellow roses.

The whole thing was soft, relaxing, and very pretty. She felt a little like she was on vacation in a French villa. This would be a good place to unwind in the evenings after a long day of doing whatever it was she'd be doing here.

Past the bed there was a short hall that had two doors, one on the side and one at the end. No doubt the dressing and bathing area.

She went to see. That's exactly what they were. Both rooms were equal to what she had at Castle Clarion, although the dressing room wasn't quite as large. More fresh flowers had been placed in each one.

One thing she spotted instantly in the bathroom, besides the large bathing pool, was the separate shower room. That was enough to make her smile. She was already looking forward to that. She was pleased to see a litter box had been set up for Benny as well.

She wasn't letting Benny out of his carrier until the footmen were done bringing the bags up, however.

She went next door to see JT's space. It had touches of deeper blue, a few nautical art pieces, and a lot fewer frills, making her wonder if the staff had adjusted the décor to something that might better suit the tastes of the visiting prince. It wouldn't surprise her. His room had no fresh flowers, but there were two potted ivy and, in one corner, a small ornamental tree.

Aunt Violet's room was the same soft blue as Ro's but with the additions of a gentle pink and pale green. The space felt inspired by a spring garden. An exuberant bouquet of flowers sat on the mantel of her fireplace. "Are you happy in here, Auntie Vi?"

She was standing by the bed, feeling the sheets. She smiled at Ro. "Oh, it's lovely. Who wouldn't be happy here? Say, do you think I should go check on Posey?"

"Absolutely. We'll make sure your trunks get put in your room."

"All right, I'll go do that then."

"I'll walk out to the sitting room with you." It occurred to Ro that she hadn't seen Edna in a while, which made her need to lay eyes on her. If Wiggy ran off, they might never find her in this place.

But she found Wiggy sitting on the couch in the same spot as when they'd arrived, staring at a reflected spot of sunlight on the wall. Ro had a moment of inspiration. "Wiggy, would you like to look at the other bedrooms? Maybe see if you'd like one for yourself? You could test the beds out."

If she could get Wiggy in one of the bedrooms, maybe she'd be less likely to dart out the door when the footmen came in.

Wiggy stared at the sunlight a second longer. "I guess."

"Come on," Ro said, clapping her hands the way she'd once done when Wiggy the cat wasn't paying attention to her. "Stop dawdling."

Wiggy sighed. "I'm coming." At least this time she got up off the couch and followed Ro.

Ro went down the other hall and found two more bedrooms, both very nice. One was done in blue and tan, the other in pastel yellow and green, both with their own dressing rooms and bathing areas. Other than the color, they were nearly identical. "What do you think?"

Wiggy sniffed around both of the bedrooms, but seemed to find something that tickled her fancy in the blue room. "I like this one. There have been rodents in here."

Ro rolled her eyes. "Let's not tell Trence that, all right?"

Wiggy lay on the bed and started rolling around as soft laughter trickled in.

Ro looked over to see Gabriel standing by the door. "I take it you heard that."

He nodded. "Would you like me to check for rodents?"

"And take Wiggy's fun away? No, sir." She left Wiggy to explore and joined Gabriel in the hall. "What did you want to show me in the bedroom?"

"Secret passageway. Leads from your dressing room out to the foyer in front of the portal."

"That's interesting. Is it secure?"

He nodded. "I spoke to Trence about it. He said it's been so long since they've had visitors, he'd actually forgotten about him himself. I made sure it was locked from the inside, though. It wasn't when I found it."

"Thanks. Is there anything I need to do that I haven't yet? I'm feeling a bit overwhelmed at the moment. Should I let the professors know where I am?"

"No. If they need you, trust me, they'll find you. There are only two royal suites in Willow Hall. The one that serves Summerton and the one that serves Malveaux. I expect them to leave you alone at least until after lunch."

"Okay." She hoped it was all right if she didn't change into a new outfit for that. Seemed unnecessary to her. "Speaking of, do we know when Queen Anyka is arriving?"

"We don't. And I asked Trence. All they know is that she's coming."

Ro sighed and started walking toward the sitting room. "I suppose that's part of her plan? Keeping everyone guessing?"

Gabriel walked with her. "It might be."

As they entered the sitting room, Trence was directing footmen with trunks. He bowed to Ro. "I have housemaids and a valet on the way up, my lady. They'll have you and your family unpacked in no time."

"Thank you." She and Gabriel stood off to the side while the footmen trooped through. "Now that I see all those trunks, it looks like way too much stuff."

"It probably isn't."

"Really? That's not what I thought you'd say."

"You are the queen. And there is a dinner every night that I'm sure most people will expect you to attend. The days here might be casual, but dinner will be more dressed up, so whatever you brought will probably get worn."

Ro sighed. "You're lucky you have a uniform."

"I know." He smiled.

"Listen, you mentioned having the guards walking patrols earlier. Is there something you haven't told me? Am I in some kind of danger?"

"No, nothing like that. Just maintaining what we do at Castle Clarion. Just because we're supposed to be on vacation doesn't mean security gets lax."

She hadn't been aware the guards patrolled at the castle. "I guess there's a lot I don't know about what you do."

"I'd be happy to tell you whatever you want to know, my lady. Just ask."

"I will."

"That reminds me," Gabriel said. "I have a question for you. What do you know about your aunt's friend Posey?"

"Not much. She runs a shop in town near where Aunt Violet had her bakery, which is how they know each other,

I guess. A place that sells tinctures and tisanes? Or something like that."

He nodded. "The Herbal Apothecary. I found out that much about her. My guess is she's got some kind of green magic."

"Green magic?"

"Magic that involves plants."

"That makes sense." Ro's eyes narrowed in sudden concern. "Why are you asking about her? You think she's up to something?"

"No, not at all. I just like to know as much as I can about anyone who becomes connected to you and because of the short notice, I haven't been able to do that yet. Not to the extent I'd prefer."

"She seems very nice. I've barely had a chance to say two words to her, but she and Aunt Violet are like two peas in a pod."

Gabriel watched the footmen, hands clasped behind his back. "I'm sure you'll get to know her more as the days go on. Vincent will apprise me if there's anything else about her I should be aware of."

"Speaking of being aware, I'd like to know as soon as Anyka arrives. I'm not going to pounce on her or anything like that. I just want to know."

Gabriel's mouth tightened into a hard line. He nodded. "That makes two of us."

# Chapter Eleven

Lunch brought Ro and her family, minus Wiggy but plus Posey, to the main dining room. The room could have easily doubled as a football field, if not in width, then definitely in length. Instead of there being one long table, as Ro had expected, there were many smaller round tables. Some sat eight, some sat six. It was, essentially, a banquet hall. "This place is huge," she whispered to Gabriel.

"And I understand it can be made bigger. Those walls at the back can be moved."

"That's impressive." She looked around. At either end of the room there was one very large round table with chairs for twelve. The royal tables, no doubt, since both of them were still vacant, and the rest of the tables had a few people at them.

All of those people had their eyes on her. She supposed that was something she'd have to get used to while she was here. It wasn't the most comfortable feeling, but she understood it. These people wanted to see the woman who'd just become their queen. It wasn't anything malicious.

At Castle Clarion, the staff didn't stare. Obviously,

because that wasn't protocol. But the lottery winners from all across Summerton sat at their tables, smiling at her.

She smiled back, feeling a bit like the blue-ribbon cow at the county fair. But smiles were good. She'd take those any day over frowns or the pursed lips of disapproval. She wondered if she should go table to table and say hello.

But if she did that today, would they expect it every day? She was the queen. She could do whatever she liked.

She lifted her hand and waved. That seemed like a decent compromise.

Then Uldamar appeared and saved her from any further decision-making. "Your highness, there you are. How are you settling in?"

"Just fine. The suite is wonderful. Perfect, really. How about you?"

"My rooms are more than adequate, thank you for asking. Have you decided who you'd like to sit with you at your table?"

"I should have known lunch wasn't going to be that easy." She realized in that moment that this stay at Willow Hall wasn't going to be much of a vacation for her. She looked at Gabriel, but he was studying the people who'd already taken seats.

"JT, Aunt Violet, Posey, and our security team. You can join us as well, Uldamar. That leaves four more seats. Bring four more professors over. Or two and their partners. Or some combination of that. Whomever you want." It was an easy out for her, but Ro was also curious to see who he'd choose.

Uldamar nodded. "As you wish, my lady."

He went off to find four more people.

She leaned in toward Gabriel. "See anyone suspicious?"

The faintest hint of a smile bent his mouth. "No, my lady. Everyone looks pleased to be here and excited to be in the same room with you."

"I hope I don't spill anything on myself during lunch. No pressure or anything." At least none of them had cell phones and would be uploading unflattering pictures to their social media. The fae realm did have some real advantages there.

"Mom," JT said. "Is that big table ours?"

"Yes. You and Aunt Vi can take a seat if you want. I'll be over in a second."

"All right. Raphaela, too?"

"Yes, the security team is staying with us."

"Cool." He tipped his head at Raphaela, who was watching the growing lunch crowd, just like her father. "You're sitting with us."

She nodded without looking at him. "Yes, your lordship."

He shook his head at his mom. "I still can't get used to that."

She smiled. "It'll take some time." She went back to speaking to Gabriel. "Don't you think it's a little counterproductive to have tables for me and Queen Anyka at opposite ends of the room? How are we supposed to get to know each other? And won't that just end up dividing the people? Grym and Radiant, each on their own side? That's not at all how I wanted this to go."

Gabriel nodded. "I'm sure Trence just thought that's

how things should be. Or maybe that's how it's always been set up. Doesn't mean it can't be changed."

"Good." She looked around. "Because I want to talk to him about it." She waved at a footman. "You there. Yes, you. Can you find Trence for me?"

The young man bowed, then nodded. "Yes, your highness. Right away, my lady." He scurried off.

"I don't like how afraid some of them act. I'm not scary."

"You're queen. That's frightening enough for some of them. Remember, this is the first time they've actually had a monarch in residence, despite how long some of them have probably worked here. No doubt they're all worried about getting everything just right."

Ro exhaled. "It's a little exhausting, all this pomp and circumstance."

Gabriel stopped watching the crowd long enough to make quick eye contact with her. "Just remember that you are queen. And you set the tone."

She wanted to ask him what he meant by that, but Trence came in. "You had need of me, my lady?"

"Yes. I was wondering about the setup of the tables. I assume that large table at the other end is for Queen Anyka and her entourage when they arrive, just like this one here is for me?"

"Yes, my lady, that's correct."

"Having us both at opposite ends will make it hard for Queen Anyka and me to get to know one another. I worry that it will also cause everyone else to sort themselves into a Grym side and a Radiant side. I was very much hoping that our time here at Willow Hall would be one of getting to know each other. Not segregation."

His brows pinched together. "Forgive me, your highness. You are, of course, absolutely correct. I merely followed the handbook provided to me by the previous Master of the House. It never once occurred to me to ask how you or Queen Anyka might want it set up."

He looked far more concerned than Ro thought necessary. She put her hand on his arm. "Trence, you didn't do anything wrong. Following past protocol makes perfect sense. But from here on out, can we have both royal tables at one end?"

"Yes, your highness. Absolutely."

"Do we eat dinner in this room as well?"

He nodded. "All meals, unless specified otherwise. And I can assure you everything will be to your liking at dinner."

"Thank you." She took her hand off of his arm, not sure what the protocol was concerning touching a member of staff like that. All she'd wanted to do was reassure him. "This is a tremendous amount of work for you and all of the staff, taking care of two different rulers from two different kingdoms. I just want you to know that I appreciate your effort and the efforts of all the staff. This is a new experience for both of us."

He smiled and his brows unpinched. "Thank you, my lady."

"We'll get through it together, all right?"

He nodded. "Yes, your highness."

"Now, I should probably take my seat. I know no one

else can eat until I start, and the dining room looks pretty full."

"Anything you need, just let me know."

"I will." She glanced at the head table, pleased to see there was a seat for her between JT and Gabriel. Uldamar was next to Gabriel, then beside him were the four other professors he'd brought along.

Everyone stood as she approached the table. Everyone. At her table and every other table in the room. A footman rushed to get her chair. She stood in front of her chair, looking out over the crowd. "Please be seated, all of you."

They did as she asked. She smiled at them. "Thank you all for coming. I'm so pleased that you're here to take part in the renewing of this tradition. I look forward to the days ahead. As you may have heard, Queen Anyka is expected."

That sent a few murmurs through the audience, telling Ro that maybe the news wasn't as widely known as she'd thought. "I don't know how many she'll be bringing with her, but my hope is that she and everyone who accompanies her will feel the warmth of our Radiant kindness and goodwill. My goal is to reunite us as nations, something I spoke of on coronation day. I meant those words. This is our first step toward that goal. It's not a path I can walk alone, however. I need you alongside me."

A decent number were nodding. More than weren't. She took that as a win. "Anyone found working counter to the goal of unification will be asked to leave immediately. Our time at Willow Hall should be one of fellowship, friendship, and relaxation. Not strife and stress."

She hoped that wasn't too harsh a message to start lunch with. "Now, let's enjoy our first meal together."

She sat down. Footmen bearing trays of plates began streaming in. She leaned toward Gabriel. "Too much?"

"Not to me. Better to set the tone now than have to explain things later. Gives you a sound reason to get rid of people, too. Not that the queen's prerogative isn't a good enough reason already, but this takes the weight off of you."

"Thanks." She was first to be served. A bowl of pale green soup was set in front of her.

"Chilled cress and cucumber soup with silver shrimp, my lady," the footman said.

She said nothing until everyone had been served, then looked over at JT. "Not the pizza you were hoping for, I'm sure."

He shrugged. "No, but I'm sure the next course will be a little more substantial."

Except the next course was a salad, followed by a selection of finger sandwiches and that was finished up with a dessert plate bearing a tiny jam tart, a single iced cookie, a beautiful strawberry, and something that looked like a cream puff filled with pink fluff.

Aunt Violet lifted the cream puff. "I feel like I've been to tea."

Ro nodded. "It was all very nice, but a little light. I have the feeling we're going to have some very hungry people roaming Willow Hall."

"Light?" JT snorted. "That was basically an appetizer in four courses. When will the actual meal be served?"

Ro sighed. "I don't think you're the only one wondering that." She was going to have to speak to Trence again. She had a feeling she and the Master of the House were going to be far better acquainted by the end of this trip than either of them had anticipated.

Gabriel cleared his throat softly. "You need a personal secretary. Someone to handle these kinds of things for you. You shouldn't have to do it yourself."

"Yeah, Mom," JT agreed. "You really need someone like that."

"I could do that job," Violet said.

Ro shook her head. "No, you're related to me. I don't think that's a good idea. And there will be plenty for you to do soon enough." Ro had been hoping Aunt Violet would help with some of the charitable concerns she'd been made aware of in Summerton.

Posey smiled. "I'm not related to you. Maybe I can help? At least while we're here? After all, I'm only here because of your generosity."

Ro thought about that for a moment. "You'd have to be vetted, I'm sure." She glanced at Gabriel, who nodded.

"What would that require?" Posey asked.

"Sit with Professor Nightborne. Answer whatever questions he asks."

Posey nodded at Gabriel. "There's nothing left to eat. Might as well get started."

# Chapter Twelve

While Gabriel went off with Posey to find a quiet corner in which to conduct his interview, Ro stood for a moment talking to the other professors who'd joined them for lunch. They were all lovely people and very happy to have been included.

Out of the corner of her eye, she saw Trence. He was supervising the footmen who were clearing the dining room, but he was close enough to make her wonder if he didn't want to see what she'd thought of lunch.

She wasn't going to lie. She smiled at the professors. "If you'll excuse me." Then she turned toward Trence. "Do you have a moment?"

"I have as much time as you need, my lady."

"There's no easy way to say this but lunch was a little light."

"Oh. I am sorry. I don't seem to be getting much right, do I?"

"It's not your fault. I know you're probably just following whatever instructions you've been left. We don't need anything that fancy, though. In fact, if you wanted to serve lunch buffet style—"

He cringed. "That would never do."

"Trence. I'm the queen and I'm telling you it would be fine. But if you don't want to do that, then why don't we try a single plate of food. Maybe with some bread and butter at the beginning and a platter of desserts at the end for each table. And something more substantial. A plate of pasta. A nice sandwich with a salad. A heartier soup and salad. Even some kind of stew or rice dish."

He seemed to be giving her suggestions consideration. "That would be easier for the kitchen. Especially when we have Queen Anyka and her people to feed as well."

"I would think so. Just let the cook know that what they produced today was lovely and delicious and very pleasing to look at, but more rustic, simple cooking would not be unappreciated, either." She gestured toward the now-empty tables. "Most of the people who filled these tables earlier are regular citizens. Farmers, shopkeepers, municipal workers. They don't eat finger sandwiches and cold soup for lunch. They eat much heartier fare."

Trence nodded. "You make a very good point, my lady. I'll take care of it."

"Thank you." So far, her vacation was more work than being at Castle Clarion. That didn't bode well for her stay here. Or any attempt she might make to befriend Queen Anyka.

Although, maybe they might bond over that. She had to be equally busy, didn't she? Or had she been queen long enough to have everything down to a smooth process?

"Probably that," Ro said to no one in particular. If Gabriel didn't think Posey was right for the job of secretary, Ro would have to find someone else. She needed help.

Aunt Violet came up to her and slid her arm around Ro's waist. "You look like you have the weight of the world on your shoulders, my dear."

Ro smiled, aware it wasn't much of a smile at that. "There's so much more to do than I anticipated."

"How did you do it all at the museum?"

Ro thought about that. Being assistant curator seemed like a lifetime ago now.

"I made lists. And I had help."

"Have you been making lists lately?"

Ro's smile improved a little. "No. And I should be. It would help get the clutter out of my head."

"Maybe that's something else your secretary can help you with."

"Maybe. Do you think Posey is up to it?"

"My dear, that woman has singlehandedly organized more community projects and charity events than I can count. All while running her own business and being grandmother to three little ones. If there's a more capable person to fill the role of royal secretary, I'd like to meet them."

Ro laughed. "And you know her how? Because you both have businesses in town?"

"That's how we became acquainted, but we became friends because she knew I needed someone. I was a bit at loose ends when I first arrived, as you can imagine. All of this was so new to me. It was a lot to take in. A lot to think about. She understood that and made herself available. Night or day. No questions asked." Violet lifted her chin slightly. "Truth be told, Posey kept me from losing my sanity a few times."

"I had no idea things were that hard for you."

Violet sniffed. "I missed you and JT so much. And to know that you were just a portal trip away…" She sighed and shook her head. "It felt like torture. Posey helped me through that. Kept me from making some very bad decisions."

"Is it true she has green magic?"

"Yes, she does. It's nothing to be afraid of."

"I'm not afraid of it," Ro said. "Just curious, really. Do you think all fae really have magic?"

"I do. Posey thinks I might have a touch of green magic myself. Not in the way she does, but in making things grow."

Ro thought about the gardens at her aunt's cottage in Rivervale. "I'd buy that, based on what I saw at your house."

"Maybe I do. Did you ask because you're questioning your own magic?"

"Just thinking about it."

"It can take a while to manifest," Violet said. "Especially when you've spent a lot of time in the mortal realm. I know that much. So be patient."

"I will." Ro looked around. JT was chatting with Raphaela, his face alight with whatever the subject was. "What do you think JT's magic will be?"

Violet glanced over at him. "Hard to say. Maybe something in the language arts. He was always so good in school. Especially with debate and student government."

"That would be the right kind of magic to have if he's going to be king someday."

Violet nodded. "Yes, it would." She took hold of Ro's arm. "Why don't we go back up to the suite and relax a bit. I know all we've done today is travel and eat, but a little rest never hurt anyone."

"I will. In a bit. I want to wait on Gabriel and see what his verdict is about Posey."

"Then I'll wait with you," Violet said. "Because if he says she's not good enough, I might just box his ears."

"Auntie Vi, I don't think attacking the most dangerous man in the kingdom is such a good idea."

"I'm old enough to make my own bad decisions."

Ro just smirked. She looked toward the door to see if there was any sign of Gabriel and realized there was a small group of citizens hovering nearby. Most likely waiting to see if they could speak to her.

She didn't want to, but then again, that was what she was here for. To get to know her people. She smiled at them. "Hello."

As a group, they bowed and curtseyed. "Hello, your highness."

"Did you enjoy your lunch? I've asked that the kitchen give us something a little heartier tomorrow."

They all smiled and nodded. Then a young man stepped forward. "Do you really think you can bring about peace between the two kingdoms?"

"I don't know," Ro answered truthfully. "But I'm going to try. Are you going to help me?"

He stared for a long few seconds, making it obvious

that he hadn't expected to be asked a question himself. Finally, he nodded. "Yes, your highness. I will do whatever you need me to do."

"Then I can count on you to be friendly to the Grym who accompany Queen Anyka? To be as kind to them behind their backs as you are to their faces? To show them the true spirit of the Radiant fae? Because that's what I need. From all of you."

An older woman beside the young man stepped forward. "I can do that. I will do that."

The older man who'd been at her side joined her. "So will I."

One by one, each member of the group gave Ro their assurances that they would do their part. It made her happy, even if she was too cynical to fully believe it. She wanted to. But so far nothing had shown her that the fae were that much different on the inside than humans were.

Sadly.

At last, Gabriel returned. Good man that he was, he didn't make her wait, giving her a quick nod as soon as they made eye contact. "She answered everything to my satisfaction. How she'll work out as a secretary, I can't say, but there was nothing about her that seemed duplicitous."

Ro looked over his shoulder. "Where is she?"

"She's waiting on a member of housekeeping to bring her a pen and notebook."

Ro smiled. "That seems like a good way to start to me."

"What's next on your agenda?"

"Nothing. By which I mean I want to go back to the suite and sit down with Posey to make some lists. After that, I might do absolutely nothing but lie on the bed and stare at the ceiling for an hour. After that, I have no idea. Is there something you need me for?"

He shook his head. "No."

"Then let's go as soon as Posey returns."

That only took a few more seconds, then Ro corralled her crew and they headed for the portal and went upstairs together as a group. They dispersed when they got to the suite. JT went to change so he could go with Raphaela to meet the stablemaster. And Violet disappeared into her room with plans for a nap.

Ro was a little jealous of that, but thankful that Posey had stepped up all the same. They settled in the big sitting room. Gabriel took a seat near the door that enabled him to keep an eye on the entrance without being so close as to be intrusive.

Not that Ro would ever think that about him. She'd grown so accustomed to him being nearby that when he wasn't, she felt his absence.

Posey had her pad of paper and pen at the ready. Both looked like they'd come from the mortal realm, but Ro didn't mind that. Nice stationery was nice stationery.

"Thank you for doing this, Posey."

"It's always good to be useful," she said.

Ro nodded. "I agree with that. I hope working as my personal secretary doesn't ruin your vacation. I'm sure there will still be plenty of time to read."

"I like reading well enough," Posey said. "But that's not the only reason I wanted to come." She smiled. "I kind of want to see if my great-great-grandmother's stories are true about Lady Cynzia's diaries being hidden in the libraries here at Willow Hall. I'm sure I'm not the only one."

Ro frowned. "Who's Lady Cynzia?"

"Only one of the most notorious women in the annals of Grym fae history," Posey said. "And her diary that tells all is supposedly hidden in one of the libraries here."

Ro shook her head. "I've never heard of her but there's a lot I haven't heard of." She looked over at Gabriel. "Do you know about Lady Cynzia?"

He nodded. "I'm familiar with the name. She was supposedly the woman who facilitated the ancient black magic ritual that created the curse Malveaux sits under. Among other things."

"The black magic ritual that one of the twin rulers underwent in an attempt to gain control of both kingdoms," Ro said. "I remember that. Uldamar told me about it." She looked at Posey again. "How do you know her diary is here?"

Posey shrugged one shoulder. "It's just always been something we've talked about in my family. My great-great-grandmother, who was half Grym, was a cook here at Willow Hall ages ago. She was the one who passed the stories down."

Ro's love for old and secret things bubbled up inside her. "What's supposed to be in this diary?"

"All kinds of magic," Posey said. "The sorts of things that have been lost over time. Not all of it good, mind you. Lady Cynzia wasn't exactly a paragon of virtue."

Gabriel snorted. "Helping one brother try to overthrow another brother through the use of black magic is a pretty big clue to that. She was a black magic witch of the highest order."

Ro was definitely intrigued. "Could her diary hold the key to removing Malveaux's curse?"

"Maybe," Posey said. "Anything's possible."

Ro's mind went wild with what that could mean toward bringing about peace. "We have to find that book."

# Chapter Thirteen

"Your highness," Gabriel started. "I don't think you understand what you're asking. There are many libraries in Willow Hall. Countless bookshelves. And this is just a rumor. A story. There's no way of knowing if it's even true."

"I get that," Ro said. "But what if it is? What if the book is here and could make everything right in Malveaux again? Don't you think that would go a long way toward reuniting the two kingdoms?"

"It would, yes. But I don't think we can put any great stock in actually locating the diary. There are a lot of myths and legends that surround Lady Cynzia. She was just that kind of figure in our history. Powerful. Beautiful. Corrupt."

"Sometimes, myths and legends begin in truth," Ro said. "I've seen it more than once when I was working in the museum."

Posey shifted position on the couch. "Which is just as much reason for her diary to be real as for it not to be."

"Maybe that's part of why Queen Anyka's coming," Ro said. "Maybe she knows about the diary, too."

Gabriel's gaze turned dark. "If she's coming to find it, it's probably to utilize whatever black magic is in there."

He got up and walked over, looking at Posey. "How strongly do you believe this diary exists and that it's here?"

"My grandmother always talked about the stories her grandmother had told her as if they were the truth." Posey shook her head. "We're honest women, Professor. We aren't tellers of tales. It's not good to be in my line of work and be known as a liar. No one will believe your products can do as you say if you aren't a purveyor of truth yourself."

"Fair point," Gabriel said. He exhaled before looking at Ro. "This presents a new problem. If that book is here and contains the kind of magic I think it does, we cannot let Anyka or anyone working for her get their hands on it. It could mean the end of Summerton."

"You think it's that serious?"

"I think...we should speak with Uldamar about this. He's the Professor of Magic. It's his job to know about these kinds of things."

"Good idea," Ro said. "Let's get him in here. Do you know which room he's in?"

Gabriel moved to the bell rope near the door and pulled it. "We can find out soon enough."

It took less than ten minutes to get Uldamar into the sitting room with them. He'd changed since lunch and was now wearing flowing robes and soft slippers. She wondered if he'd been napping, too. His outfit looked very comfy.

Once he'd taken a seat, Ro launched into the reason he was there. "What do you know about Lady Cynzia?"

"Many things." Uldamar's brow furrowed. "Why are you asking about her?"

"Because according to a story that's been passed down through Posey's family, Lady Cynzia's diary is hidden in one of the Willow Hall libraries."

Uldamar didn't react at first. He glanced at Posey before letting out a sigh and bringing his attention back to Ro. "Are you asking me to help you find it?"

"Does that mean it's true? The diary is here?"

Uldamar seemed to choose his words carefully. "I don't know if 'diary' is the right word. It's rumored to be more of a grimoire. Her personal spell book."

"But it's true?"

"There is a real possibility it exists. I've heard rumors it's here. I've also heard it's locked away in the depths of the Malveauxian vaults. But if anyone in Malveaux could lay their hands on it, they would have nullified the curse years ago. Much more likely they have no clue where it is, either. Or that it's been lost to time."

"But if it were here?"

His eyes narrowed. "If it were here and Queen Anyka were to get her hands on it...maybe she'd use it for good. But she might also use it to claim Summerton for her own once and for all."

Ro collapsed back against the cushions. "So we could have a situation on our hands."

"Perhaps," Uldamar said. "But you're talking about something that's been missing for centuries. The chances of us finding it are small, your highness."

Posey made a little noise and pursed her lips.

"What haven't you told us," Ro asked.

"It wasn't just stories that were passed down," Posey answered. "There was a little poem my great-great-grandmother used to recite. We all learned it. My sister and I used to jump rope to it."

"Go on," Ro said. "If you remember it."

"Sure I do," Posey said. "Lamp lights flicker, pages fall. Darkness heeds the witch's call. One for the queen, fallen in a heap; one for the king, taking a leap; one for the heir and the people weep.

"Close the books, put out the lights, hide the words in plain sight. Blue in mourning, red in sleep, shadows stretch and move and creep...oh, bother. What comes after move and creep?" Posey blinked a few times and shook her head. "I have it written down somewhere."

"Keeping quiet their secret so deep," Uldamar finished.

"That's it." Posey nodded.

"That's a cheery little ditty," Ro said. "Do either of you know what any of that means?"

"Some of it," Uldamar said. "Lady Cynzia was rumored to have killed off an entire royal family at some point in her history. The rest I don't know."

"I think it's all clues," Posey said. "Lamp lights flicker, pages fall. That's obviously a library."

Gabriel snorted. "That could be a lot of things. It could be any place. Any room with a lamp and book qualifies."

"But it says pages and books," Posey argued. "To me that means more than one book. So a library."

"Could be," Ro said. But she really wasn't sure. "This doesn't seem like much to go on." She looked at Uldamar.

"Is there any way to scan the books in the libraries and see if any of them have magic in them? Or attached to them in some way?"

"That's not going to turn out the way you think, my lady." Uldamar clasped his hands, then spread them out, palms up. "But maybe it would be better to show you rather than try to explain."

"Show me what?"

"Good idea," Gabriel said.

"What is?" Ro asked.

Uldamar stood. "Come, your majesty," he said. "It's time for you to see one of Willow Hall's libraries."

She didn't really know why they couldn't just tell her what this was all about, but if she'd learned anything about the fae, it was that they loved a little drama. Clearly this was a show-don't-tell situation.

"Okay." She got to her feet.

"Which one?" Posey asked.

"Any one will do," Uldamar said. "Whichever one we come to first. I believe that might be Non-Fiction. Or General Literature. Either one is a good enough place to start. But we must agree to tell no one why we're there. If word of this diary spreads—"

"Agreed," Gabriel said. "We'll have a free-for-all on our hands."

"Not a word," Ro said.

"Not a word," Posey repeated.

"I need to tell Vincent he's on duty," Gabriel said as they went out into the hall. He slipped into one of the guest rooms across the way and came back out trailing the other guard. "We can go now. Vincent will keep an eye on your aunt."

"Thank you," Ro said. She was so curious about what they were going to show her in the library that she was almost itchy.

They went downstairs using the portal, then down the long hall past the dining hall and kept going until they came to a set of double doors. Gabriel opened one a few inches and looked in. "This'll do."

He held the door for her, and Ro went in. Posey and Uldamar followed.

The room beyond was, indeed, a library. A very big library with books all the way to the tall ceilings. Rolling ladders gave access to the heights. Tall windows fitted with insets of stained glass let in light, but sprinkled prisms of color across the space, too.

In the corners of the room were small booths with glass doors. The booths looked like they might hold three people max. No one was in any of them, but then it seemed they were alone in the library.

Here and there were glass display cases with either books or objects in them. She took a better look at the one closest to them. The little note card inside announced that the quill pen on display had once belonged to Fleur Littlefeather and had been used to write her masterpiece, *Songs of Quiet*.

Ro made a mental note to find that book and read it.

An older man in a robe not that different from Uldamar's approached them. Ro wasn't sure where he'd come from. He stopped a few feet away and bowed. "Good afternoon, your majesty. Welcome to the General Literature Library."

"Thank you."

He put a hand flat on his stomach. "I'm Kernon Bookbinder, Willow Hall's Master Librarian. Anything you need, I can find."

She wondered if that included a black magic diary. "Thank you. My friends really just wanted to show me the library."

"Look as long as you like. That's what the books are here for." He drifted back to wherever he'd come from, leaving them alone.

"This is a great library," Ro said. "What exactly did you want me to see? And don't you think we could just ask him about the book?"

Uldamar shook his head. "The staff pride themselves on showing no bias toward any particular ruler, but I think you know fae nature better than that by now. Not saying I think he would side with Anyka, but I still believe it's best if we keep this to ourselves."

She understood Uldamar's point, but if the Master Librarian didn't know about this book, then what hope did they have? "I'm all right with that for now. But I still think he might be a great resource. Even if he is biased, which could be toward the Radiant side, you know."

"I know, your highness. But I worry about news of this spreading."

"Understood. And so do I."

He rubbed his hands gently together. "Now. As to what I wanted you to see. That would be the reason I can't simply conjure up a spell to find a book that's been touched by magic or contains magic or has magic within its pages."

He pulled his hands apart and strings of green light stretched between them. "Alight every book that carries the presence of magic." Then he held his palms in front of him and blew across them, sending little threads of green light into the air like dandelion fluff drifting on a breeze.

The threads danced in the air currents, floating and gliding along without any discernable purpose. Until they reached the nearest bookshelf. Then the threads untwisted, making more and more of themselves. Each one attached itself to a book like a little stem of supernatural fungus, glowing and pulsing with magical light.

Book after book after book gained a thread. They spread through the library in a blaze of cool green fire, until Ro was surrounded. She turned slowly, unable to spot a single spine that didn't have a strand of magic on it. "All of these books have been touched by magic? How is that possible?"

Uldamar wiped his hands through the air and the green threads winked out and disappeared. "Because we are fae. And the fae are magic. More than that, magic is how the books are filed and accessed."

"Meaning?"

Posey stepped up. She held her hands out, palms flat and open. "I call for a book about gardening in the Victorian era."

Ro watched Posey's hands, but nothing happened. Then movement caught her eye and she realized there was a book drifting toward them from one side of the library. It landed on Posey's palms. The title read *A Year In The Victorian Garden*.

Ro looked at Uldamar. "Can anyone do that?"

He nodded. "They should be able to. The books are cataloged with the most accessible magic available. The spells are designed to work with whatever magic the user has. Try it."

Ro held her hands out like Posey had. "I call for a book about fae tapestries."

Twenty seconds later, a book came to rest in her hands. "*The New School of Tapestries*," Ro read off the cover. "That's amazing."

She sighed. "But it is definitely going to make the search harder."

# Chapter Fourteen

If it weren't for everyone else who was going to Willow Hall, Anyka might have already left. But getting Beatryce to leave now would mean rushing her, something that rarely went well. And Bea wouldn't want to travel at night. Anyka knew that without asking.

Unfortunately, there was nothing left for Anyka to do. Everything she could possibly need had been packed. She'd sent out a few letters so that her correspondence was caught up, including the one to the trolls letting them know she would be in residence at Willow Hall until further notice.

She'd even been to see the kitchen and housekeeping staff to let them know she expected them to maintain standards during her absence.

They would still slack off, she knew that, but it couldn't hurt to remind them of their duties.

She stood in her quarters, looking out at the village of Dearth below and thought about taking a long, hot soak before the evening meal. Dinner would be in the dining room again with Beatryce and Ishmyel, and Nazyr would be joining them. The Minister of Magic had been rather occupied lately and Anyka wasn't sure what he'd been up to. This would be his chance to explain himself.

She was mostly curious because whatever he'd been spending his time on wasn't something she'd given him to do. He was certainly allowed to do his own things, but he answered to her. She wanted an accounting of his time. Tonight she also wanted to talk about what she expected from him on this trip.

As appealing as a bath was, if she took one now, it would seem silly to take another after dinner. Maybe she'd walk in the garden instead. It was only just coming to life this time of year. "Galwyn, would you like to go to the garden with me?"

He squawked at her and fluttered his wings. Of course he'd want to go to the garden. Any chance to catch a snack.

She changed into trim black pants tucked into black boots, added a blood-red blouse and her black fitted jacket that hung to her knees in a soft swirl of fabric. She twisted her hair up and secured it with two pointed sticks. Then she reached out her arm to Galwyn.

He came to rest on her shoulder. She stroked his back. "Pretty boy. Let's go see what's come to life out there, shall we?"

She took the main steps. The castle was so quiet this time of day. Well, most times of most days it was quiet. She didn't like noise and the staff knew that. But there was almost an eerie stillness to the place at times, and that she didn't like, either. She found it unsettling.

On more than one occasion she'd thought she heard familiar voices whispering to her. Voices long gone.

She picked up her pace, going through the main ballroom and using those doors to access the gardens. Once upon a time, before the curse, she imagined they'd been bright and beautiful, overflowing with color.

That wasn't exactly the case now. The gardens still had some color, but it was more subdued. Most of what grew here did so because it was hardy enough to survive the dreary days and inclement weather. There were the greenhouses, but those didn't feel real to her and so she tended to stay away from them.

The greenhouses felt like exactly what they were. Artificial environments. Yes, they served their purpose, providing fruits and vegetables for her table and brilliant flowers to adorn the castle's rooms, and she was grateful for that, but it wasn't enough to endear them to her any further.

It didn't help that they reminded her of her mother. And what Malveaux no longer was.

She left the castle behind and crossed the yard for the pair of sculpted topiaries that marked the entrance to the formal garden, Anyka's favorite place to walk. Some years ago, she'd had the original dragonfly topiaries replaced with ravens in a tribute to her very first pet raven, Trylla.

Her father had raised the intelligent birds, so she'd always been around them, but until his death, she'd never kept one for herself.

After losing him, she'd hired a ravenmaster from Dearth to care for her father's birds. Galwyn was a descendant of those birds, and the great-grandson of Trylla. Understandably, he was dear to Anyka for many reasons.

He cackled softly as they walked past the topiary ravens and into the garden. A tall hedge of boxwoods surrounded the first section, hiding it from view. She wandered through, studying the ground in the various beds. Here and there, green shoots were poking through, some taller than others. Some already sporting leaves.

"By the time we get back from Willow Hall, this place will look very different."

The next section of garden had some color by way of early flowers. Small purple crocus and snow-white anther drops, ivory winter lilies with their white and green lace-variegated leaves. The lilies really stood out against the deep crimson and evergreen of the blood ivy climbing the trunks of the pines behind the bed.

Galwyn shifted back and forth on his claws, doing the little dance that meant he was excited. She understood why, too, because she could hear the low thrum of the thin waterfall at the far end of the garden. That's where they were headed. To sit on the bench there and just watch the water. There were electric arakoo in the water, as well, a kind of large black carp capable of giving small shocks.

Galwyn would probably take a bath in the shallows, maybe look for tadpoles or minnows. She'd had a large flat rock put near the shore just for him to stand on. He'd be safe from the fish there, because it wasn't deep enough for them to reach him.

She walked on, starting to feel a slight chill as daylight dimmed. All around her, the things that made their own light began to take on a subtle glow. The phosphorescent moss on some of the trees, the tiny starflowers that bloomed on the fast-growing vines used as ground cover, even some of the lichen on the rocks.

She made her way to the bench, then lifted Galwyn off her shoulder. "Go on. I know you want to get in the water."

He hopped down to the grass, digging with his beak. After two tries, he came up with a wriggling black beetle that disappeared down his throat. Then he went to the water's edge and stepped into the shallowest part, dipping his beak in, then raising it toward the sky to drink. From there, he hopped onto his flat rock and stood with the water just covering his feet.

In the depths of the large pond, she could see subtle shapes drifting by. Now and then, a tiny spark would crackle over one of the arakoo, outlining the fish temporarily.

She leaned against the back of the bench and watched Galwyn splash. "It's probably time we found you a mate." Ravens mated for life. Galwyn deserved to find a partner and raise a family. One of his children would be her next companion eventually.

The thought of that companionship brought to mind Sebastyan, Anyka's late husband. What a strong, brave man he'd been. Captain of the royal guard. He'd saved her life by knocking the poisoned cup of wine out of her hands just as she was about to drink. What would he think of her life now? Would he wonder why he'd saved her if this was where she was? Alone?

Yes, she had Beatryce, but eventually her daughter would marry. Something else that ought to happen soon.

But as for Anyka...there was no man she'd ever trust the way she'd trusted Sebastyan. He'd proven himself that terrible day and that wasn't something that could be repeated. Nor should it be. Ever.

Darkness continued to fall, and the garden's soft glow increased. Maybe she should take Wyett as her consort. It was a decision she'd talked herself out of as many times as she'd had the idea.

It always came down to Wyett being too valuable as her valet. She trusted him almost as much as she'd trusted Sebastyan. But she needed Wyett more as her right hand than she needed him in her bed. Any man could fill that spot. No one else could take Wyett's place.

But the truth was, she was lonely. The idea of having a man to keep her company felt like a dream that would never come true. Who would that man be? Someone from Dearth? One of her guards? There was no good answer.

Mostly because the perfect man didn't exist. She was destined to be lonely. She'd had offers of marriage. Men from distant kingdoms, sent to her as a way of making a treaty. The goblin king had sent his brother, a bloodthirsty hooligan who'd tried to bed her before dinner had ended.

She'd thought about sending back the cretin's head as an example, but refrained, not wanting to go to war with the goblins just because Davunk couldn't keep his roaming hands to himself.

The hill people, or wyverns, might be an option. One of their warriors. They were big, silent types. But the wyverns rarely mixed with outsiders and had never entered into a treaty with anyone. They kept to themselves. So much so that in another hundred years, they might not even exist anymore.

Perhaps she'd send them a letter, just to see if they were interested in sending a few young men to serve in the royal guard. Anything was possible.

The mountain elves weren't an option. They had no love for the Grym, despite the many attempts Anyka had made to reach out to them.

Galwyn caught a minnow and gobbled it down. The light was nearly gone now. At least the clouds would part to give them a glimpse of the moon and let some stars shine through. They almost always did.

"We should get back for dinner," Anyka said. She held out her arm to Galwyn.

He came out of the water, hopping a little and shaking his feathers, then flew back to her shoulder. He leaned his head against hers.

She smiled. He was damp but she didn't care. "There's my boy. Maybe you're the only man I need, hmm?"

She went back inside, back to her quarters, and fed Galwyn some dried fish. While he ate, she changed into a simple gown of burgundy silk with matching slippers and a long black duster in beaded black organza. She left her hair up but changed out the simple wooden sticks for decorative black enamel ones tasseled with raven feathers and faceted garnet beads.

She leaned near Galwyn's perch. He sidestepped his way onto her shoulder. Together, they went down to dinner.

Nazyr, Beatryce, and Ishmyel were all just taking their seats. Ishmyel was helping Beatryce with her chair. They stopped and stood as she entered.

Nazyr bowed. "Your highness. So good to see you. You look as beautiful as ever."

She gave him a tight smile in return. If he thought cheap words were going to get him back in her good graces, he was a fool. A very handsome fool but there was no way he would ever warm her bed.

She was lonely, not desperate.

"I'm pleased you could join us this evening, Nazyr. I expect you have much to say."

His brows rose and his lips pursed in amusement. "I'm sure you're referencing my recent absence. For that, I apologize, but I'm sure you'll forgive me when I tell you what I've been working on."

"Well, then, let me take my chair. I'm eager to hear this news."

He pulled her chair out for her. She settled in, Galwyn took his usual perch on the back, and she lifted her hand to let the footmen know they could begin service.

Tonight's soup was pumpkin, one of her favorites. That gave her hope for the rest of the meal. She sipped her wine and waited for Nazyr to explain himself. "Go on then. What have you been working on?"

"When I heard the new queen was reopening Willow Hall, I must admit I was thrilled at the news. I've been trying to find a way to spend some time there for a few years."

"As I'm aware." It was true. He asked her at least once a year if she'd consider going. She'd turned him down every time, mostly because it wasn't as simple as just visiting.

If she went, those in Summerton would either see it as an act of aggression, since they had no ruler to attend, or as an attempt to meet them halfway in certain diplomatic areas. Which she had no intention of doing.

Queen Sparrow deciding to reopen the Summer Palace had basically forced Anyka's hand. Another reason to dislike the woman more than she already did.

Beatryce frowned. "I didn't know that." She looked at Anyka. "Why didn't we go then? We could have had a nice little visit."

"And how do you think the pompous professors of Summerton would have responded to me going to Willow Hall?"

Ishmyel nodded. "Your mother's right, Bea. It would have created...issues, at the very least."

Beatryce seemed satisfied with that, making Anyka grateful for her uncle's support. "Well," Beatryce said. "I'm glad we can go now."

"So am I," Nazyr said. "You see, there's something very precious at Willow Hall. Something more valuable than you can imagine. Something hidden away in that vast palace that might change life in Malveaux as we know it."

Anyka frowned at him. Nazyr was known for making grandiose statements sometimes. She had no doubt this was another of those. "What might that precious, valuable, life-changing thing be?"

Nazyr smiled. "The grimoire of Lady Cynzia."

# Chapter Fifteen

As the sun sank lower, the colors coming through the library's stained-glass windows didn't so much dull as they changed, taking on a curious glow.

"What's going on there?" Ro asked, indicating the windows.

"It's Moonfire Falls," Gabriel said. "Go look out the window, my lady. You'll see."

Ro walked over. The waterfall was aglow from top to bottom with pale blue light. Her jaw dropped. "What am I even looking at? How is that possible?"

"Bioluminescent algae that lives in the water. It's only activated by vigorous movement, so the churning of the water over the falls brings it to life," Gabriel said. "Quite a show, isn't it?"

"It's one of the most beautiful things I've ever seen."

Posey had joined her at the window. She gasped when she saw the falls. "I have to show this to Violet."

"Definitely," Ro said. This world never ceased to amaze her. She hoped that remained true for many years to come.

Kernon reappeared, along with a few others, and they lit the chandeliers in the library with spells.

"Those aren't candles or gas lamps," she said. "It's all

magic?" A small bedside lamp was one thing, but several large chandeliers seemed like a much bigger deal. But then, Ro still had a lot to learn about fac magic.

"That's right, your majesty," Uldamar said. "They're magic lights and the magic will last until dawn. The libraries are open constantly that way."

"Interesting. I like that." She glanced at him. "But I suppose we should get back to the diary. If we can request any book come to us, why can't we ask for Lady Cynzia's diary?"

"If it was truly hidden, then it won't have been catalogued," Uldamar explained.

"No, of course not." Ro shook her head. "I should have realized that."

"That would have made things a lot easier, though," Gabriel said.

"Wouldn't it have?" Ro stared at all the books around them. "So how are we going to find this thing? Split up and look at each book? That's going to make it pretty obvious that we're searching for something."

Gabriel nodded. "It will. And I'm not sure it'll do any good anyway. We don't know if the diary is even in this library."

"You keep saying 'libraries,' plural," Ro said. "How many are there?"

Gabriel shrugged and looked at Uldamar.

He shook his head. "I confess, I'm not sure myself. Perhaps we could ask the Master Librarian?"

Ro cleared her throat softly and called out for the man. "Kernon? Are you around?"

He appeared from between two tall shelving units. "Yes, your majesty? How may I be of service?"

"We were wondering something. How many libraries are there in Willow Hall?"

"There are nine in total."

"Nine?" Ro almost laughed. "Wow, that's a lot. Are they all this big?"

"No, my lady. The Children's Library is quite large, as is the History Library, but the Horror Library is the smallest. The others are not this large, but still well stocked, I assure you."

"What are the other libraries?"

"They're divided by genres so that guests can more easily find their favorite kind of books. To that end, there are libraries for science fiction, romance, mysteries and thrillers, non-fiction, and magic."

At the last word, little bells went off in Ro's head. That had to be it. "Where is the Magic Library?"

"They're all located off this corridor, which is known as the Hall of Libraries. The Magic Library has green doors. It's the fifth one down. I would be happy to escort you, if you'd like, but I'm sure you could find it."

"No, that's all right. It sounds easy enough to get to. Thank you for your help. I'll be seeing you again."

He smiled and gave another bow. "I look forward to it, my lady."

Without waiting for the others, she went back into the hall. They followed her out. She looked at them. "That has to be it, don't you think?"

"It's a little obvious," Gabriel said.

"Which is why it would be the perfect hiding place. No one would think it would be in there *because* it's so obvious."

Posey laughed. "That's actually sort of clever. I say we at least go have a look."

Uldamar nodded. "I would very much like to see the Magic Library. I will gladly join you."

Gabriel just looked at Ro. "I go where you go."

"Then we're off to the Magic Library."

It was as easy to find as Kernon had told them it would be. The green double doors trimmed in burnished gold showed some signs of wear near the handles. A popular location, she thought. And why wouldn't it be? If everyone in this realm had magic, then the subject would interest everyone.

Gabriel opened the door, and they all went in.

The space was smaller than the General Literature Library but not by much. The ceilings were just as tall and the shelves just as packed. Magic chandeliers were glowing in here, too, lighting the room with a soft warm glow that was plenty to see by.

The bioluminescence coming off the waterfall was evident in how the stained glass windows were lit up.

There were more conversation chambers in the corners, just like there were items in glass display cases that she assumed must have magical significance. One appeared to be a wand, something she hoped to have a better look at later. But just like in the first library, there were books in some of the cases. No doubt more first editions or books signed by important authors.

She loved how the displays mixed historical and important objects along with books of cultural significance. It was a winning concept and she wondered why more libraries didn't do the same.

Ro glanced at a few of the cases, then looked around. As best she could tell, they were alone. "Uldamar, what if you cast a spell to look for a book that didn't belong? Or a book that wasn't placed here by a librarian?"

He nodded. "Yes, I see what you mean. Try to find it by means of it being an outlier. It might work. Provided the universe thinks a book about magic doesn't belong in a magic library. And that it wasn't put here by a librarian."

She sighed. "Okay, maybe not the best examples but something along those lines."

"Or," Gabriel said. "You could just cast a spell to look for a book by Lady Cynzia, could you not?"

"I could," Uldamar said. "But I believe whoever hid it would have crafted some kind of concealment spell, making that aspect of the book moot." He held up a finger. "Worth trying, though. Worth trying."

He rubbed his hands together as he'd done before, this time pulling them apart to reveal a luminous dragonfly. "Find me a book that contains the words of Lady Cynzia."

The dragonfly, a purely magical creature comprised of delicate lines of pale blue light, took flight. It circled twice overhead, slow, lazy loops that nearly skimmed the ceiling. On its third time around, it swooped lower and began darting in and out of the bookshelves.

On the fourth pass, it landed on a book. Then it split in two, becoming a second dragonfly, and the new one took off to continue flying around. Moments later, that dragonfly landed on a book, and again split off another version of itself, which kept on flying.

"What does that mean?" Ro asked.

Gabriel answered before Uldamar. "I'm guessing it found more than one book with Lady Cynzia's words in it."

Uldamar nodded. "I wondered if that might happen."

Posey shrugged. "We should at least have a look at those books, don't you think?"

"I do," Ro said. She headed for one of the rolling ladders.

"Your majesty," Gabriel called out. "Please, let me."

"I'm not going to fall off the ladder."

"No, you're not. Not while I'm on duty." With a little smirk, he went ahead of her, climbed the ladder, brought the first book down, and handed it to her. "Be right back with the second one."

"There are two more now," Posey called out. She pointed. "Look."

Ro lifted her gaze to see the new books that had been selected. "I really didn't expect that."

"I did," Posey said. "Regardless of what anyone thinks of Lady Cynzia, she was a very talented woman. Sadly, she used those talents for some terrible things, but it doesn't surprise me that she's still being referenced."

"Then you don't think any of those books are actually her diary?"

Posey shook her head. "I don't think it's going to be found as easily as casting a spell. Lady Cynzia would have seen to that herself."

"I'm afraid she's right," Uldamar said.

"Well, that kind of sucks," Ro muttered. She opened the book Gabriel had given her and shook her head. "I don't even know what I'm looking for." She handed it to Posey. "You probably do, though."

Posey paged through it. Gabriel returned with the second book and held it out to Ro. She shook her head. "Give it to Uldamar."

While Gabriel continued to get the books the dragonflies had selected, Ro wandered over to the windows. Just like in the first library, the stained glass didn't make up every single panel of glass. Those in the center had been left clear to allow a good bit of natural light in.

In the first library, there had been stacks of books depicted in the stained glass. The carefully crafted panels here showed little showers of sparks. The kind of thing that might accompany a magic trick. Or fae magic being done.

It made her curious to see the other libraries and what the glass in those spaces held.

She looked out the window, glancing at the falls again. She hadn't seen much of the grounds around Willow Hall except for what she'd seen on their way here. The falls provided some light outside, but there were other soft spots of luminescence around the landscape that told her Willow Hall had some of the same kinds of plants the royal gardens did.

Or maybe those sorts of glowing plants were just a standard fae thing. Something else she needed to learn more about.

"My lady?"

She turned to see Gabriel behind her. "Find anything?"

"No. I'm sorry."

She sighed. "Do you think this was all a wild goose chase?"

His eyes narrowed. "Why would I chase wild geese? I don't follow."

She laughed softly. "It's an expression. It just means a waste of time. A worthless endeavor. That sort of thing."

"Nothing that keeps you and the kingdom safe is a wild goose."

She was still disappointed. "Thanks."

"There are seven more libraries to search." He looked around. "Even this one could still be gone through with much more precision."

"Sure. But what are our chances of actually finding this book?"

"I don't know. Seems worth an attempt, though. If it really contains such powerful magic."

She nodded. "I agree. I just wish we had more to go on."

"So do I. I know we've agreed not to tell anyone else about this, but it might be worth bringing Professor Cloudtree in."

"The Professor of History." She liked Spencer Cloudtree and his wife, Althea. They were nice people. "You think he'd know something about Lady Cynzia that might help us?"

"It couldn't hurt to speak to him."

"That's a fantastic idea. Thank you."

Gabriel smiled. "Happy to help."

"Any further news on when Anyka might be arriving?"

"Nothing yet. I'm sure Trence will let us know as soon as he finds out."

"I hope so," Ro said. "I really don't want to be caught off guard."

"We'll do our best to make sure that doesn't happen."

"How long before dinner?"

"I believe we have two hours."

"All right. Are we going to look at the rest of the libraries?"

"We will do whatever you want."

She glanced past him to where Posey and Uldamar were chatting. "I don't want to wear anyone out."

He smiled. "You won't. They both seem eager to keep looking."

"Then let's get moving. Where to next?"

"Horror is to the right, Science Fiction is to the left."

"I say go right until we reach the last one, then we'll come back and do the rest."

As a group, they moved on through the rest of the libraries and had the same luck in each one. They found nothing.

Ro was feeling a little defeated by the time they were done. "We tried the obvious. Now we're going to have to try harder. Thanks to Gabriel's suggestion, I'm going to speak to Professor Cloudtree and see what else he can tell me about Lady Cynzia. If any of you have any other ideas that might bring us some clues, please come forward with them."

Posey gave Ro a comforting smile. "If the book was easy to find, it would have been found a long time ago. We'll figure it out."

"I hope so," Ro said. "I have no idea when Anyka will arrive, but once she does, it's going to make our search a whole lot harder."

# Chapter Sixteen

Ro was happy to discover dinner was a much more robust affair than lunch had been. Maybe that had always been the plan, or maybe Trence had spoken to the kitchen staff, but things were looking up. After a nice bowl of fish chowder, they were served roasted game hens with an orange glaze, roasted vegetables, and whipped potatoes with butter and gravy along with pumpkin biscuits and honey.

Uldamar had arranged for Professor Cloudtree and his wife to sit at the royal table, which had been moved slightly to accommodate the addition of the second royal table previously at the other end of the room.

She said nothing about the diary, however, because there were other people at the table, and she wanted to keep the diary's possible existence quiet. Instead, she waited until after dessert, a lovely berry crisp served with vanilla custard, to ask the professor and his wife up to the royal quarters.

Before leaving the dining room, she stopped a footman and requested coffee, tea, spiced cocoa, and a plate of cookies to be sent to the royal suite. She didn't know how long they'd be talking but she wanted to be prepared.

She'd already given JT and Violet the short but thorough update on Lady Cynzia's diary. They were full of ideas instantly, and she could tell they'd been about bursting at dinner not being able to talk about it.

Now, as they all took seats in the large sitting room, there were a lot of furtive looks and sideways glances.

At Ro's request, Gabriel, Raphaela, and Vincent were present, too. Ro felt it was important that they be up to speed on the diary situation, since the three people they'd be guarding would be searching for it. That would enable them to work as teams, something that should make the hunt easier.

Spencer and Althea Cloudtree showed up about fifteen minutes after Ro and her crew had returned. The refreshments had been delivered and were on the side table where anyone could help themselves. Ro stood as they came in. "Thank you for coming."

Spencer nodded. "Thank you for inviting us. I'm sorry for the delay, your majesty. Several people stopped me to chat. I got away as quickly and politely as I could."

"No problem," Ro said. "Please, help yourself to something to drink, if you'd like, then take a seat."

He and his wife each made a cup of tea for themselves, then came over and joined the group.

Ro had already gotten a cup of spiced cocoa, which she held on her lap. "I'm sure you're wondering why I've asked you here. I must first say that this conversation is to be kept absolutely confidential. Do you both understand?"

They nodded and said yes.

"Good. Now that that's out of the way, we can get into it. What do you know about Lady Cynzia?"

Spencer's brow furrowed and he jerked back slightly. "She's a dark figure in our history, my lady."

"I've been made aware. What else can you tell me about her? I thought you, of anyone here, might know something more than just rumors and conjecture."

He sipped his tea, then set the cup on the table. "There *are* certainly a lot of rumors about her. That's generally what happens to people like her as time marches on. Or they're completely forgotten. But Cynzia was too evil to disappear completely."

"Why do you say evil?" Ro wanted to hear his account for herself.

"She was what most would consider a witch. A very powerful one. And especially skilled in the kind of magic most fae shun. Dark magic. The black arts. Blood spells and death curses. She was the originator of the curse that befell Malveaux."

"So I've heard."

Spencer cleared his throat and seemed to consider his next words before speaking. "No one can be certain if the curse on Malveaux was intentional or just a side-effect of the spell she was attempting to cast, but the power of that curse is unquestionable. You can see its effects by just looking across the grounds of Willow Hall to the Malveauxian border. That kingdom is a dark, dreary place. The light went out of it the day Ramus Moorehill traded his soul in an attempt to gain the power he thought necessary to overthrow his brother."

Ro leaned forward. "That brother was sitting on the Radiant throne, right?"

Spencer nodded. "Arnus Moorehill was king of Summerton. The brothers were twins, as I suspect you know."

"I do. Uldamar told me about them. So Lady Cynzia was behind the magic that basically destroyed everything."

"She was," Spencer confirmed. "She was Ramus's Minister of Magic and most likely his consort."

"So she had a dog in the fight," Ro said more to herself than anyone else. Still, Uldamar and Spencer both gave her curious looks. "What I mean is that she had motive to want to help him. She would have wanted him to succeed."

Uldamar ate one of the cookies he'd taken. "She did, very much so. If he'd become the ruler of both kingdoms, her power would have increased as well. Which is why I don't think the outcome of her magic was intentional."

"What do you think happened, then?" Ro asked. "You know more about magic than the rest of us. What's your educated guess?"

Uldamar's eyes narrowed. "She was dealing in black magic. It is never predictable. What happened was that the spell was either too much for her to control or she got some small piece of it wrong, or simply that the darkness she brought forth took what it wanted and returned the same. Her first mistake was being foolish enough to believe she could control something like that."

Made sense to Ro. "Do you think the diary might really hold the key to undoing it all?"

"What diary is that?" Spencer asked.

Ro answered him. "Allegedly, Lady Cynzia's diary."

He paled. "I've heard rumors. Is it real, then?"

"That's what we're trying to determine," Uldamar said. "And why you were asked here. Right now, rumors and legends are all we have."

Posey nodded. "It's been considered true in my family for a long time."

Ro glanced at her, then back at Spencer. "Posey is the one who brought the diary to our attention. Her great-great-grandmother worked here at Willow Hall and always told her family the diary was hidden in one of the libraries here."

"If that's true…" Spencer glanced at his wife.

Althea shook her head. "It's not good. Not if Queen Anyka is really coming here."

"That's what we've been told. I guess we won't know for sure until she actually arrives," JT said.

Spencer moved toward the edge of his seat, like he might get up. "She shouldn't be allowed to have that book. We need to find it."

Posey nodded. "We've tried. We did a preliminary scan of all nine libraries. Uldamar used his magic. We found nothing."

"Unfortunately," Ro said. "But we have a rhyme that's been passed down in Posey's family. One of you might have heard it as well. It might be a clue, it might not be. We really don't have a lot to go on."

Spencer nodded. "I know the rhyme you speak of. Or at least I think I do. Maybe just a version of it."

"Posey?" Ro looked at her. "Can you recite it again? And maybe we should have you write out a few copies, too. For the sake of being able to study it."

"Sure." She got out her pen and paper and rested them in her lap. "Lamp lights flicker, pages fall, darkness heeds the witch's call. One for the queen, fallen in a heap; one for the king, taking a leap; one for the heir and the people weep. Close the books, put out the light, hide the words in plain sight. Blue in mourning, red in sleep, shadows stretch and move and creep, keeping quiet their secret so deep."

When she finished, she started writing.

"That sounds like the version I've read." Spencer sighed. "If this diary is real and if it is here, we must do everything in our power to keep Queen Anyka from laying her hands on it."

"That's our intention," Gabriel said.

Ro nodded. "It definitely is. As far as the poem goes, do you have any ideas about what it could mean?"

"The queen, king, and heir reference a royal family she allegedly killed off. The queen was poisoned, the king was spelled to believe he could fly and, as a result, he jumped from one of the castle's highest towers, and their son, the heir, was also poisoned."

"Were these Grym or Radiant royals?"

"Grym," Spencer replied. "She made way for the one who'd employed her, a distant relative of that family and the one who was next in line for the throne."

"And did that person get the throne?"

"They did," Spencer said. "They didn't last long, though. A year, I believe."

"Wow."

"The history of Grym royalty is much more turbulent

than that of the Radiant."

"Apparently," Ro said. "Anything else you can tell us about the poem?"

"You obviously figured this out already, but it sounds very much like that book has been hidden in a library. That would make sense to me. Cynzia had quite a library of her own. She loved books, but then most fae do. As for the rest…" He glanced at Posey. "Is that a copy of the poem?"

"It is." She tore off the top sheet of her notebook and handed it to him.

"Thank you." He read it over before he looked up at Ro again. "I'd have to return to my books in Summerton to properly research this, but I'm sure the blue in mourning and red in sleep mean something. Something that would probably help you locate the book."

"Then I would like you to return to Summerton and do whatever research you need. Althea, you are welcome to stay and help us here. Or you can return with Spencer, whichever you prefer." As Althea looked at her husband, Ro turned to Gabriel. "Can they go by portal or will they have to return by carriage?"

"They can go by portal."

"Good," Ro said. That would be quicker. "Can you spare a guard to accompany them home? I'd feel better knowing they had a guard with them."

"Yes, your majesty. I'll see to it."

"Thank you." She smiled at Spencer. "I'm sorry to send you back, but this is very important."

"I understand, your highness. And I agree. This is

urgently important." Spencer smiled at his wife. "Althea will stay here and help you in whatever way you need. That way, we can both be working toward the same goal more efficiently."

"Perfect. Thank you both. Gabriel, how soon can you have a guard ready to travel with Spencer?"

"I should think within an hour or two."

Ro nodded. "Spencer, take that copy of the poem with you. Posey, make a few more copies of it so we can all have one, but remember, all of you, this isn't to be discussed with anyone outside of this room. If you have a copy of the poem, I expect you either to memorize it and burn the paper or hide it very carefully. In fact, it would be better if it stayed on your person instead of somewhere in your room where it could be found. Maybe that seems overly cautious but humor me."

Uldamar shook his head. "It's exactly the right amount of caution. There is more at stake here than just the Radiant throne. If Anyka gains power, those of us in this room will be among the first she imprisons or executes." His face was as solemn as Ro had ever seen it. "I, for one, do not wish to spend the remainder of my days on Tenebrae."

Spencer shuddered and Althea let out a ragged sigh. He took his wife's hand. "It would be better to be executed."

"Tenebrae?" Ro asked.

Uldamar nodded slowly. "You might say it is the fae equivalent of Alcatraz."

Ro grimaced. "Heard and understood."

# Chapter Seventeen

After everyone left, Ro returned to her chair in the sitting room and just sat there reading the copy of the poem Posey had given her. She kept hoping she'd have a lightbulb moment and it would suddenly make sense, but so far, it hadn't.

Posey and Violet, accompanied by Vincent, had gone downstairs to listen to a string quartet. JT and Raphaela were off to do some close-combat training. Uldamar and the Cloudtrees had probably gone to their rooms.

Frustrated that her brain wasn't doing what she wanted it to, Ro looked up, her gaze immediately going to Gabriel.

He was close, having positioned himself by the door again. He'd already sent word that he needed a volunteer from the guards to accompany a professor back to Rivervale.

She sighed at the paper in her hands. "I really want to make sense of this poem but I'm not coming up with anything."

"May I speak freely, my lady?"

"Of course. You can say anything you want to me whenever you want." She really disliked how formal things had gotten between them.

He nodded, but she doubted he'd actually do anything

she hadn't given him direct permission for. "You might be thinking about it too much. I find that to be the least productive kind of problem-solving."

She laughed softly. "You're right about that. I know nothing's going to come of reading this poem over and over, but I can't help it. I want answers so badly."

"Then do something else. Give your subconscious a chance to work on the problem."

"That's a good idea. Any suggestions about what else I might do?"

"We could go for a walk. I've been told the gardens here are beautiful. They'd be the best place to see the falls. But I know the lake is not to be missed in the evening. You can see for yourself why they call it Celestial Lake."

"That sounds like just what I need. Some time outside. This is a great suite of rooms, but I'm not here to just sit around. Let's go see the lake. I'm going to change into something more casual and I'll be right out."

He smiled. "I'll be waiting."

Poem in hand, she went to her room and put on a slim pair of pants that tucked into soft boots, along with a tunic and cape of velvety marula wool in dark teal that had been embroidered with a trim of silver dragonflies along the hem.

Then she heeded her own words, folded the poem in four, and tucked it into her boot. In the other boot, she tucked a dagger. Not because she had any fear about going out at night, certainly not with Gabriel at her side, but because it had become habit. It was just what the fae did.

Most would probably have another dagger at their waist, too.

But she had Gabriel.

She went back out to the sitting room. "I'm ready."

"Perfect." He smiled. "Are you up for a little adventure?"

She had no idea what he had in mind, but she was game. "Absolutely."

"Then let's go."

They left the suite. Gabriel gave a nod to the guard at the door, who hadn't been there when they'd come back from dinner. They walked down the corridor in the opposite direction of the portal elevator, as Ro had come to think of it.

The corridor was nothing but door after door leading into guest suites. The passage was lit with what looked like gas sconces, but then Ro realized it was more magic light like she'd seen in the library.

Finally, they came to a large foyer with seating and stairs that connected the second floor with the first and third. There was another portal elevator, too.

They went down the stairs. She expected to see the same grand hallway they'd been in when they were searching the libraries, but that wasn't where they came out.

Instead, it was a sturdy-looking room with a set of heavy wood and metal doors where the hall should have been.

"This isn't where I thought we were going to end up."

"Did you think we'd be by the libraries?"

"I did."

He nodded. "So did I the first time I came down here. Apparently, there's both some crafty architecture and a bit of fae magic at work in the structure of this building." He went over and opened one of the big wooden doors. "This is what we're here for."

She walked over and looked out at a scene illuminated by two more magic lamps. "That's water."

"The river, to be precise. This is the very center of Willow Hall where it crosses the water."

The river was flowing at a slow but steady pace past the enormous stone supports that held Willow Hall up. Steps led directly to the water, where all along the stone bank, small boats were tied. The scent of damp rose up, but it wasn't unpleasant. Behind Willow Hall, the soft glow of the luminescent falls lit the night.

"Come on," he said. "Let's take a little boat ride so you can see exactly how the Celestial Lake earned its name."

She hesitated by the door, pointing at the boats. "Anybody can just take those?"

"Yes. Although I'd like to remind you that you aren't just anybody."

"No, I suppose not."

"You're not afraid of the water, are you?"

"No." Even if it was dark outside and the water was black, and she couldn't really see much beyond the pools of light cast by the magic lamps. "But those boats look pretty small."

"They're very safe. And I promise, the trip will be worth it."

"All right," she said. She didn't see any life jackets, though. She walked through the door. It was cooler out than she'd anticipated, but her cape was plenty warm. "This is the point that divides Willow Hall into Summerton and Malveaux."

"It is. Everything past those stone supports is Malveaux. There's a boat station over there, too."

"Will we still be in Summerton when we're on the lake?"

"Technically, the lake is neutral ground."

"That's interesting."

Gabriel shut the door behind him, then went to the centermost boat. She followed him down the steps. She could see now that the boats had small lateral supports on each side. Nothing as large as the traditional Hawaiian outrigger canoes, but similar. That would definitely help their stability.

He untied the first boat, then held it fast. "Take the middle seat, my lady. I'll sit in the back so I can paddle."

She nodded and approached. There was nothing to hold onto. Some kind of railing would have been nice.

"Put your hand on my shoulder," Gabriel said.

Of course he would know exactly what she was thinking. She used him for support and carefully took a seat. The boat sat low so that she felt like she was floating directly on the surface of the water.

He got in behind her, barely moving the boat. She glanced over her shoulder. He picked up the single oar and pushed off from the stone dock.

"The current will do most of the work until we reach the lake," he said.

They drifted out from underneath the hulk of Willow Hall. The Summer Palace blocked the light from the falls now, casting them in deeper darkness. Her eyes began to adjust, helped along by the abundance of stars.

She glanced toward the other side of Willow Hall. The Grym side. There were no lights on in the second floor. That would change soon enough. "Where does all this water go once it's in the lake?"

"You mean how does the lake not overflow? A lot of the water is siphoned off by underground streams that feed springs. Some of which empty directly into the Whistling Sea."

A few sweet scents reached her, some kind of night-blooming flower maybe, and there was a curious chorus of sounds. Insects and something else. "What's that sound? That chirping? Frogs?"

"Frogs, bladder crickets, moon sparrows. Probably a mix of nocturnal critters."

The river wound past some tree-lined banks, but most of them were grassy. Curious to think that one bank was Summerton, one bank was Malveaux.

The lake was just ahead. Gabriel picked up the paddle and made a few strokes on either side. They picked up some speed but he'd already returned the paddle to its holder. They were entering the lake now, gliding across the water and away from the few trees that had darkened the sky above them.

"Behold Celestial Lake," Gabriel said.

In that moment, as they left the trees behind, the sky seemed to expand. She lifted her gaze in an attempt to take it all in. Watching the sky made the movement of the boat seem to slow. Or maybe it actually did slow. But she was too fascinated by the sparkling heavens above to give it more thought.

"It's really something, isn't it?" Gabriel said softly.

"You never see stars like this in the city. Too much light pollution." She smiled as she looked up. "I keep thinking I recognize a constellation, but then there's one or two stars different."

"The brightest star overhead? That's the tip of the tail of a constellation we call the Fox. He's always visible, no matter the time of year. And just next to him is the Dragonfly. See those two slightly green stars?"

She nodded. "I do."

"Those are the Dragonfly's body. But to see the most amazing thing, you'll have to bring your gaze back down to Earth."

"What? Why?" But even as she asked, she dropped her gaze and understood.

The lake was flat and still, the black water reflecting the sky so that it was virtually impossible to tell where the sky ended, and the water began. It was as if they were sitting inside the stars, completely surrounded.

She sucked in a little breath of air. "Oh, wow."

"Celestial Lake."

She took it all in, trying to lock the image into her memory. "This is one of the coolest things I've ever seen.

And I've seen the Northern Lights." She looked over her shoulder. "Thank you for bringing me out here."

He smiled. "My pleasure, your majesty."

She sighed. "Gabriel, it's just us. You can call me Ro."

His eyes narrowed. "If you'd like, we can dock the boat and walk along the shoreline. There's a path that goes all the way around."

So much for regaining their casualness with each other. She looked straight ahead again. "That sounds nice."

He rowed them to a dock that wasn't far from where the river joined the lake. She was happy to see it was firmly on the Summerton side. He steadied the boat. "I'll hold it."

She climbed out, using a handhold on the side of the dock.

Then he got out and tied the boat up.

"You can just leave it there? You don't have to return it?"

He shook his head. "There are boat tenders who do that as a convenience for the guests."

"It's really beautiful out here."

He looked at her for a long moment, then back out at the lake. "It is. I can see why it was the retreat of choice for both kingdoms for so many years."

There was a bench nearby built of wood and stone. She took a seat. "You can still see the stars on the lake from here. It's not quite the same as being in the middle of it, but it's close."

He walked toward her but stopped short of sitting.

She looked at him, then patted the empty bench beside her. "I don't bite, you know."

He sat.

Sitting in the dark gave her new courage, although it took a few moments for her to form the words. "I miss you, Gabriel."

"I'm right here, my lady."

She exhaled. "I miss the Gabriel who I sat on the bench in the royal gardens with. The one who...told me all kinds of truths." She'd been about to say "kissed me," but her courage didn't extend that far, apparently.

"I have never spoken anything to you that wasn't true."

"I know. It's not what I meant to say. I meant to say I miss the version of you who kissed me." She glanced at him. His eyes were focused on the lake.

"You weren't queen then."

"Why is that such a big deal? I get when there are other people around. I understand royal protocol. But when it's just us? Why does it matter then?"

He didn't answer for a moment, making her think he wasn't going to. Then he spoke. "Did you know there's a law in Summerton that makes touching a royal without their consent punishable by death?"

"No, I didn't know that, but it seems a little harsh." She turned to see him better. The lake was beautiful, but so was he. "So you're worried that if you touch me without permission, you'll get in trouble? If it's just us, who's going to say anything?"

"There are eyes and ears everywhere. I've been in charge of palace security long enough to know that." He tipped his head. "Some of those eyes and ears were put in place by me."

"Okay, maybe that's true. Maybe someone would say something. But how would they know you didn't have my permission?"

"They wouldn't. But if someone wanted to hurt me, all they'd have to do is make an accusation." His whole body seemed to tense. "Regardless of the truth, I would be tried in the court of public opinion."

"Some things never change." She shook her head. "This is a very lonely job, you know. If I didn't have JT and Violet, I'd be having serious second thoughts. But the truth is…" She hesitated to tell him what she was really feeling, but if she didn't say it now, she never would. "I sort of thought I had you, too."

# Chapter Eighteen

Ro's emotions were a jangled, jumbled hot mess of confusion. She was glad to have such an honest conversation with Gabriel, but at the same time, it was like stripping naked, standing in front of him, and waiting to be judged.

And she wasn't a hundred percent confident about the way she looked with clothes *on*.

He stared at the water. His lips parted, but he didn't say anything and closed them again. Then he sighed. "You do have me. Maybe not in the way you anticipated, but I am here for you. I swear to you that I am."

She crossed her arms. "Thanks." She knew there were all sorts of layers to that one word, layers he was smart enough to interpret, but she didn't care. She was hurt and disappointed and unhappy.

"I know that's not the answer you wanted but it's the only one I can give you." He sighed. "I like you. Liked you. I still do. But now I can't. Taking the throne made you off-limits to me. I don't know how else to explain it. It wasn't because I suddenly lost interest, I swear on my sword."

"I wish I'd known that ahead of time."

Looking genuinely curious, he slanted his eyes at her. "Would it have kept you from taking the throne?"

She thought about that. "Probably not. But we could have at least had this conversation sooner. I would have better understood that I was setting myself up to be alone the rest of my life."

"You don't have to be alone."

"Really? Because it seems that way to me." She rolled her eyes. "It's nothing I haven't dealt with already in my life. I've been alone for most of it. I just didn't think I'd be alone for the rest of it."

"You don't have to be alone," he repeated.

She looked at him. "Meaning what?"

"Meaning you could take someone as your consort."

She said nothing. Just stared. And thought that through. Finally, she spoke. "I know what that means. Or at least I think I do. I'd basically be announcing to the kingdom that I'd decided to officially take a man into my bed. Is that right?"

He chuckled. "Well, that would be part of it. But the Queen's Consort is essentially her husband. Sharing a bed would be neither scandalous nor unexpected."

"Oh." Ro sat back. Would she actually want to get married? Maybe. But there was a lot that would have to happen first. And how could it? "How am I supposed to get to the point of having a consort if no one can touch me without my permission? How do I date? Or meet a man?" She didn't honestly care about any of that. She'd already met the man she liked. He was sitting right next to her.

"Generally, an official announcement is made. The queen formally announces her courtship with the honorable Lord So-and-So. That kind of thing."

"Wow, that's romantic."

He laughed. "Royal protocol seldom is."

"Doesn't matter. I don't want to date or meet a man."

He went solemn again as he finally looked at her. "No?"

She shook her head. "I've already met a man. One I just want to get to know better. You. Can't I do that?"

"You're the queen. You can do anything you want." A subtle gleam played in his eyes. Interest? Attraction? Did her frankness amuse him?

She didn't care what it was so long as he kept looking at her like that. She lifted her chin slightly. "I suppose that means I could order you to kiss me, and you'd have to obey."

"I would. Or risk being thrown in the dungeon."

"Is there a dungeon?"

"A small one, yes."

She leaned in just a little. "Do you want to kiss me?"

His gaze raked her mouth before he went back to looking into her eyes. "I haven't stopped wanting to kiss you since the last time I did it, standing on that street in the middle of the city."

He'd appeared out of nowhere and saved her from a possible mugging that night. "Good. Because I don't really want to send you to the dungeon. Oh, and I give you permission to touch me. Now, do I really need to order you to—"

His mouth was on hers, making her forget whatever she'd been about to say next. He moved closer, one hand wrapping around the back of her neck. His palm was warm and rough and his touch sent a shiver through her.

She put a hand on his chest and grabbed hold of his leather vest, like he might try to get away. She inched closer, enjoying the kiss with every fiber of her being.

She'd thought everything between them was gone. She was thrilled to find out that wasn't true. Thrilled to feel like a woman again and not just a head of state. She kissed him back with as much eagerness as she dared.

His mouth was soft and gentle, but insistent, telling her he'd been thinking about doing this just as much as she had. That alone gave her hope that this would not be the last time such a kiss happened.

When the kiss ended, he tipped his forehead against hers. They stayed that way, just breathing and absorbing the moment.

Something splashed in the water, and they moved away from each other as ripples spread across the surface of the lake. But she caught his hand in hers and held onto it. "Thank you."

He grunted. "I'm sorry things are so complicated."

"It's not your fault. It's that stupid royal protocol. Can we please just be us when we're together?"

He nodded. "As you wish, my lady."

She laughed. "Stop that right now. That's an order."

He lifted her hand to his mouth and kissed the back of it. "Since we're being so honest with each other, I must tell you that I can never be consort."

She frowned. "Why not?"

"The Queen's Consort shares a certain amount of her power. They can't rule, unless they're declared Regent, but they still wield a lot of influence. It's just not a position I can hold, because I'm Grym fae, but worse than that, I'm Malveaux born."

"JT is half Grym. He'll sit on the throne someday and he wasn't born in Summerton. I don't see why it should matter where the next ruler is from or what his bloodlines are."

"But he's your son and so his birth makes him eligible. For the record, I don't think a fae's place of birth or bloodlines should matter, either, but there are laws about these things."

"I'm the queen. Can I change those laws?"

"You can. But you have to know it might hurt your popularity if the people don't agree with you."

That touched a nerve. She'd come here to Willow Hall to show the people how important the long-standing traditions were to her. To get them to like her, even if she wasn't Summerton born and raised.

Changing a long-standing law might undo whatever progress she'd made.

She sighed. "This is a really hard job."

"It is. I don't envy you at all. But I will always be here if you want to talk about any of it."

She squeezed his hand. "Thank you. I hope you're always by my side."

"I have no plans to be anywhere else, Ro."

That pleased her. They sat for a few minutes longer just

holding hands and watching the water. Then she yawned without meaning to, letting go of his hand to cover her mouth. "I guess we should go back. Can we do this again?"

He nodded. "We can do anything you want. I don't expect we'll have it all to ourselves again, though. The rest of the guests will want to see this for themselves, too."

"I'm sure they will. And they should. It's really beautiful."

"Not as beautiful as their queen."

She smiled. "That will definitely keep you out of the dungeon a while longer."

He grinned as he stood. He offered her his hand. She didn't need it, but she took it anyway. Any excuse to touch him again.

Together they walked back to Willow Hall and went in through the same entrance they had when they'd arrived from Summerton. Footmen stood on either side of the door.

Strains of music drifted toward them from deeper inside the palace. No doubt some of the evening's entertainment.

Gabriel walked her to the portal and got in after her, closing the doors behind them. "I'll see you to your suite, then I need to make sure Professor Cloudtree gets off all right."

"That definitely needs doing. And I'm probably going straight to bed anyway," Ro said. "Thanks again for tonight. I really needed that." She felt alive inside. Renewed by time with him. Capable of facing whatever nonsense Queen Anyka might bring with her. Which was hopefully none, but Ro would deal with whatever happened.

"I will endeavor to do better. To not let royal protocol get the best of me." He turned the portal wheel, aligning the gemstones for the second floor.

"Good," Ro said as time and space shifted. She hoped the evening meant they were back to where they'd been before, but time would tell.

The guard was still at the door to the royal suite. Gabriel questioned him as they approached. "Anyone in or out?"

"No, sir."

Gabriel looked at her. "I'll come in with you anyway, your majesty, if that's all right with you. I'd just like to run one last security check."

"Absolutely, Professor Nightborne." She did her best not to smile but talking to him like this now felt like playing a game.

He opened the door, and they went in. He didn't go any farther than a few steps. "I'm only across the hall if you need me."

Facing him, she nodded. "How is the room?"

"Not as nice as this, but still far nicer than I need."

That pleased her. "Good."

Emboldened by the evening's events, she cupped his face and kissed him. Just a short, sweet, to-the-point kiss, because she could. Even so, his hands slipped to her waist for a second before it ended. She was very pleased with herself as she gazed up at him. "See you in the morning, Gabriel."

He nodded, a smile twitching the corners of his mouth. "See you in the morning, Ro. Sweet dreams."

She smiled. There was no way they wouldn't be now.

# Chapter Nineteen

Anyka rose before dawn, wrapping herself in a thick robe and pulling the hood up over her head. Only embers remained in the fireplace, the maid having not yet been in to stoke it or bring Anyka coffee.

For Galwyn's sake, Anyka tossed a piece of split wood on the embers and fanned them to spark flames. Then she went to his perch and added seed to his dish before sitting by the windows to watch the day arrive.

She hadn't slept much. Nazyr's news about Lady Cynzia's grimoire had made sleep nearly impossible.

There was too much to think about. Too many possibilities. If the book even existed. Part of Anyka wondered if this wasn't mostly a creation of Nazyr's, meant to justify his recent behavior. But Lady Cynzia wasn't a myth, so why would her grimoire be?

The woman's history led Anyka to believe that she must have had a book of spells at some point. Whether or not it still existed, that was really the question.

And whether or not Anyka believed it had been hidden at Willow Hall.

If it had, there wasn't a better hiding place than a

palace no one had visited in centuries. Finding it wouldn't be easy, no matter what Nazyr thought.

Anyka snorted. His idea was that the grimoire would show itself to her because of a magic amulet he was creating from a few bits that had once belonged to Lady Cynzia. Would it work? Anyka had no idea. Nazyr appeared to think it would, but Anyka wasn't convinced.

Magic was a powerful thing. She knew that to be true. Which was why she didn't think that Lady Cynzia would have left her grimoire behind without using her own magic to protect it. Simply wearing an amulet made from Cynzia's things wasn't going to fool a spell into thinking Anyka was Cynzia.

But Nazyr seemed confident they'd find it in a matter of days once they arrived.

Galwyn ate some of his seed, then jumped down to stand on the arm of her chair. She stroked his sleek feathers. "Good morning, my handsome boy. Are you excited about traveling today?"

He let out a little trill.

Once the book was hers—because it would be hers—she would decide what to do with it. And how to proceed with whatever was inside. No matter what part Nazyr played in finding it, the grimoire would belong to Anyka.

If it contained the means to lift Malveaux's curse, she would consider that very carefully. Magic that strong would undoubtedly come at a cost. But if it also contained the means by which to take control of Summerton, Anyka would be dutybound to use that spell. No matter what the price.

Summerton was the reason her parents were dead. Not avenging them would be cowardly. Avenging them was not only the right thing to do, it was what her parents would want. What the citizens of Malveaux expected. Probably what the citizens of Summerton expected as well.

She would hate to disappoint anyone.

She heard a soft knock and the door to the outer chamber swept open. The maid, come to stoke the fire and leave breakfast. "Put it on the table," Anyka called out.

A little shriek answered her. "Sorry, my lady. I didn't realize you were up."

Anyka didn't bother turning around, just waved her hand. She could smell coffee and warm bread. There had better be honey or preserves and butter on that tray as well. "Stoke the fire. It went out last night. I had to put wood on myself this morning."

"Sorry, my lady."

Galwyn cawed at the young woman. Hurrying her along, maybe. Anyka smiled. "Are you hungry, my pet?"

Once the chamber door shut, Anyka went to the breakfast tray. There was a shallow dish of flaked, smoked fish for Galwyn. She put the dish on his stand. "There you go. Eat your breakfast."

Then she went back and poured a mug of coffee and slathered a thick slice of seeded bread with butter and pear chutney, which would have to do. What she wouldn't give for a pot of blackberry jam.

Willow Hall would probably have it.

But then, so would Malveaux if she could lift the curse

and return the proper amount of sun to this forsaken kingdom.

She carried her coffee and bread back to her chair and returned to watching the dawn arrive. The horizon line had just begun to lighten, but the clouds seemed heavy. Much as they always did.

She sipped her coffee and ate her bread while Galwyn demolished his fish. She was ready to leave for Willow Hall. Ready to get on the road. It wasn't because Anyka was looking forward to meeting the Radiant queen, but she *was* curious about the woman. To see how weak she was. Where her vulnerability lay. If she was in any way a threat to Anyka. Or Malveaux.

But Anyka also wanted the chance to be somewhere else for a while. To have some interactions with people outside her daughter, her ministers, and her household staff. Perhaps there would be real conversations.

And maybe even a man who might not be completely intimidated by her status and power.

She took another bite of bread. There was little chance of that. She wasn't an idiot. She knew very well how men saw her. And there would only be Grym and Radiant there, neither of which would dare think about approaching her without her direct consent.

She ate the last of her bread, then carried her coffee into the bathing room. The temperature had risen a few degrees now that the fire was properly built up and crackling away. She would bathe, dress, then head down to see what she could do about hurrying everyone else along.

She took her time, knowing how early she was. She

rang for a maid before getting into the bath.

The young woman appeared a few minutes later. "Yes, my lady?"

Anyka sank down to her neck. The hot water felt good. "Send the hairdresser up. And clear the breakfast tray but leave the coffee."

"Yes, my lady."

Anyka soaked until the hairdresser arrived. The hairdresser was traveling with them. Anyka wasn't about to do her own hair at Willow Hall. "Refill my mug."

"Yes, my lady," the woman said.

While the hairdresser did that, Anyka got out of the water, wrapped herself in a towel, then put her robe back on and sat before the mirror.

The woman returned, putting Anyka's mug nearby. "Would you like anything particular today?"

"Hair that will last through traveling."

"A smart choice," the woman said. She went to work drying Anyka's hair, then oiling it and, finally, braiding it.

Anyka nearly drifted off during the process. When the woman was through, Anyka inspected the final result. Pleased, she sent the hairdresser away. She dressed herself in trim dove gray pants with a cutaway gown of dove gray silk lined with deep purple. She wore gray slippers and some of her nicest amethyst jewelry. A wide choker of the gems, a pair of dangling earrings, and a ring with a fat oval stone the size of a quail's egg. All accented with diamonds and trillianites.

On one hip she sported a matched set of gleaming silver daggers with mother of pearl handles in twin sheaths. As decorative as they were deadly. On the other, she wore a chatelaine bag that contained certain necessary items. A small pot of lip rouge, a powder compact, a paper packet of dried meat for Galwyn, a handkerchief, a small vial of headache powder that in large quantities, such as the entire vial, could double as poison, and tiny scissors.

She took one last look around, but there was nothing else she could think of that needed to come with her.

Except for Galwyn.

She walked over to his perch where he was watching her. "Ready to go?"

He cocked his head and let out a little warble.

She patted her shoulder. He jumped up.

Together, they went downstairs, followed by Trog, who'd left his post by her door. Unlike the previous day, when it had been as quiet as a tomb, the palace was bustling with activity.

The grand carriage had already been brought around, all the metal bits polished to a high shine. Trunks were being stacked onto some of the other carriages and on one wagon designed specifically for hauling larger loads.

She glanced at Trog. "You may go and get your horse and whatever else you need."

He nodded. "Trog be back."

She knew he would be. He'd ride alongside her carriage, ensuring her safety. She caught sight of Wyett. He was supervising the handling of her things.

He bowed when he saw her. "Good morning, your highness."

"Good morning, Wyett. Are we close to being ready?"

He hesitated. "I've not yet seen Princess Beatryce."

Anyka pursed her lips. "And my uncle?"

"He was here but had to run back to his quarters for something he forgot."

"Have you seen Minister Nazyr?"

"Yes. He's in his own carriage." Wyett leaned back to look down the line of conveyances. "The sixth back, my lady."

"Good enough. I'd like to leave as soon as Princess Beatryce and Lord Ishmyel arrive."

"Then that is what we'll do."

He'd be riding up front with the driver. They'd have one royal guard on the back, plus one riding alongside as well as Trog. They would be well protected, although she couldn't imagine running into any kind of trouble on the way.

Now, coming home, if they were in possession of Lady Cynzia's grimoire? That might be a different matter altogether. But it wouldn't do to add too many extra guards on the return trip. That could draw unnecessary attention.

She'd cross that bridge if and when they came to it.

Ishmyel walked out of the palace, dressed in an embellished robe and slippers along with a few choice pieces of jewelry. "Morning, my lady niece."

"Good morning. Are you ready to leave?"

"I am." He looked around. "Any sign of Beatryce?"

"No. I'm about to send a footman to fetch her." She stepped closer to him so she could speak without being overheard. "Have you given Nazyr's information any deeper thought?"

Ishmyel nodded. "I have. But it's led me no closer to belief. How can we know for sure? I don't think we can."

"Neither do I." She sighed. "Which means we will be forced to search."

"And forced to do it in such a way that we arouse no suspicion."

She nodded. That was the bigger issue. If word got out, Willow Hall would be torn apart by all those under its roof. "We cannot let Queen Sparrow know."

"Agreed. This *item* must not fall into Radiant hands."

She groaned softly. "What chance do four of us have? Everything I've ever heard about Willow Hall says it is vast."

"We can always bring a few more people in. Only those you trust, obviously."

"There are very few of those."

"There must be someone."

"None of the other ministers, I can tell you that. They are all far too self-serving."

Ishmyel nodded. "I understand, but perhaps you could treat it like a test of their loyalty? It would be easy enough to search their belongings should one of them suddenly become more proficient with magic than they were."

"True."

Wyett walked by, speaking with Chyles, her scribe, who was jotting things down on paper with a pencil.

Anyka watched them for a moment. "I'll give that idea some thought, but I believe there are at least two more right there that I can enlist for our hunt."

# Chapter Twenty

Ro had no idea when JT or Violet returned to the royal suite, because she'd fallen asleep not long after saying good night to Gabriel. She woke with a sense of calm and peace that she hadn't felt in days.

She lay motionless, staring up at the coffered ceiling. Watery light spilled through the seam where the drapes met, an indication that it was still early.

She'd dreamed last night. Now she tried to remember what about. She'd been in a field of flowers, beautiful, colorful blooms that smelled heavenly. She'd stood in the midst of them, enjoying the sight and scent, when a dark cloud had appeared out of nowhere.

The cloud spread and grew, covering every inch of blue sky.

In the shadow of that cloud, which had growled with thunder and crackled with lightning, the flowers had withered away and their perfume disappeared.

She frowned. Without knowing why, she understood what that dream meant.

She got out of bed immediately, pulled on her robe, and went out to the small sitting room. There was no one there. She went through to the larger sitting room and found Gabriel pouring himself a cup of coffee from a tray on the sideboard. Next to that tray was a platter of pastries, each one prettier than the last.

"Hey," she said softly, tightening the belt on her robe. She really should have taken a look in the mirror before running out here. There was no telling what her hair looked like.

He turned and smiled. "Good morning, your majesty. Coffee?"

"Yes, please. And I thought we were not going to do the formal thing anymore?"

"I'm working on it." He handed her the coffee in his hands, then poured himself a cup.

"Have you heard anything about Anyka arriving today?"

He shook his head. "No. I don't think anyone knows when she's getting here."

"It's today." She added cream and sugar to the cup. "I can't explain it, but I had a dream and that's what it told me. She's arriving today."

Gabriel looked at her, brow furrowed. "Have you had dreams before that told you things?"

There was nothing about his tone that said he was anything but serious. "No. This is the first one. Although JT told me about one of his dreams on the way up here, and that seemed to have a pretty clear explanation, too. At least to me."

Gabriel leaned against the sideboard. "Last night I dreamed that I was tested repeatedly in swordplay. Every opponent I fought had *Merediem* as their weapon. Would you like to tell me what that means?"

She smiled as an idea filled her head. "Did you win or lose?"

He frowned. "I lost every battle until the very last one. I didn't care for it at all."

"Are you sure you really want to know what I think it means?"

"Yes, of course."

"All right. Our visit to the lake last night had quite an impact on you. Your subconscious isn't sure it's up to the test of being with me. Somewhere, deep down inside, you don't feel equal."

His eyes narrowed. "That doesn't sound promising." Then he sighed. "Sadly, I don't think you're too far from the truth. That feeling isn't so deep down, either."

His honesty was sweet. "Gabriel, you are absolutely equal to me. Probably more than equal. The only thing I have going for me is being queen. You, on the other hand, are a genuine catch."

"That's not remotely true," he said. "You have more good qualities than I can name."

"How about we agree that we're well-suited, then?"

He smiled. "I can agree to that." He sipped his coffee. "I guess we know what kind of magic you have then."

She'd been thinking about taking one of the delicious-looking pastries arranged so nicely on the platter. Not the most nutritious way to start the day, but they looked and smelled so good. "What's that now?"

"Your magic. It's the interpretation of dreams."

She squinted at him. "I think it's a little early to say

that's actually my gift. We have no idea if Anyka's really going to arrive today."

"We'll soon see, won't we?"

She settled on a small, square pastry with ruby jam in the center and a drizzle of white frosting. She put that on her plate, then picked her coffee up with her other hand. "We will. I should go get ready for the day."

"If she does arrive today, which I believe she will, you can expect me to be at your side all day."

Ro smiled. "I won't mind that." Then she realized what he was saying. "Do you think she means me harm?"

"I don't know. But I don't want to give her the chance to attempt anything, either. Please, wear all your blades today."

Ro nodded. "Okay. I will. I'm going to need Luena and Helana today to get ready." She went over and pulled the bell rope. "If I'm going to meet Anyka, I want to look as put together as possible."

He nodded, still drinking his coffee. "Of course. Which reminds me, do you want me in uniform today?"

"I don't know," Ro said. "Might be better to keep her guessing as to who you are. Not that she can't ask and find out, but I think I'd prefer you in street clothes." He looked good in anything. He looked especially good in his uniform. But for reasons Ro couldn't quite name, she wanted him to seem more approachable.

"Whatever you want."

"Thanks. When the staff answer my call, send them for Helana and Luena, please."

"I will."

She took her coffee and pastry back to the bedroom. Her decadent plan was to have her pre-breakfast in the bathing pool, which was exactly what she did. It was the perfect way to start the day she would meet the woman who could be considered her archrival.

Ro didn't want to think of Anyka that way, but she understood that was probably how Anyka saw her. Ro would have to do her best to convince the woman otherwise. Ro wasn't all that confident that her best would be good enough.

Not with the years of bad blood that had passed between the two kingdoms.

But if Ro could get her hands on Lady Cynzia's diary and lift Malveaux's curse, wouldn't that be about as grand a goodwill gesture as existed? It seemed to her that such an act would be the most foolproof way of proving she had only good intentions toward Malveaux. And Queen Anyka.

"My lady?" a voice called out. "Helana and I are here."

"Luena? I'm just finishing up," Ro called back. "Please come in." There was more than enough steam to provide some modesty, but at the same time, Luena was Ro's seamstress. She was already pretty familiar with what Ro looked like under her clothes.

Luena and Helana entered, curtseyed, then stood almost as if they were at attention.

"Good morning, ladies. I have every reason to believe I'll be meeting Queen Anyka today. I want to look appropriate for that occasion. A nice gown, good shoes, the right jewels, and, of course, hair and makeup that make me look kind, approachable, but also a little like someone not to be messed with." She grinned. "Can you do all of that?"

The two smiled. Helana nodded. "We can do anything."

"I love that confidence." Ro looked at her hands. "Okay, I'm wrinkling. Time to get out and get ready. If you two haven't had coffee, go help yourselves. Then we need to get me dressed and primped. Thanks in advance. I know you have your work cut out for you."

"It's our pleasure," Luena said.

They left. Ro got out, wrapped her hair in a towel, then dried off and put her robe back on. She could use another cup of coffee, but she knew she'd be going down to breakfast in the dining hall when she was ready.

She went into the dressing room. Luena came in a few minutes after her, coffee in hand. Ro smiled at her. "Any idea what I should wear today?"

Luena nodded. "There are three options I was thinking of." She set her coffee on the small center island full of drawers, then went to the racks of clothing. She took out something slightly unexpected, mostly because it wasn't a gown.

Luena held out the dark teal pants and long fitted jacket trimmed with dark teal braids of silk. Ro liked the way it was so nipped in at the waist. "I know you said gown, but this outfit, especially with boots, has a very strong look. It's almost a little military, which I was thinking might work for what you were going for. At the same time, because of the drape of the top, the length of it, and the way the waist is emphasized, the outfit still feels feminine. Plus, we can pair it with some really strong pieces, like the suite of trillianites and diamonds in platinum."

"Definitely not something I would have considered, but I can see what you're saying about it. What's another of the options?"

Helana came in, but said nothing, just watched.

Luena pulled out an ivory gown. The full skirt and bodice were both embroidered in gold with dragonflies, small beetles, and bees. The insects were all accented with gemstones, giving the gown a surprising amount of color and life. "This is the most royal gown we brought for you. The only person who would dare to wear a dress like this would have to be a queen."

"That is stunning and I agree with you, but I think I'd like to save that for an evening event. What's the third choice?"

Luena hung the ivory gown back up and pulled out another gown, this time in a medium blue with a lighter blue chiffon overskirt and flowing sleeves. Trillianites flashed electric blue from the neck, waist, and all over the underskirt, where they'd been scattered randomly. "Very feminine, cut to accent your figure beautifully, and catches the light."

"I do love that one." Ro had yet to wear any of these. They'd all been made especially for this trip. "Let me try on the first one, then Helana, I want to hear your ideas for hair. Then I'll try that last one and you can tell me what you'd do for it."

Helana nodded. "Of course, my lady."

Ro thought about modeling both looks for Gabriel, but there was no logical explanation for doing that. Helana and Luena would think it odd and the last thing Ro wanted to do was start a rumor about herself and her personal guard.

That wouldn't do either of them any good.

She tried both options, listened to Helana describe the hair and makeup to go with it, then Luena's ideas for the accessories, and ultimately decided on the first outfit of pants with the fitted jacket. It had a powerful look to it, and Ro liked that.

She also liked that while trying the outfits on, Luena determined that Ro had lost some weight since the outfits had been made. She was definitely more active in the fae realm than she'd been in the mortal world.

When Ro was finished, her hair had been braided back at the sides and teased slightly through the top and crown, giving her a nice bit of added height. It also gave something for the platinum, diamond, and trillianite circlet she was wearing to grip onto.

Helana did a smokey eye with a soft cheek and lip. Besides the circlet, Luena gave Ro bold, dagger-shaped platinum earrings and a wide platinum cuff in the shape of a dragonfly set with trillianites and diamonds.

Ro added two daggers, one at her hip, and another in her boot. She took a final look in the dressing room mirror and shook her head at the fierce creature staring back at her. "I don't know how you two do it. Well done, both of you. And thank you."

They both nodded. Luena smiled. "Our pleasure, my lady."

"I hope you both enjoy the rest of your day. I may need you for dinner, but until then, the time is yours. Have fun."

"Thank you," Helana said. They both curtseyed and took off.

Ro walked out after them. She hoped Gabriel was still in the big sitting room. He was. So were JT, Raphaela, Violet, and Vincent. They were having coffee and all looked dressed for the day. Gabriel had changed into a dark shirt tucked into black leather pants, which were in turn tucked into boots. A single braid dangled from each temple and a sword hung at his hip. There was no telling how many daggers he had on his person.

He nodded and smiled when he saw her.

JT's brows lifted. "Wow, Mom. You look like you're going to some kind of fashion battle."

Ro laughed. "I hope that's a good thing."

He nodded. "You look great. Very queen-like. And a little off-with-their-heads."

"I'm going to take that as a compliment."

Violet set her cup back on her saucer. "You look fantastic, my dear. Where are you going?"

"Just down to the dining hall for breakfast, but I wanted to be prepared." She looked at Gabriel. "Did you tell them?"

He shook his head.

She looked at her family again. "I fully expect Queen Anyka to show up today. I had a dream that told me she would."

Violet gasped softly. "Is that your magic? It is, isn't it."

Ro smiled and shook her head. "I don't know. All I can tell you is this dream left me feeling utterly convinced Anyka would arrive today. Now, who's going with me to breakfast?"

JT got to his feet. "I am. I could eat a horse."

"My lord, we don't eat horses," Raphaela said.

JT snorted. "It's just an expression. Which I will not be using again."

Violet set her cup and saucer on the table. "You go on. I told Posey I'd wait for her."

"You'll have seats at the table, so no rush. After breakfast, I expect all of you to spend some time in one of the libraries, having a serious look around. Finding that book before Anyka does is very important."

They all nodded in understanding. Ro just hoped it was actually possible.

# Chapter Twenty-One

It had taken much too long to get moving, as far as Anyka was concerned. All because of Beatryce, who had apparently gone back to her quarters to fetch a gown she just couldn't leave behind.

Waiting for Beatryce had tried Anyka's patience, but she did her best not to let it show as they were finally in the carriage and underway. Instead, she tried to concentrate on the most important matter at hand.

Lady Cynzia's grimoire.

Anyka spoke to her daughter and her uncle, her two companions for the trip. "I've told Wyett and Chyles about the book and sworn them to secrecy."

Beatryce rolled her eyes. "Wyett, sure, but Chyles? He's a boy. What makes you think he'll keep his mouth shut?"

"Because he will," Anyka said. She had no doubts about either of them. "He is very loyal to me. And he doesn't want to spend the rest of his life on Tenebrae. If I don't decide death is a more suitable punishment."

Beatryce looked unconvinced. "I hope that's enough of a threat."

"It will be," Anyka snapped. She took a breath, forcing herself to relax, but it angered her that Beatryce didn't trust her mother's judgment of the people who served her.

"As it happens, Wyett already had heard rumors of the book. He knew the poem, too. Said he very much believed it could be in one of the Willow Hall libraries."

"That's encouraging," Ishmyel said. "Did he know anything about what the poem meant? Or have any insight as to how we might find the grimoire?"

"No, but he promised to give it serious attention." Anyka had the utmost faith in Wyett, that he might come up with something. He rarely failed in any task she gave him. And when he did fail, it was generally because she'd asked him to do the impossible.

Ishmyel shifted in his seat across from Anyka and Beatryce, stretching out a bit on the leather upholstery. "Do you think this amulet of Nazyr's has any chance of working?"

Anyka sighed and smoothed out her skirts so that they wouldn't wrinkle. "That really is the question, isn't it? I don't know. He's got strong magic, I don't doubt that part. But trying to fool the grimoire into thinking I'm Cynzia? Just because I'm wearing an amulet made of things that once belonged to her? It seems like a gamble at best."

Beatryce ate the last of the pastry she'd had on a cloth on her lap, then shook the cloth out the window to be rid of the crumbs. "I hope it does work. I don't want to spend all of my time at Willow Hall hunting for this old book. I want to have fun. I want to participate in all the activities."

"You will, Beatryce, but you have to understand how important this book will be for us. It will change our lives. It will protect Malveaux."

"I understand all of that," Beatryce said. "And I want

you to have the book. I really do. I just don't know if I actually believe it exists. Or if it ever did."

This was the first time Anyka had heard Bea say such a thing. "Why don't you think it's real?"

Beatryce shrugged one shoulder. "It's a lot to believe. That this super powerful book of magic has been hidden away in Willow Hall for centuries and no one, not one of the staff that live and work there, has ever come across it? Don't they employ entire teams of librarians to maintain those libraries? And what about the staff that does the cleaning? How has one of them never found it? Aren't the books dusted? It just seems unlikely to me."

"Not to me." Ishmyel cocked his brows and spoke one word. "Magic."

Anyka looked at him. He wasn't without his own gifts and powers, which gave him a thorough understanding of such things. More than she did, but then, he had time to study and practice. She had a kingdom to run. "Meaning?"

"Meaning the book won't be found until it wants to be found. Not until the magic protecting it senses that the time is right." He leaned forward. "Nazyr might be on to something with that amulet of Cynzia's. It might be just the thing to make the magic believe you are the right person at the right time."

Beatryce made a face. "You really think so?"

"I do." Ishmyel nodded. "Your mother has some pretty strong magic of her own. There's no reason so think Cynzia's grimoire won't recognize that and reveal itself."

"Well," Beatryce said. "That would be something."

Anyka nodded. Ishmyel's words had given her new

confidence. "I pray you're right, Uncle. I pray that is exactly what will happen. I trust it will. Otherwise, Nazyr's labors will have been in vain."

Ishmyel smiled, but there was a slyness to it. "The trick will be to keep Nazyr from claiming it for himself."

Anyka snorted. "May he rot in Tenebrae. That will not happen."

"I hope it doesn't," Ishmyel said. "But you said it yourself. He's got powerful magic. If he gets his hands on it, there's no telling what he might do. My guess is that he will suddenly disappear, taking the grimoire with him."

Anyka's hand went to the daggers at her side. "I'll kill him if he tries to take it."

Ishmyel mouth hardened. "Not if I do it first. That book belongs to you." Then he sighed heavily. "But my fears go beyond him taking the book." He stared out the window, like whatever he had to say was more than he could deal with.

"What is it?" Anyka asked. "What do you think he's going to do?"

"I don't know anything for sure. But I fear that he might...harm you to get the book." He swallowed. "You and Bea are my only family. If something were to happen to either of you, I would..." He looked out the window again.

Beatryce had her needlepoint out and was slipping a thimble onto her finger. "We'll be just fine, Uncle Ishmyel. Don't you worry."

Anyka was touched by her uncle's concern. The tension around his eyes spoke volumes. "I have Trog and

Wyett to protect me. And Beatryce now has two royal guards assigned to her. We will be fine. And if I am able to find the book, we will devise a way to keep it secret from Nazyr." She touched Ishmyel's hand. "I promise you."

"You're right. You are both well protected." He didn't look convinced, however. "I just do not trust the man."

Anyka couldn't argue that. She didn't trust him, either. She never trusted anyone more powerful than she was, and Nazyr certainly qualified in the area of magic. But what could she do? She couldn't send him back to Malveaux now. It would cause an uproar amongst the other ministers. And doing so would definitely make an enemy out of the skilled wizard.

As it was now, he still obeyed her. Mostly.

She stared out the window. She had so much to think about. Lady Cynzia's grimoire was really only a piece of what lay before her. Meeting Queen Sparrow occupied another large part of Anyka's mind.

What kind of woman was she?

Anyka wished she knew. As soon as she'd heard about the new queen, Anyka had tried to meet the woman by crossing over into the mortal realm and going to Sparrow's place of work, but Anyka had been too late. Sparrow had already left the mortal realm behind by then, deciding to take the crown after all.

Anyka tried to suss out the woman based on what she knew about human nature, which had to apply to Sparrow, since she'd only just found out she was fae.

Humans were capricious. They had short attention spans. They often lacked commitment and loyalty.

For a woman to give up the only life she'd ever known to take charge of a kingdom like Summerton meant... what? That Sparrow's life in the mortal world had been lackluster and unfulfilling? That she'd had few attachments to keep her there? No loyalty to the job she'd held for so many years?

If those things were true—and as far as Anyka knew, they were—it would mean this Sparrow was of weak character, perhaps not the most interesting or likeable person, and easy to manipulate. Possibly with material goods or the promise of great wealth.

Wasn't that why she'd come to Summerton? To bask in the riches of the kingdom and live the kind of life she knew she'd never achieve in the mortal world?

It seemed very plausible to Anyka, and that filled her with hope. Even if Sparrow somehow stumbled onto the grimoire first, Anyka believed she could talk the woman into giving it over.

Anyka would explain that it belonged to Malveaux. That it was part of Grym history. She would further emphasize that returning it to Malveaux would ensure a better chance at peace for the two kingdoms.

Of course, that would be a lie, but such things were necessary at times. Especially when it came to survival, be it of the kingdom or herself.

And if Sparrow refused to give up the grimoire, Anyka would send Nazyr to retrieve it. Let him use his magic then.

That would give her the perfect excuse to make a scapegoat of him and sacrifice him in the name of justice.

Assuming he killed Sparrow to get the book. Which Anyka presumed he would do.

She exhaled. This was all going to work out. She wasn't sure exactly how, but it would. And when it was all over, she'd have the grimoire, *both* kingdoms, and one less rival to worry about.

# Chapter Twenty-Two

"Professor Cloudtree got off all right last night," Gabriel filled Ro in as they walked toward the portal elevator. "I sent a royal guard with him and he's going to stay to escort him back as well, but I also requested ten more guards be sent to us here. They should arrive late this afternoon or early evening. They're coming on horseback, not by portal, so that they'll be able to provide additional protection when we eventually return home.

"I'm glad about Spencer, but ten more guards?" Ro blinked at him. "That seems like a lot."

"In light of the news about the diary, I don't think it is."

They stepped into the portal. He closed the doors and dialed the first floor.

Ro wasn't going to argue safety measures with him. It was his job, and he was very good at it. "I'm sure you're right. You're the head of security for a reason, after all. Thank you for being proactive."

"You're welcome." The doors slid open. "Your majesty."

They stepped out into a soft wave of noise, almost all of it coming from the dining hall. There were a lot of people, and staff, milling about. More than Ro had seen so far, although if she'd come down for the music last night, she'd have probably seen them all then.

Ro's brows lifted. "I guess we're not the only ones who've shown up for breakfast."

"Safe guess. I'll be right here if anyone gets too close."

She cut her eyes at him. "Don't run anyone through, all right? These are still citizens of the kingdom. If they want to talk to me, that's to be expected."

There was amusement in his eyes as he nodded. "Heard and understood."

"At the same time, I would like to actually eat something. We have a long day of library searching ahead. I don't want to waste too much time sitting around the table, so if someone does come to talk…"

"I can handle that."

She smiled at him. "I know you can."

She started forward. He stayed at her right shoulder about a half-pace back. As soon as she entered the dining hall, the buzz of conversation dropped in volume and all eyes turned toward her, except for the staff, who went right on about their business.

Ro gave a nod and polite smile to those already in their seats, then headed for the royal table, which was set with several carafes. Probably coffee, tea, and that delicious spiced cocoa, but there were too many other good aromas to pick out any particular ones.

An older man stepped into her path. "Your majesty, please forgive the intrusion." He bowed.

Gabriel moved in closer.

Ro might not have known every single line of royal

protocol by heart, but she knew that it was generally considered inappropriate to address a monarch before they addressed you. However, she understood that if someone really wanted to talk to her, their best chance was to seek her out and hope she'd forgive them. "What can I do for you, sir?"

He rose. "I am Sam Silversmith, my lady, and I must first thank you for returning us to the tradition of Willow Hall."

She smiled. "You're welcome. I'm glad you could join us." When he didn't say goodbye, she understood that he wasn't done. "Is there something else, Sam?"

He nodded. "My lady, I come from a long line of metallurgists, and I have a gift I would love to present to you. A dagger. Made by my own hands."

"That is very kind of you, Sam."

"It's a very special dagger, my lady. One imbued with magic. One designed to protect you."

Ro could practically feel Gabriel bristle at her side. She smiled at Sam. "How thoughtful. I promise you I am well protected, but—"

"You *are* well protected," Sam said, glancing a little nervously at Gabriel. "I didn't mean to imply otherwise. But this dagger is special. The magic embedded in it causes the blade to increase in temperature when dangerous magic is nearby."

"Oh. Isn't that interesting?" She looked at Gabriel, who was too busy staring Sam down to respond. "It does sound handy. And not like anything I have already. Do you have the dagger with you?"

"I do, my lady." He reached into the small satchel clipped to his belt and took out an object wrapped in a scrap of leather. He unwound it to reveal a beautifully tooled sheath of dark blue leather containing a dagger. He held it out to her in both hands.

She took it and pulled the dagger free by its hilt, which was some kind of dark blue stone flecked with silver and carved to look like twisted rope. The blade itself was brightly polished silver and perforated with a series of tiny stars all along the blade. Ro smiled. "It's lovely. It reminds me of Celestial Lake. Thank you so much, Sam."

Sam grinned and nodded. "Thank you, my lady."

As he left, Ro turned to Gabriel. "A very nice gift."

"One you should turn over to Uldamar for vetting."

She barely contained her smirk. "You think Sam might be a secret Malveauxian agent of doom?"

Gabriel was clearly unamused. "My lady, I am serious. No gift to royalty goes unvetted. It's standard royal pr—"

"Protocol, I know."

"Actually, procedure. But I grant you, they're very similar."

"Then when Uldamar joins us, he can have a look at it. All right?"

Gabriel nodded. "That's all I'm suggesting."

She narrowed her eyes at him, fighting not to laugh. "Was that really a suggestion, though? It sounded so much more forceful than that."

He sighed, mouth nearly bent into a frown. "If I overstepped—"

"I'm just teasing."

"Your safety is no laughing matter to me."

"And I am very grateful for that." He was awfully serious this morning. Maybe to balance out the kissing they'd done last night. But if she could have kissed him now without causing a scene of epic proportions, she would have.

"Mom."

She looked toward the door to see JT, Raphaela, Violet, Posey, and Vincent walking in. "Hello there." Then she said to Gabriel, "I guess we should take our seats."

They did and as everyone was joining them, Uldamar showed up with Althea Cloudtree. She curtseyed. "Good morning, your highness."

"Good morning, Althea. I'm so glad you could join us."

"I am very appreciative of the invite."

"I'm equally appreciative of your willingness to stay back and help."

"It's good to be useful."

Footmen came over and started filling cups. One stopped near Ro. "What would you like, your highness?"

"Half coffee, half cocoa."

As he filled her cup, Ro held out the dagger toward Uldamar. "This was a gift from a citizen this morning. Gabriel would like you to make sure it's not some kind of magical boobytrap. Although it does have magic in it."

Gabriel took the sheathed blade and passed it on. "According to the man who made it, the blade will heat up when dangerous magic is nearby."

JT looked up. "That's pretty cool."

"I thought so," Ro said.

"A bespelled dagger. How curious," Uldamar said. He accepted the dagger and removed it from its sheath to have a better look at it. "Marvelous piece. Just marvelous. Looks like Silversmith's work to me."

"It is," Ro said. "If you mean Sam Silversmith."

Posey nodded. "The Silversmiths are a very talented family."

"Yes, they are," Uldamar said. "Been around a long time. Good people. They do excellent work with metal and magic. As you can see." He carefully turned the dagger in his hands, then he just held it and closed his eyes.

Ro could have sworn light danced across the surface of the blade.

Uldamar opened his eyes and returned the dagger to its sheath before passing it back to her. "Seems perfectly safe to me. A generous gift, my lady."

"Great. Thank you. I'm happy to hear that." She set the dagger on her lap to be dealt with later.

"So am I," Gabriel said.

The footmen brought platters to the table, and one announced what was on them. "Cheese and egg pie with sausage and onion. Potatoes fried in duck fat. Broiled tomatoes. Wine-braised mushrooms. Potted beans."

JT grinned. "That's my kind of breakfast."

As plates were being filled, more platters arrived. These were put directly on the table and were piled high with little pastries, muffins, and biscuits. Pots of jam and preserves were added, too, along with delicate plates of butter pressed into the shape of a crown.

It was very fancy, and Ro appreciated all the work

the kitchen was going to. "This is quite a spread." She looked at JT. "Wiggy is going to wish she hadn't overslept."

He shrugged. "I tried to wake her up. She said she was up late chasing rodents and wanted to sleep."

"As long as she's enjoying herself." Benny had been asleep on the bed when Ro had left.

Althea leaned in. "Are there really rodents? I can't say I'm a fan of those."

Uldamar smiled. "My good lady, it's an enormous palace that's been here for centuries, straddles a body of water, stores immeasurable amounts of food, and boasts a stable capable of housing over a hundred horses. Of course there are rodents."

Ro just rolled her lips in to keep from laughing, but beside her Gabriel chuckled.

He looked down the table at Althea. "Maybe you should borrow the queen's cat, Benny, to inspect your room."

Althea nodded, her expression absolutely serious. "If that's an actual offer, I would definitely take you up on that, your majesty."

"Sure, Benny can come over and have a look around. But Mrs. Wigglesworth seems to care more about rodents than anyone I know, feline *or* fae."

"I would be grateful for any assistance," Althea said.

"I'll send her over." Hopefully, the Cloudtrees' room didn't have too many rodents or Wiggy wouldn't want to leave.

At the end of the meal, during which Ro had tried not

to overindulge, they sat for a few moments, discussing their plans.

Ro drank the last of her second cup of mixed coffee and cocoa. "I'll be in the History Library today. How about the rest of you?"

Althea raised her hand. "I can take the Children's Library. I'm always looking for new books to read to the grandbabies."

Posey and Violet looked at each other, then simultaneously announced, "Mysteries and Thrillers."

"Perfect," Ro said. "Uldamar? The Magic Library?"

He nodded. "Of course, your highness."

She looked at her son. "That leaves you, JT. Where do you want to go?"

He glanced at Raphaela. "How about Science Fiction?"

She gave him a nod. "Wherever you wish, my lord."

"That works," Ro said. "All right, let's see what we can find. Anyone who does find something, you know where the rest of us are. Locate whoever's nearest to you and share your discovery. No matter how small. We need all the clues we can get."

With that, she got to her feet, effectively dismissing them. Gabriel joined her, taking up his usual spot of half a pace back.

As they walked, she looked for a way to attach the new dagger to her person. "I don't know what to do with this."

"May I suggest your other boot? That sheath should nestle in there fairly well."

She nodded. "Yeah, I could do that. Although I must

look like I'm ready for battle now. A dagger at my hip and one in each boot." She laughed.

"You might be glad you have all of those when Anyka arrives."

She stopped as they reached the library door. "True enough." She glanced down the hall. People were wandering about, looking for their day's activities. "I wish my dream had been a little more specific about when she'd arrive. I feel a bit like I'm waiting for the other shoe to drop, you know?"

His eyes narrowed. "Why would a shoe be dropping?"

"I just mean waiting for her is making me antsy."

"Ah." He opened the library door for her. "In that case, I'm ready for the shoe to drop, too."

# Chapter Twenty-Three

Anyka leaned her head against the window and studied Willow Hall as it came into view. Beatryce and Ishmyel had both fallen asleep. She'd wake them in a bit, but for now, she was content to enjoy this moment alone.

Galwyn tucked his head against hers as if reminding her she wasn't truly alone.

"No, my pet," she said softly. "I have you, don't I?"

The Summer Palace was quite a sight to behold, even if the Grym side was shrouded in gray because of the cloud cover that hugged the boundary line of the river. Once it curved toward the lake, the sun reached every inch of it.

She squinted at the Summerton side. It was so *very* bright. But if she was able to find the grimoire and follow the ritual to remove the curse, that was exactly what Malveaux would look like once again.

Hard to imagine it had ever looked like that. She'd never known it that way. Just the way it was now. Dark and dreary, cold and often rainy. She didn't love the weather. In fact, she generally despised it and found it hard to stay warm.

But all this sun...that would take some getting used to.

"Are we there?"

Anyka looked over to see Beatryce had woken up and Ishmyel was coming around. "I was just about to wake you two. We're nearly there."

They both moved to look out the windows.

"I love it," Beatryce said. "I cannot wait to be out in that sun."

Apparently, Beatryce had none of Anyka's reservations.

"Take a parasol," Ishmyel said. "Or you'll be burnt to a crisp."

"He's right," Anyka said. "You've never had to worry about the sun before, but you'll have to be mindful of it here."

"I didn't bring a parasol."

"I'm sure the palace has one you can borrow." Anyka went back to looking out the window. They were arriving now and their carriage was pulling through a covered area where two long rows of staff awaited to greet them.

That was a nice touch, considering all Anyka had told them was that she was coming. No day or time. She'd done that partially because she hadn't been sure and partially because she wanted to see how they handled it.

So far, she was mildly impressed.

The carriage came to a stop directly in front of the palace's grand double doors. They were open, giving her a quick glimpse of the interior.

The carriage rocked slightly as a footman came down off the back. Wyett descended next. She saw them through the windows as the footman opened the door. Wyett stood waiting, his hand extended to help her out.

She smoothed her skirts, hoping she wasn't a wrinkled

mess, then took a breath and touched Galwyn. "Here we go, my pet." She placed her hand in Wyett's to descend the carriage steps.

As soon as she was out, Wyett let go of her hand and announced, "Her royal highness, Queen Anyka Blackbryar of Malveaux. And Galwyn, the Royal Raven."

It pleased her to have Galwyn announced. Those in attendance would do well to remember the importance of her pet.

A man stepped away from the rows of staff and bowed. "Your highness. Welcome to Willow Hall. We are extraordinarily pleased to have you here. I'm Trence Underwood, Master of the House. Anything at all that you need, my staff and I will see that you get it. You have only to ask."

"Good," Anyka said. "Thank you." Behind her, Beatryce and Ishmyel got out.

Wyett announced them as well. "Princess Beatryce Blackbryar and his Lordship, Ishmyel Blackbryar, uncle to the queen and great-uncle to the princess."

Trence bowed to them. "It is our pleasure to have you here."

He returned his attention to Anyka. "Is there anything I can offer you now? A refreshment of some kind? A tour of the grounds or palace? Or would you like to go directly to the royal suite?"

"The suite." She knew Beatryce would probably want the tour, but Anyka needed to see what kind of space they'd given her. Just because they were calling it the royal suite didn't mean it would be up to her standards.

"As you wish," Trence said. He clapped his hands twice

and footmen came out of the ranks to collect baggage. "Right this way."

She glanced over her shoulder at the carriage. Chyles hovered near the back of it. She nodded at him. "Come along."

She motioned to Trence. "Go on."

He led them inside, where there was a wide, sweeping staircase and a grand hall. A few people wandered about, paying no attention to her.

Trence directed them to a small room. "This portal will allow you to travel to any of the floors in Willow Hall without a ring. It's built into the portal. Rather old-fashioned, I know, but it works for our purposes."

He showed them how to dial it, then closed the doors and set the ring for the second floor. When he opened them again, they looked out onto a new area. It was carpeted with a thick, botanically patterned weave in midnight blue, ice blue, emerald green, mint green, lavender, and royal purple.

The walls were midnight blue accented with trim in gold. The wall sconces were gold as well and flickered with cold flames that were clearly magic. Anyka preferred real flames in Castle Hayze, because they contributed some heat as well.

Trence led her directly to an alcove with another set of double doors. These were glossy emerald, trimmed in gold, with small accent lines of midnight blue.

He gestured to the other side of the hall. "There are guest suites on this side for anyone you wish to keep close." Then he opened the doors to the royal suite. "There are five bedrooms available here, each with their own private bathing and dressing rooms."

Anyka walked in through the small foyer and found herself in a generous sitting room. The colors in the hall continued through but the sitting room had walls paneled in warm, dark wood. The picture that hung over the fireplace was of Castle Hayze, but it had obviously been painted long before the curse had befallen Malveaux, because sunlight streamed across the canvas.

She said nothing and walked through to a more private sitting room. There was a perch set up for Galwyn. That pleased her. Several doors led off of the space, but through an arched opening at the very end she could see a dining room. It was good to know she wouldn't be expected to take every meal in a common dining hall.

She looked at Trence. "Which would be my bedroom?"

"Of course, any bedroom you'd like would be yours, but the grandest of the three in here would be the door all the way to the left."

Anyka went through that door. The room beyond was nearly as large as her personal quarters at home. It was done in shades of green and purple with accents of snake print, gold leaf, and feathers.

As much as she hated to admit it, the space was slightly better decorated than her current quarters. That made her realize she was overdue for a change at home. Another perch sat near the fireplace. "What do you think, Galwyn?"

He cawed softly as she walked on to inspect the dressing room and bathing room. Both were more than adequate. She came back out to the smaller sitting room. Beatryce and Ishmyel were standing there, obviously waiting on her decision.

"That will be my room. Take whichever ones you want for yourselves." She'd thought about sending her uncle across the hall, but in light of the news about the grimoire, she'd decided it would be better to keep him close.

She walked out to the big sitting room. Wyett, Chyles, and Trog were there, as was Trence. She spoke to Wyett. "You and Chyles may take one of the suite's other bedrooms. Have a look now and decide which you want but come back here when you've sorted that. Trog, you may have one of the bedrooms across the hall if you think you'll need it."

Trog grunted and went to stand by the door, his usual spot. Wyett and Chyles went nowhere. Wyett cleared his throat softly. "That is very generous of you, my lady. Where might those bedrooms be?"

She realized she didn't know herself. She looked at Trence. "You did say there were five bedrooms in total?"

"Yes, your highness." He went over by the fireplace and pushed on one of the wood panels. It opened with a soft snick. "Down this hall are the other two."

She nodded. "There you are, Wyett. Chyles. Go have a look."

They went to make their selections.

"Trog, will you need a bedroom?"

Trog grunted, and Anyka understood him well enough to know he'd said he wouldn't.

"Well, if you must, you can always rest in here."

Under normal circumstances, she never would have considered housing Wyett, Chyles, or Trog so close to her, but these were not normal circumstances. Somewhere in this palace was the Radiant queen and all of her guards.

Anyka wasn't going to take any chances. For all she knew, Queen Sparrow had orchestrated this entire trip as a way to draw Anyka out and put her in a vulnerable spot. This might be an elaborate ambush. A way for Queen Sparrow to eliminate Anyka.

She sucked in a breath as that realization settled over her. Had she just willingly walked into a trap?

"Anyka," a voice said softly.

She turned to see Ishmyel at her side.

"Are you all right? You looked pale for a moment. Not quite yourself."

She swallowed, still a little lost in her mind's wanderings. "I…"

"Perhaps something to eat and drink would help? It's been a while since breakfast, hasn't it?"

She nodded, grateful for the excuse. "Yes, it has."

Ishmyel looked at Trence. "Queen Anyka needs a meal and something to drink. We all do. Surely you can see to that?"

Trence gave a quick nod. "I can. I should mention, lunch will be served in the dining hall shortly. I can have the kitchen send up something light to tide you over until then, if you like."

"No," Anyka said. "I'll take my meal here. Now. In the private dining room."

Just then, Wyett and Chyles returned to the sitting room.

"Very good, my lady," Trence said. "Unless there's anything else, I'll go now and let the kitchen know."

"Nothing further," Anyka said. She knew the footmen would be arriving with their trunks shortly. "Wyett, deal with the footmen when they bring our things."

"Yes, my lady."

She grabbed her uncle's arm. "I would like to speak to you in private. My room. Now."

She didn't say another word until they were in the bedroom. She closed the door and sat on the bed, her uncle standing nearby looking slightly unsure. She clasped her hands together. "I fear I've made a grave error."

"How so?"

"By coming here! What if this is just a trap set by Summerton's new queen? What if getting me here was the first step? She could kill me and make it look like a thousand different kinds of accidents. I could be murdered in my sleep. I could—"

"Anyka."

She looked up at him. She knew her mind was getting the best of her. She'd heard whispers that her mother had suffered from the same kind of strain. "What?"

"You are surrounded by protection. Not just the royal guard, but Wyett and Trog and me. Even Chyles. None of us will let harm come to you. You know that."

She did. She nodded. "I do. I just can't help but think this was a foolish mistake."

"It wasn't. It was brave and courageous and it's going to

change the course of Malveaux once you find that grimoire."

She exhaled. The grimoire. She needed to keep her focus on that. "*If* I find it."

"You will. Just like you will meet the Radiant queen and show her that she is the one who should be afraid. Not the other way around."

He came closer, eyes full of fierce light. "You are Anyka Zaryna Blackbryar. Ruler of Malveaux. She who wears the Grym crown. Wielder of the royal sword, *Mourning Hawke*. You cheated death when you were sixteen and the dark specter learned its lesson that day. You are not a woman to be trifled with. Anyone foolish enough to cross you deserves what they get."

She nodded. He was right. She got to her feet. "Thank you, Uncle." Spirits renewed, she lifted her chin. "I think the traveling tired me more than I realized."

He smiled. "A little refreshment will do you good." His eyes narrowed. "Then an introduction must be made. It cannot seem that you are avoiding this new queen."

"No, it can't. You're right." She rested her hand on the daggers at her waist. "I believe we'll go down to lunch after all."

# Chapter Twenty-four

Ro and Gabriel sat in one of the conversation chambers in the History Library. She had a book in her hands. He was staring out into the library, keeping watch. Even with the glass doors, it was quite cozy and if it had been any other day, she would have been thrilled to be in such a small space with him.

But two things were ruining her joy.

One was that she'd walked the entire library three times in her supposed search for the right book to read and found nothing that remotely seemed Lady Cynzia-related.

The second was that with each passing minute, she knew the arrival of Queen Anyka drew closer.

"You haven't read a page of that, have you?" Gabriel asked.

"Yes, I have," Ro said. "I've read the same page at least four times. Did you know that the term 'Radiant' comes from an ancient fae word meaning light-bearer?"

He smiled. "Yes, I did know that."

"You did not." She bit her lip. "Did you?"

He nodded. "When we escaped Malveaux and resettled in Summerton, my parents drilled Radiant history into us. They wanted us to be as knowledgeable about our new home as our native neighbors."

"Not a bad strategy."

He nodded, his concentration on the library beyond the conversation chamber's glass doors. "It worked well enough. No one could ever say we were ignorant of our new kingdom's ways."

"When you say 'we,' does that mean you have siblings?"

"I have a sister and a brother. My brother lives in Yarne, the goblin kingdom. He manages one of the trillianite mines. My sister...I haven't spoken to her in a while. She lives in France. At least she did the last I heard."

"She's in the mortal world?"

"Yes. She left years ago." He shrugged. "She had a taste of it and decided instantly that was the life she wanted."

"Does she come back to visit?"

"No."

Ro let it drop. It saddened her to think Gabriel had family he never got to see. She would have killed for a brother or sister. Being an only child was lonely sometimes. If she'd been in a different position as an adult, she would have given JT a sibling.

That opportunity just hadn't presented itself to her. Thankfully, he seemed to have turned out just fine. Well-adjusted. Liked by everyone who met him. No lasting defects from being a single.

"Should we cross off the History Library as a possible location for Lady Cynzia's diary?"

"I don't know," he said. He shifted to see through the

doors better. "Do you think you've searched it as thoroughly as it can be?"

"Not even close. To do that, I'd have to spend hours in here, look at every book, flip through pages…" She sighed. "It seems impossible, honestly."

He glanced at her. "Hopefully, when Professor Cloudtree gets back, he'll have some clues for us to follow."

"I really pray that's true."

A soft, dulcet chime sounded.

She looked through the glass doors. "What was that?"

"Not sure." He got up. "I'll go find out. Don't let anyone in unless you know them."

"Yes, sir."

He made a little face. "Please." Then he slipped through the doors.

She went back to her book and read a brand-new page before he returned.

He opened one door and stood halfway in. "That chime was the announcement that lunch is now being served in the dining hall."

"I suppose we should go, then. Be a good chance to see how everyone else did, although no one came to share any news, so I'm pretty sure I already know how they did." She closed her book. "Same as us."

He held the door for her as she came out. She placed her book on a table to be reshelved by one of the librarians and walked with Gabriel to the dining hall. They found Uldamar and Althea on the way.

"Any luck?" Ro asked.

Althea answered first. "It would take days to properly search that library."

Ro nodded. "That's going to be the same with all of them, I think. Uldamar, how about you?"

"Some very interesting books, to be sure, but nothing like what I was hoping to find. There is another matter, however." He glanced around, looking slightly anxious about whatever he was going to say next. "Your majesty, I have it on good authority that Queen Anyka is here."

Ro stopped walking. The news pinned her feet to the floor and, for a few seconds, made it impossible for her to process any further thoughts. It had happened. The shoe had dropped. "You're sure?"

He nodded. "Trence told me himself."

Ro blew out a breath, then rolled her head around trying to release the tension that had suddenly settled into her neck and shoulders. "Why does this make me so nervous?" She put her hand to her stomach, which was tying itself in knots.

"Because you perceive her as a threat," Althea said. "And while she might be, in the immediate here and now, you have nothing to worry about. We will do everything in our power to protect you."

Ro smiled down at the petite older woman. "Thank you. How did you get to be so perceptive?"

Althea smiled. "I used to teach psychology at Summerton University."

Ro laughed. "So you're technically a professor, too."

"I was," Althea said.

Gabriel had somehow gathered two royal guards while

Ro and Althea had been talking. "Your highness, you'll have an escort now. One guard ahead of you, me at your side, another behind."

JT and Raphaela joined them. He said, "Hey, what's up?"

Gabriel spoke to his daughter. "The raven has landed."

She nodded in understanding and looked at the guards he'd called over. "Flank formation?"

"Yes."

"Your lordship," Raphaela said to JT. "If you could walk into the dining hall at your mother's side, I'll be just behind you."

"Sure, I can do that," JT said. "But we're not going in without Aunt Vi and Posey, are we?"

Ro shrugged. "They might already be in there. Unless you want to go down to the Mysteries and Thrillers Library and see if they're still in there."

"Yeah, let me do that." He nodded and tipped his head down the hall as he looked at Raphaela.

"Coming," she said.

Gabriel called after them. "We'll be right here." Then he focused on Ro. "Don't be nervous. She might be a queen, but so are you. You're her equal. Regardless of how long you've been on the throne."

Ro smiled. "Good point."

Uldamar stroked his beard, bushy brows raised. "I'd like to add that while Queen Anyka might have ascended to the throne because she was next in line, the magic of Summerton *chose* you."

Ro laughed softly and reached out to touch his arm. "Thank you. I needed to be reminded of that."

JT and Raphaela reappeared in the hall with Violet, Posey, and Vincent. Once they were all back together, they formed up. One of the royal guards in front, then Ro and JT with Violet and Posey directly behind them and Gabriel and Raphaela just to the sides of them. Behind them was Vincent, then Uldamar and Althea. The last royal guard brought up the rear.

Ro felt like she was in an impromptu parade. Before they could move forward, she shook her head. "No, this is silly. I don't want to look ridiculous, and this is too much pomp and circumstance for *lunch*."

JT turned toward her. "How do you want to do it then?"

"Gabriel can walk me in first. Then the rest of you come."

Gabriel grunted, the expression on his face telling her he didn't approve of her change in plans.

She addressed him. "Send the guards in ahead. They can stand on either side of the door or table, whichever you prefer, so long as they're out of the way of the staff who are serving lunch."

"And if Queen Anyka is already in there?"

Ro thought about that. "Then I'll go over, introduce myself, and say hello. There's no reason not to keep things simple. Overthinking it is what's making me nervous. She's probably a lovely woman."

Gabriel's sharp glance at Uldamar wasn't lost on Ro.

She faced her aunt, because she knew Violet would tell

her the truth. "How do I look? Everything straight? No weird flyaway hairs or smudged makeup?"

Violet took a hard look at Ro, then shook her head and smiled. "You look every inch a queen. And a very beautiful one at that."

"Thank you, Auntie Vi." Then Ro spoke to Gabriel. "Come on. Let's just do this. If I stand around any longer, I'm going to lose my nerve." She started forward, relying on a lot of willpower to keep her going. Gabriel stayed beside her.

Ro clung to what Gabriel and Uldamar had said. She was Anyka's equal. And the kingdom Ro ruled had actually chosen her to be in charge.

That seemed like a pretty good qualification for being queen.

Gabriel cleared his throat softly and spoke in a low voice Ro knew was meant only for her. "Your aunt is right. You look very beautiful."

Ro smiled and whispered back, "Thank you." Those words gave her another boost of confidence. She would have loved to be able to hold his hand in that moment but knew it wasn't possible.

Footmen opened the doors to the dining hall as they approached.

She took a breath, fixed her smile in place, and walked through. Her gaze went straight to the second royal table.

Every seat was filled but it wasn't hard to find Queen Anyka. She was beautiful in a cold, slightly terrifying way. The sharp angles and pronounced bone structure of her body and face made her look like she wasn't exactly flesh and blood, but rather carved of glass and stone and then animated.

The tips of her ears poked through her long, dark, perfect hair. She had eyes that glittered like chips of glacial ice. She was talking to a younger, softer version of herself, seated just to her right. She hadn't seen Ro yet, so Ro stayed where she was, staring, even though she knew she shouldn't.

Gabriel, still at Ro's side, let out a quiet, muttered curse.

"What's wrong?" Ro asked without looking at him.

"The woman to the left of the queen, two people away from her."

Ro looked at the woman in question. Also very beautiful, but with emerald green eyes and deep auburn hair that flowed in soft waves where it wasn't caught back in braids. "What about her?"

He snorted out a hot burst of air. "That's Lystra."

The name was familiar to Ro, but she couldn't quite place it. Not while her mind was so occupied with Queen Anyka. She had to go over and introduce herself. Had to make a good first impression. She would be strong, but nice. "Who is that again?"

Gabriel grunted. "My ex-wife."

# Chapter Twenty-Five

Anyka felt eyes on her. She turned in time to see a woman coming toward her. A woman in a crown and beautiful clothing, daggers at her hip and in both boots. A woman who carried herself as if she owned the world.

Anyka envied the woman's sun-kissed skin and generous curves even as ice sluiced through her own veins at the sight of her rival. Anyka forced her legs to straighten and pushed to her feet, realized Queen Sparrow was smiling at her, and made herself smile back.

"You must be Queen Anyka," the woman said. She extended her hand. A portal ring adorned it. Her nails were short but buffed to a high shine.

Anyka shook the woman's hand carefully, oddly aware of how stark her own black-lacquered nails looked against her pale skin. How prominent the bones of her hand were. "I am. And you must be Queen Sparrow."

"The one and only," Queen Sparrow replied. "It's a pleasure to meet you. I'm so glad you came. I wasn't sure you were going to after your answer to my invitation."

"Yes, well, I wasn't sure I was going to, either."

"No worries. You're here now and that's all that

matters." The trillianites in Queen Sparrow's circlet were breathtaking. "How was your trip?"

Anyka did her best to pay attention to what Queen Sparrow was saying. Were all Radiant fae this...chatty? "It was fine. Thank you for asking."

"Wonderful. Your jewels are gorgeous. I just love amethysts."

"Thank you. Yours are also...very nice." Whatever Anyka had expected, it wasn't this.

"I'll let you get back to your meal, but I look forward to speaking to you again and getting to know you better during our time here. I really feel like this is the dawn of a new era for our kingdoms, don't you?"

Anyka didn't know how to answer that without saying something she'd regret. So she lied. Her pulse was elevated for some unfathomable reason. "Yes."

"That's fantastic. I know we'll talk soon." Queen Sparrow kept on smiling. "Enjoy your meal."

Anyka blinked, feeling slightly blindsided, as she'd been utterly unprepared for such mundane small talk. "You, uh, do likewise."

"Thank you." Queen Sparrow went to her table, which was mercifully far enough away that neither group could overhear the other's conversation.

Anyka sat and stared at her place, which held a small plate filled with a dressed salad of greens, vegetables, cheese, and nuts. She replayed the conversation in her head, trying to make sense of what had actually just happened. Was Queen Sparrow genuinely being nice? Was she clueless? Or was it some ruse to distract Anyka from whatever Sparrow's true intentions were?

Regardless of the real answer, Anyka was definitely distracted.

"She's fat," Beatryce said.

"Be quiet," Anyka snapped. "You can't say things like that when we're amongst so many people."

"Well, she is," Beatryce said. She stabbed a slice of radish with her fork.

Anyka glared at her daughter. "Regardless of what she looks like, you will keep your opinion to yourself unless we are behind closed doors. You are the next in line for the throne. You cannot speak openly about people that way. At least not people who rule the neighboring kingdom."

Beatryce rolled her eyes, but at least lowered her voice. "You're going to overthrow her. Why are you so concerned with what she..." Beatryce trailed off as her gaze shifted toward the door. "Who is that?"

Anyka looked over. A tall, handsome Grym man had just walked into the dining room. "I have no idea. He must have come with us, but I don't—" The young man had a female royal guard at his side. Also Grym. But dressed in Summerton's colors.

He went and sat at Queen Sparrow's table and Anyka was able to read his lips just enough as he spoke to the queen.

"How did it go, Mom?"

The Grym man was Sparrow's son? The prince of Summerton? Anyka stared. Hard. How was it possible that the new queen, the one who'd been able to free *Merediem* from the stone, had a Grym son? How?

"Are you seeing what I'm seeing?" Ishmyel asked.

Anyka nodded. "I am. I don't understand it, though."

"She obviously took a Grym lover at some point in her life. Maybe even married him, although I don't recall anything being said about her having a husband, so he either left her or is deceased."

Anyka stopped staring. "I cannot believe the people of Summerton didn't riot against this."

He shook his head. "I agree with you. It is very curious."

Anyka sipped her water and snuck one final look before changing the subject. "Any news from Nazyr?"

"Not yet," Ishmyel said. "He claims he needs more time to perfect the amulet and give it the precise adjustments it needs now that we're finally inside Willow Hall. He requested his next three meals be sent to his quarters."

"Fine with me," Anyka said. "Just so long as he gets it done. And it works."

Ishmyel frowned. "I hope he's not just stalling."

A new fear lit through Anyka. "You don't think he's using this time to search for the book on his own, do you?"

"I hope not. But he'd be seen if he was. Willow Hall is well populated now."

"Perhaps." Anyka nearly growled in frustration. If Nazyr proved to be disloyal, she would treat him appropriately.

Beatryce nudged her. "Is that Grym man related to Queen Sparrow?"

Anyka nodded. "Yes. I believe he's her son."

"Seriously? How can that be? She's Radiant." Then Beatryce gasped and laughed. "Oh, but her personal guard is also Grym, isn't he? Seems the queen has dark tastes. And doesn't care who knows it."

Again, Anyka glared at her child, who had suddenly lost the sense she'd been born with. "That guard has only recently been assigned to her. How would he have *anything* to do with her son's heritage?"

Beatryce blinked as if she were processing the question but unable to find an answer. "I don't know. Maybe they knew each other before. Maybe he helped her pull the sword from the stone because they're lovers and he wanted her to be queen."

Anyka stared in speechless wonder at her daughter. Then she grimaced. "Stop speaking unless you have something valuable to add to the conversation."

Beatryce sniffed and went back to her salad.

Anyka glanced over at Queen Sparrow's guard. He was indeed Grym. She didn't recognize him, but she knew who he was supposed to be, if rumors were correct.

Gabriel Nightborne. A refugee to Summerton. A traitor to Malveaux. A man Anyka thought might turn out to be very useful, with a little persuasion.

Anyka shifted her gaze to a woman at her own table, one of her invited guests. "Lystra, is that him?"

Lystra turned to look. She stared for a few long seconds, then faced Anyka again. There was a brief flash of pain in the woman's eyes, but it was quickly replaced by steely resolve. "Yes, my lady. That's him. And my daughter, too."

Anyka pursed her lips. "When do you plan to begin?"

"Soon. This evening, perhaps."

"You will keep me aware of any progress you make."

It wasn't a question, but Lystra answered anyway. "Yes, your highness."

Anyka pushed the leaves of salad around on her plate. She needed to eat. She was hungry. But her appetite had waned since meeting Queen Sparrow.

The woman was nothing like what Anyka had expected and yet, somehow, more than at the same time.

She pierced a small hunk of cheese as a realization struck her. Was this sense of uncertainty about the new queen actually Sparrow's magic at work? Could one so newly arrived to this realm already have magic?

Anyka's lips parted in shock at the thought. She snuck a look at the woman again.

Sparrow was laughing and smiling with those at her table. As if meeting Anyka hadn't fazed her a bit.

To Anyka, that settled it in her mind.

Queen Sparrow's magic was far greater than any of them understood.

# Chapter Twenty-Six

Under cover of the table and the long cloth that draped it, Ro reached for Gabriel's hand and gave it a squeeze. She just needed to connect with him for a moment. To be reassured that all was well.

He squeezed back, brightening the smile she'd been clinging to. She released his hand and brought hers back to the table, even though she would have preferred to hold onto him. They did both need to eat, after all.

"So, is that her daughter?" JT asked.

"I don't know," Ro answered. "I guess so. She didn't introduce anyone at her table. Then again, I didn't introduce any of you, so I guess we'll just get to that part later."

Posey, who was seated facing Anyka's table, had been watching the young woman next to Anyka. "She's very pretty."

Ro nodded. "They both are."

Aunt Violet leaned in. "Do you think food is scarce in Malveaux? They're all so thin, aren't they?"

Ro had noticed but didn't want to speculate on the cause. "Maybe that's just what's in style in Malveaux. She reminds me of some of the ballerinas that used to come into the museum. They were built a lot like that. Thin as a whisper with those knife-edge cheekbones and collarbones, but at the same time, muscled." Her brow furrowed. "Maybe the queen was a dancer. Or is."

Gabriel snorted. "I doubt it. As far as I know, the queen has never been anything but the queen."

Uldamar nodded. "Her entire life has been spent in service to her kingdom. It's all she's ever known." He glanced toward Anyka's table. "It is, I believe, one of her faults. A broader experience makes for a much better ruler. One with compassion and understanding. One who cares for more than just furthering the power she wields."

The table went quiet. Ro hadn't been expecting that response and neither had anyone else, judging by the silence.

"Well said, Uldamar," Ro said. "I will do my best to keep that in mind for my own governance."

"Your highness, you have already shown compassion and understanding in the few days you've worn the crown." His eyes narrowed. "In my humble opinion, Malveaux would be better served with a fae like you at its helm."

Again, the table went silent.

Then Gabriel lifted his glass. "To Queen Sparrow."

They all put their glasses in the air. "To Queen Sparrow."

A moment after that, every Radiant fae in attendance did the same, filling the room with the words and making it obvious that Queen Sparrow's table had been overheard.

Ro felt her cheeks warm. She wasn't embarrassed for herself so much as she was embarrassed that Anyka had been present for that. There was something...awkward about another ruler hearing your praises being sung.

It was sweet, too. Ro wasn't about to tell them to stop. But she didn't dare sneak a look at Anyka. Instead, she asked Gabriel to do it. "Did Anyka freak out about that? Or did she take it in stride?"

He shifted his gaze across the way. "She looks moderately perturbed, which is about what I'd expect. I imagine she pretty much always looks that way."

Then she broached a much trickier subject. "Are you going to speak to your ex-wife?"

"No reason to."

"Does Raphaela know she's here?"

"Probably."

"You seem bothered by it." He did, actually. When he gave those kinds of short answers, Ro understood he was upset.

The muscles in his jaw twitched. He sat back as a footman cleared the empty salad plates while another came behind him and served the next course: cold sliced chicken and ham, potato salad, an assortment of pickles, fresh fruit, and bread with butter.

He spoke when the footmen were gone. "I can't say I'm thrilled by it." He sighed. "It seems to me Anyka had to know who she was, which tells me she was brought along for a purpose. What that purpose is, I don't know, but there isn't an ounce of me that believes it's something good."

"Maybe you should talk to her, then. Get it over with. Or see if you can figure out what she's up to."

"No. I'm not digging up that grave until I absolutely have to."

"Digging up that grave?" Ro shuddered even as she laughed. "In the mortal realm, people say opening a can of worms."

Gabriel's eyes narrowed. "How is that better? Or, frankly, different?"

"Good point."

They went back to eating and chatting about insignificant topics. No one, it seemed, wanted to discuss the hunt for Lady Cynzia's diary when Anyka was over at the next table. Ro didn't think there was any chance of anyone eavesdropping. There was more than enough distance between the two tables, not to mention the ambient noise of the dining hall that made deciphering individual words and who'd spoken them impossible.

All the same, she was happy to leave that topic alone. She didn't want anyone figuring out what they were up to. Not other Radiant in attendance, not any of Anyka's people, not even the Willow Hall staff.

It just needed to be kept to their own group.

When dessert arrived—individual vanilla layer cakes with chocolate icing and raspberry sauce drizzled over it, along with a handful of fresh berries—Ro was ready to get back to the hunt. She had no grand ideas that any of them would be successful. But Anyka's presence had stoked the fire in her, urging her to get the book before the other queen did.

Gabriel's cake was half gone. He leaned over. "You were right, by the way."

"About what?"

"Your dream. About her arriving today."

"Oh, right, I was." She laughed. "Maybe that *is* my magic."

"What's that, Mom?" JT asked.

"Gabriel thinks that dream interpretation might be my magic."

JT nodded. "You were right about that dream I had about Raphaela."

Raphaela looked at him. "You dreamed about me?"

He laughed. "Yeah, you were a wolf."

She grinned. "Seems about right."

Violet nodded. "Dream interpretation would be a marvelous gift to have."

Posey looked thrilled by it. "Maybe we should start telling you our dreams in the morning and letting you tell us what they mean so you'll know if it's true or not. I had a dream last night that I was being chased through the forest by awful, candy-colored monsters."

Violet snorted. "*I* can tell you what that means. It means you ate too many bonbons at the recital last night."

Posey's brows went up. "I didn't see you turning them away."

Ro smirked and took another bite of cake. She swallowed, looking at Gabriel. "Maybe we should take a break from the library to practice sword work again."

"Whatever you'd like, my lady." He made a face like he had more to say.

"But?"

He took a breath. "But I think there are more pressing matters."

She nodded. "You're right. I guess I'm feeling a little like we're searching for a needle in a haystack, you know?"

"Now *that* I understand. And I do know. But that needle will be found. It *will* be."

"You seem very sure."

"Because not being sure is like saying that not finding it is okay. Which it isn't. We are potentially talking about the survival of our way of life." His gaze softened, completely focused on her. "For some of us, it's our own survival. We have no choice but to find it."

"Then I guess we need to get back to work, don't we?"

He nodded. "Yes, my lady. We do."

She looked around the table. "All right, everyone. Time to resume Operation Needle, as in 'needle in a haystack.' Let's all take up where we left off. I'm hoping, as I'm sure we all are, that Professor Cloudtree has already uncovered some valuable information and will be headed back to us very soon."

Althea smiled. "I'm sure he's doing his best.

Ro nodded. "I know he is. Spencer is a good man." She set her napkin alongside her plate, then rose to her feet. "Same instructions as before. Happy hunting, my friends."

As they were all getting up, she and Gabriel headed out. "Thanks for the pep talk," she said.

"Anytime."

They went back to the History Library. Ro stood in the center of it, having a look around for what felt like the millionth time and trying to see it with fresh eyes. Gabriel stayed close but let her be. She walked toward the tall, stained-glass windows present in every library.

These depicted scenes from fae history, none of which she really understood. She would someday, but right now she was content to admire them for the beauty of the craftsmanship. She glanced back at Gabriel. "Has this stained glass always been here? Or were they added later?"

He shook his head. "I don't know. I'm sure the librarian would."

As if on cue, the librarian, a woman named Deanna Sweetwater, appeared. "Is there something I can help with, your majesty?"

"I was just wondering if this stained glass is original or if it was added later?"

"Those are the original windows. Aren't they beautiful?" She gazed up at the scenes on display. "We had a terrible storm nearly fifty years ago that damaged some of them, but they were all repaired."

"Willow Hall is beautiful," Ro said. "And those of you who work here and look after the place do an amazing job."

Deanna smiled and dipped her head. "That is so kind of you, your majesty. Thank you."

Ro decided to ask a question she'd been hesitant to previously. "Maybe you could help me find a book?"

"I would love to, my lady. What did you have in mind?"

"As you know, I'm new to the throne. This is my first time meeting Queen Anyka. I'd love to understand more about Malveaux." Ro lowered her voice. "I'd very much like to read about the curse that changed everything for that kingdom. About how it all happened, who was involved, that sort of thing. Do you have any books that would cover that?"

Deanna nodded. "I believe we do. If you'd like to find a spot to sit, I'd be happy to bring them to you."

Ro pointed toward the conversation chamber she and Gabriel had been in before. "We'll be over there."

"Excellent. I'll bring the books over as soon as I've collected them."

"Thank you." Ro and Gabriel went to sit in the conversation chamber.

He closed the doors. "Well done. Asking for books about Lady Cynzia without using her name."

Ro smiled. "I know it was a little risky, but I thought it was worth a shot."

"I agree." He sat where he could see through the doors and keep an eye on anyone approaching them.

"Might not lead to anything, but then again..."

"Agreed." His gaze was focused outward, as usual. "Library is busier now than it was this morning. A good number of them are Grym."

"Good. I hope our people and the people of Malveaux make friends and understand there are no enemies on either side."

He slanted his eyes at her. "There *are* enemies."

"Yes, I realize that, but you know what I mean. We're all fae. We all bleed the same color."

"Something I hope no one has to find out anytime soon," he muttered.

Deanna returned several minutes later with an armful

of books. Gabriel opened the door for her, and she handed him the books. "I believe all of those will cover the time and events in question. Some of it might overlap, but each author will undoubtedly focus on different aspects with varying levels of detail."

"Thank you so much," Ro said. "If there are some I'd like to hang on to, is it permitted to check the books out and take them back to my suite?"

"Absolutely, your majesty. Just let me know and I'll take care of that for you."

Ro smiled at the woman. "I appreciate that, Deanna. You've been a big help."

The woman curtsied and left, smiling.

Gabriel closed the door again. "You're good at winning people over. I wouldn't be surprised if she comes back at some point with a few more books on the subject."

"I'd be all right with that. Anything that can lead us closer to finding our needle, I'm for."

"I agree."

"Good, because I need you to help me go through these or we'll be hauling them all back to the suite." She picked off the top book and opened it, hoping there was a table of contents to help her find a starting place.

"You realize I'm supposed to be keeping an eye out for potential danger."

She sucked in a breath as she looked up through her lashes. "You just made me remember something."

He sat up a little straighter. "What?"

"When I was over at Anyka's table, speaking to her, the dagger in my boot warmed up. In all the excitement, it sort of slipped my mind. In fact, I think when it happened, I dismissed it, because I'd forgotten about the dagger and what it could do. But you said potential danger and it came back to me. What do you think it means?"

Gabriel's face went stony. "I think it means that Anyka and her party are a threat to you, and you should by no means be alone with any of them."

## CHAPTER TWENTY-SEVEN

Anyka retired to her suite after lunch. Beatryce and Ishmyel returned with her. She sent Ishmyel to bring Wyett and Chyles in and they were soon all assembled in the large sitting room. Trog was at his spot by the door.

Anyka faced them all. "I know we need to begin looking for the grimoire, but I can't imagine we'll have any kind of success until Nazyr finishes the amulet."

"When might that be, my lady?" Wyett asked.

"I wish I knew." Everyone else was sitting, but she was too wound up to be still. Instead, she paced. "But I can't stay in the room. Not when Queen Sparrow is out and about. I have to be seen."

Wyett coughed quietly. "There are activities day and night, my lady. Perhaps doing a few activities now, before you have the amulet, would balance out the time you'll be spending in the libraries later."

She stopped pacing to consider that. It wasn't a bad idea. "What kind of activities are there?"

He pulled a scroll of paper from his jacket. "Watercolor painting, poetry reading, garden tours, a guided walk around the lake, boating, archery, trail riding up to the waterfall, fishing, birdwatching, still-life drawing, cake decorating, a talk on the history of fae weaponry, a tour of Willow Hall that includes all of the most important art—"

Anyka put her hand up. "I understand. There is a lot to do."

"I'm going to take the tour of Willow Hall," Beatryce announced as if it were a foregone conclusion.

Anyka frowned. "Really?"

Beatryce nodded. "That way I can learn the layout of the palace while being seen and seeing others."

Anyka laughed. "That's actually a good plan." Just when she'd started to think her daughter had lost her way, Bea came through. "Why don't we both do that? Trog will accompany us, of course, but then that leaves the rest of you to peruse the libraries and possibly see what our Summerton friends are up to."

Ishmyel rubbed his chin as if thinking. "I wouldn't mind having a look through a few of the libraries."

"Then go, do that," Anyka said. "Wyett, Chyles, I don't mind if you look around the libraries as well, but I'd like you to see if you can mix in with the staff a bit. Maybe see if there's anything to be gleaned about Queen Sparrow from them."

Wyett nodded. "We can do that. Chyles might have more success. My position as your valet is fairly well known."

"Whatever you can find out will be welcome." Any information would be helpful, since they basically had none. "I believe that Queen Sparrow has great magic. Far more than we've been led to believe. See if anyone can confirm that."

Wyett got up. Chyles scrambled to follow. Wyett nodded. "We will, my lady. We'll do the best we can."

"I know you will." She looked at Beatryce. "I need a few minutes and then I'll be ready to go."

Ishmyel got up. "Enjoy your tour. I'll see you this evening."

"Goodbye, Uncle. Good hunting."

He smiled. "If only it were that easy."

She laughed softly. "Indeed." Then she went off to check on Galwyn. She'd requested a dish of fish for him. He was on his perch, which she'd moved by the windows so he could look out. His water bowl was full, but his fish had all been eaten.

"Hello, my darling. Did you enjoy your food? I'm sorry I can't take you with me. I worry that you might be frightened by something and fly off and if anything were to happen to you, I would not forgive myself."

He shifted back and forth on his perch, one foot to the other, cocking his head to see her better. She understood. He wasn't happy.

She stroked his back, then scratched his neck. "Maybe I'll see about taking you to the library with me when I go there. What do you think about that?"

Why shouldn't he be able to come? She was queen, after all. No one should deny her the ability to have her dearest companion with her.

She took out the raspberries she'd carefully tucked away in her chatelaine purse and placed them on his perch. She taken them from her dessert, knowing instantly how much Galwyn would like them. Fresh berries in

Malveaux were a rare treat. "There you go. You enjoy those and I'll be back before you know it."

Galwyn snatched one up in his beak.

"Mother, are you ready?" Beatryce called out. "The tour will leave without us if we aren't at the meeting spot in the next half an hour."

They hadn't even left yet, and Anyka was already irritated by the activity.

She sighed. "Coming." She ran her fingers down Galwyn's back once more. "I'll see you soon, my pet."

She went to meet Beatryce, who was waiting by the door. Trog stood at the ready. "Where do we go for this tour?"

"We meet by the grandfather clock in the East Foyer."

"You mean the Summerton side." Anyka rolled her eyes. Of course they had to traipse all the way over there. "Very well. Off we go."

"We could take the portal. There's one that will transport us directly to that side," Beatryce said.

Anyka made herself shake her head. "You want to see and be seen, don't you? Very hard to do that when traveling by portal. We'll walk."

The walk took nearly fifteen minutes and Anyka was surprised by how many cautious looks and sideways glances they got on the way there. She did her best to keep a pleasant expression on her face, even nodding civilly at a few folks who made direct eye contact.

Wouldn't do to have the Radiant fae all muttering about how the Grym queen seemed haughty or glared daggers at them.

Shockingly, Anyka had learned something from Queen Sparrow today, and that was the value of being underestimated. There was power in not being what someone expected you to be. It was clearly a way to gain an advantage.

Because of how Sparrow had surprised Anyka, she'd decided to do the same and let people think she was just like Queen Sparrow. Approachable, chatty, a woman of the people, and filled with a sense of happiness so profound it flowed out of her.

It was, however, harder than she expected not just to *do* but to maintain. She tried to settle into her new character of the contented queen and hoped that the tour would allow her to sink into the background a bit and just observe.

When they reached the grandfather clock, a young man in a gray and white Willow Hall staff uniform bowed to both of them. "Queen Anyka, Princess Beatryce. What an unexpected pleasure to have you with us today. I am honored by your presence."

*As well he should be.* Anyka looked at the others in the group. Two Grym and two Radiant. The Grym also bowed. The Radiant, as expected, did not.

Anyka ignored them and smiled at the young man, even though the expression was starting to make her cheeks ache with the effort. "We look forward to getting to know Willow Hall better."

Beatryce nodded enthusiastically. "We so do."

"You will know a great deal more about this place when I'm through, I promise. I'm Daniel Newlight, one of the stewards here at Willow Hall. I'll be leading you on the tour today and helping you get to know this beautiful palace. Please feel free to ask any questions you might have."

Anyka looked around. There had been more people out and about directly after lunch but not as many now. She guessed that was because they'd all gone off to their next activity.

Daniel went on. "I'll start by telling you about our meeting point. The Hopewell Clock. Crafted exclusively for Willow Hall by one of the premier clockmakers of the day, the Hopewell Clock …"

Anyka was already bored, but Beatryce seemed to be listening intently. Anyka imagined this was as much of a vacation for Beatryce as a trip could be. She'd never been anywhere, outside of their recent trip to the mortal world. It was no wonder she was interested in everything.

From the clock, they moved on through various rooms, saw and heard about particular pieces of art, even got a lesson in how the floors were laid.

Anyka had to stop smiling. It was either that or break something to alleviate the agonizing dullness of it all.

She brought her smile back into place whenever anyone passed or glanced in her direction, however. Tedious. And somewhat idiotic. But she liked the idea of the ruse she was perpetrating, so she kept it up.

They made their way to the start of the libraries. Daniel named off the nine and gestured to where they were all located. Nice of the palace designers to put them all together in one hall. Very convenient.

Anyka had a question. "What hours are the libraries open?"

"They never close, your majesty," Daniel said. "We want our guests here at Willow Hall to be able to access these books whenever they want. That is essentially the reason people come here. To immerse themselves in reading and books and knowledge."

"That is good news."

He smiled, pleased that he'd made her happy. Of course, he had no idea what she was really happy about. It would be much easier to search the library after most people had gone to sleep.

There was always the possibility that a few night owls would be about, but Wyett could deal with them. Or Trog, depending on how much persuading they needed.

"We won't actually be going into any of the libraries today," Daniel continued on. "We maintain a fairly strict quiet zone in all of them, so obviously, bringing a tour through wouldn't be a very quiet thing to do." He laughed.

So did everyone else.

Anyka did her best, but she hadn't found his words funny. Doing the polite thing was incredibly hard. Keeping this up was going to give her a headache.

Daniel rubbed his hands together. "Moving on now, I'd like to take you to the very center of Willow Hall, where the palace spans the river. There you'll find skiffs and small boats are accessible. Anyone can use them to go boating on Celestial Lake, which I highly recommend you do at night at least once. But from this center point, you'll be able to see exactly where the dividing line is between the kingdoms. Right this way."

Beatryce glanced at Anyka and grinned. Anyka smiled back. That was easier to do. She was genuinely happy that her daughter was enjoying herself. Anyka hoped Bea made a lot of memories and absorbed the experience thoroughly.

Because Anyka doubted this was ever going to happen again.

# Chapter Twenty-Eight

Ro wasn't sure Gabriel was really helping her read. Every time she looked up at him, he was peering through the windows of the conversation chamber. She tipped her head. "Maybe we should just take all of these books back to the suite."

He frowned. "I'm sorry. I know you want help. But after you told me your dagger warmed up, I'd be remiss in my duties if I didn't keep a watchful eye out. Taking the books back to the suite would mean I'd be free to help."

"Then let's do that."

He closed the book he hadn't really been looking through and got up. "I'll let the librarian know."

He opened the door and leaned out, then waved.

Deanna came over. "What can I do for you?"

"Her majesty would like to take all of these books back to her suite."

"I'll get them checked out and find a runner to transport the books for you. Won't be a second." She went off to take care of things.

Ro closed her book and returned it to the stack. "You think anyone else has had any success?"

"I hope so."

Deanna came back with a young man holding a basket

with leather straps attached to it. He bowed to Ro. Deanna gestured toward him. "Roddy will take your books up for you. And you're all checked out. I hope you enjoy them."

"Thank you. I'm sure I will," Ro said.

She and Gabriel left the conversation chamber, then Roddy stepped in and loaded the books into the basket.

Once it was full, he slipped his arms through the straps like a backpack being worn the wrong way. Then he followed after them.

They used the portal elevator to go upstairs. The guard outside the suite doors came to full attention as they approached.

"At ease," Gabriel said.

The guard opened the door. Ro went in first.

Mrs. Wigglesworth was sleeping on one of the couches in the big sitting room, but she woke up at the sound of the door. "Did you bring me a rodent?"

"Nope," Ro said. "And I'm not ever going to bring one, so you can stop asking."

Wiggy sighed like Ro had just ruined her life. She definitely needed something to occupy her time. Ro looked at Gabriel. "What are the chances you could get one of the more energetic royal guards to accompany Wiggy on an exploration of Willow Hall?"

He nodded. "I can do that. Let me speak to Jason at the door."

As he stepped out into the hall, Ro directed Roddy where to put the books. "Take them through to the dining room and put them on the table, please."

"Yes, your majesty." He went off to do that.

Gabriel came back in. "Jason's willing to take her. He's due to be replaced in about half an hour anyway."

"Perfect. Wiggy, wake up. You're going out. You need to get some exercise."

Wiggy popped up again. "Rodent hunting?"

"You can do anything you like, so long as you don't go into areas you're not supposed to, and you don't cause trouble."

Wiggy snorted. "I don't cause trouble."

"I'm serious," Ro said. "We are guests here."

"I know," Wiggy said. "I won't cause trouble." Although her expression said she wasn't happy about it.

Ro figured she'd forget all about being unhappy when she got to explore. "Good. Thank you."

Roddy came into the sitting room, basket empty. "Your books are all on the table, your majesty."

"Thank you, Roddy."

With a little bow, he left.

Gabriel walked Wiggy out and introduced her to Jason, then they took off, too.

He closed the door behind him, but stayed near it.

"You really want to stand out there and guard the suite until the next guard shows up, don't you."

"Is it that obvious?"

"Pretty much. Why don't you just lock the door? I'm sure the new guard will knock to let us know he's arrived."

Gabriel took a breath but said nothing.

Ro smiled patiently. "Whatever you want to do is fine with me. I'll be in the dining room, hoping one of those books can shed some light on Lady Cynzia. After I check on Benny."

She didn't wait for an answer, just went to her bedroom, where she was sure she'd find Benny. She did. He was curled up in the chair by the fireplace, which had no fire in it, but he didn't seem to care.

"Hi, baby." She ran her hand from the top of his head down his back. "You sure seem to be a happy camper, huh?"

Benny let out a little chirp and rolled so that his head was upside down and his tummy exposed. Ro gave his belly fur a little ruffle. He started to purr. He was so adorable. "Enjoy your nap. I'm off to work."

She went to the dining room and found Gabriel at the table with a book in front of him.

"The next shift showed up early."

"Great," Ro said. She sat in the chair adjacent to his, which put her at the head of the table. She took the top book off the stack and opened it, looking for a table of contents. Instead, she found chapter listings and headers.

The third chapter had a heading that read, "The Curse." That seemed like a good place to start. She turned to the page and began to read.

It was interesting stuff.

She stopped two paragraphs in and looked up at Gabriel. "Find anything?"

"Nothing that's mentioned Cynzia by name, but this is a pretty detailed account of what led up to the curse. The ritual that created the curse is skimmed over, but that's to be expected. You?"

"This book uses her name. Listen to this." Ro read, "The king's Minister of Magic, a woman of nobility, Lady Cynzia Marwood, was a controversial figure well before she was appointed."

"Marwood? One of the books I read said her surname was Ashdown."

"I've read that last name for her, too." Ro shrugged. "That happens a lot in historical documents. Details get lost or confused as the years pass."

"Go on," Gabriel said. "Keep reading."

Ro picked up where she'd left off. "Known for her love of black magic, her questionable morality, and her thirst for power, it was no wonder King Ramus gave her the position. He was nearly as ambitious as she was."

Ro stopped reading. "Pretty interesting. Cynzia wanted power more than the king?"

"I feel like that should be surprising, but it isn't really."

"I agree. Says a lot that this author thought to include that bit of info."

Gabriel nodded. "What else does it say?"

Ro glanced down at the book again. "Besides her talents and ambitions, Lady Cynzia was known for her love of riddles. In fact, many scholars believe that's how King Ramus came to draw the curse down on Malveaux. That Lady Cynzia presented the power ritual to him using riddles he didn't understand, which led him to believe what he was about to do was safe. As we now know, it was not."

Ro stopped again. "That poem is obviously a riddle. Do you think it's possible Lady Cynzia wrote it herself?"

"Sure," Gabriel said. "Why not? Do you think Posey has any idea of the origin of the poem? By which I mean, how did her great-great-grandmother learn it to pass it down? Did she read it somewhere? Or learn it from someone else? It might help us to know that."

"We'll ask her as soon as she gets back," Ro said. "But if Lady Cynzia wrote it, then we need to read it with that in mind."

"Every line has to be picked apart."

She nodded. "Yes. All the clues we need might be right in front of us."

"If we can figure out what they are."

She looked at her book again. "We'd better read everything we can about her."

They got back to it. Ro's book continued to be full of little tidbits such as Lady Cynzia's favorite color was purple and how she enjoyed feats of subterfuge. Ro took that to mean magic tricks, which was both random and on brand. And while Ro had no idea how things like that might be helpful, they were at least aiding in the formation of the picture of the woman in Ro's mind.

She was sure that if she could really get to know Lady Cynzia, the poem would start to make sense. She finished the section she was reading, set that book aside, then moved on to the next.

That book just skimmed the events of the curse, referring only to Lady Cynzia as the king's Minister of Magic.

She kept working her way through the books as Gabriel did the same. She was on her fourth book when he looked up. "Find something?" she asked.

"Maybe. If you believe it. This book talks about Lady Cynzia's death."

"Which was?"

"She was imprisoned at Tenebrae, where she was able to escape her cell and fling herself to the rocks that surround the prison."

Ro grimaced.

"Yes," he said. "But this book claims that Lady Cynzia actually faked her own death and escaped to the mountains, where she might still live."

"She'd be..." Ro couldn't quite do the math. "Really old."

"Ancient. But she supposedly had a tremendous amount of power and, generally, the more magic a fae has, the longer they live."

"Really?" Ro narrowed her eyes. "Then you think it's possible?"

After a moment of hesitation, he nodded. "I do."

She sat back, surprised. But if he believed it, she did, too. Gabriel was one of the most rational fae she knew. "Okay, then. We have to consider that."

"We do?" He seemed taken aback by her trust in him.

"Yes." Ro saw the feats of subterfuge in a different light now. "Because if she's still alive, this could be a very different thing than we believe it to be. She could be setting one of us up. I mean me or Anyka. I don't really mean us specifically, I mean us as in we're the rulers of our kingdoms. Anyway, I just read about how Cynzia enjoyed 'feats of subterfuge,' which seems like a fae way of saying boobytraps."

Gabriel nodded. "That would be how I'd interpret that, too. And if she's alive, she could want revenge. Who put her in Tenebrae? I haven't read anything that's made that clear yet. If it was a Grym, by default she'll be after Anyka. And if it was a Radiant, she'll be after you."

Ro exhaled. That's what she'd been thinking, too. She just hadn't wanted to put it into words.

# Chapter Twenty-Nine

At the end of the tour, which had been far longer than Anyka expected, she decided to do a little exploring on her own. Namely in the libraries. She wasn't unhappy she'd taken the tour, however. She had a much better understanding of the palace layout now, and that would aid her in the days to come.

"Wasn't that fun?" Beatryce said. "Daniel was very informative, wasn't he?"

"He was," Anyka said. Beatryce had thanked the steward profusely, having obviously enjoyed the tour the most. "It was very educational," Anyka added. "Now, you may do whatever you want, but not until you have one of your guards with you."

Beatryce sighed. "But that means I have to go back upstairs."

"No, it doesn't." Anyka looked around, then snapped her fingers at an approaching footman. "You there."

He bowed and came over. "Yes, your highness?"

"Fetch one of the Malveaux royal guards from wherever they're being housed, tell them they're required to guard Princess Beatryce, and bring them here, ready to work."

"Yes, your highness." The young man hurried off in the direction he'd been coming from.

Anyka looked at Beatryce. "You are a princess. Act like it. You are always surrounded with those willing to do your bidding."

Beatryce smiled. "You're right. I need to remember that more. I'm just all out of my element here. It's much different than being at home, you know."

"I know," Anyka said. "But the Willow Hall staff is here to take care of us. That is part of their purpose. They are essentially replacing the staff that we've left behind at home."

Beatryce nodded. "I can't believe I didn't think of it that way sooner. That helps."

"Good." Anyka sometimes worried her child wasn't cut out to wear the crown, but she was going to have to be. She was the next in line.

Thankfully, a royal guard found them after a few more minutes. "You called for a guard, your highness?"

Anyka nodded. "Guard the princess wherever she goes until you're relieved."

"Yes, your highness."

Anyka glanced at her daughter. "I'll expect to see you for dinner."

"You will," Beatryce said.

Anyka made her way out of the hall where the tour had ended. The space was filled with priceless works of art, including paintings, ceramics, and sculptures, and Anyka had enjoyed looking at them, but she had some ground to cover to return to where the libraries were. At least a five-minute walk. Maybe more. She glanced over her shoulder, confirmed Trog was behind her, and kept going.

When she reached the library she had in mind, her plan was to get a little background on Lady Cynzia *without* Nazyr realizing what she was doing. She knew he thought she'd rely on him to educate her. She was counting on that belief. Counting on him to do the same thing to her that she'd done to Queen Sparrow.

Underestimate her.

Finally, Anyka arrived. She walked into the History Library, Trog just behind her, and looked around to find the librarian in change. There were a few people reading but none who looked like staff. She called out, "Hello?"

Several of those reading cut their eyes at her until they realized who she was. Then they went back to minding their own business.

A woman came out from between some shelves. "Your majesty. Hello and welcome." The woman's voice was barely louder than a whisper. "Can I help you?"

"Yes. I want every book you have that references Lady Cynzia." Anyka lifted her chin, defying the woman to say something about Anyka's topic of choice.

"Oh, I'm so sorry, your majesty. I can't help you with that. I—"

"You can and you will," Anyka commanded, indignant that the woman had challenged her request. How dare she? "Not only is it your job, but I can read about anyone I choose to read about. If you don't help me—"

"Forgive me, your majesty." The woman looked slightly

panicked. "I just meant there are no books to give you on that subject. I've already checked them out to someone else."

Anyka's anger turned to confusion. Had Wyett already been here? Or perhaps Ishmyel? "Who took them?"

"I'm sorry, again, your majesty, but protocol doesn't allow us to share the names of those who've taken books out." The woman nervously clasped her hands and took a long look at Trog. "I'm sure I could find you some books on Larmyn the Cruel. He was quite an interesting wielder of black magic. Some say he was Lady Cynzia's inspiration, but I don't—"

"No. I don't want any other books." Anyka spun around, frustrated but unsure if it was warranted or not. If one of her own staff had taken those books out, she couldn't be cross with them for doing what she'd asked. If Nazyr had taken those books out, however, she might have every reason to be furious.

Especially if he'd done it as a blatant attempt to undermine Anyka's intentions. She would not stand for that. She was so incensed that her emotions pushed her to a breaking point. She would see for herself what he was up to.

With Trog in tow, she stormed back upstairs via the portal, and went straight to her quarters. She pulled the rope to ring for a footman. As soon as he showed up, she met him at the door. "What room is Minister Marwood in?"

"Suite Fifteen, your majesty." The footman pointed.

"Trog." She pushed past the footman and went down

the hall. She stopped at the door to Suite Fifteen and knocked loudly. After a long wait, there was no answer. She knocked again.

Finally, a voice called out, "I am not to be disturbed."

Anyka glared poisoned arrows through the door. "I will disturb you whenever and wherever I please."

The door opened and Nazyr appeared on the other side, smiling apologetically. "Begging your forgiveness, my lady. I did not realize it was you."

She did not smile back. "Invite me in, Nazyr."

He bent his head as he moved out of the way. "Of course, your highness. Please, come in. You're welcome anytime."

She doubted that was true. Nazyr dealt in secrets, and he liked his privacy, often disappearing to who knew where for days on end.

She walked in. His suite had a small sitting room with a dining area off to one side, then a door that must open onto the bedchamber and bathing room. The décor was similar in color and style to the royal suite, but not nearly as grand, which pleased her. "What have you been doing all day, Nazyr?"

"I thought your uncle would have told you. I've been finishing the amulet. I wanted to finetune it once we were here to take advantage of any residual magic in the air, which I assure you I've found plenty of."

None of that meant anything to her. "Then you weren't in the library today? You didn't have books sent up here?"

She looked around and saw none, but they could be in the bedroom.

"No, my lady. I've been in my suite all day. I haven't even left to eat. All my meals have been sent up."

There was evidence of that on the table. She still wasn't satisfied. He was up to something. She could feel it. "Then with such dedication, the amulet must be done."

He smiled. "Very nearly. I need to add one final spell to the piece and then, yes, it will be complete. I had planned to present it to you before dinner this evening, but if you'd like to wait…"

She hadn't expected that answer. Was he bluffing? There was only one way to find out. She crossed her arms. "Fine. I'll wait."

He nodded. "Very well. You're welcome to sit if you like. It won't take me too much longer."

"Take as long as you need." She settled into a spot on the sofa, with a nod at Trog to stay close. Just because Nazyr said he was about to apply a spell to the amulet didn't mean that spell would be completely harmless. Better to have Trog nearby. He moved behind her.

Nazyr came over to the seating area and took the chair at the end of the small table that served the sitting room. At the end of that table sat a folded piece of fabric on the polished wood surface. The fabric had a small lump in it, but not enough to indicate what was inside.

He picked the fabric up, putting one hand under it and one hand over it. Then he closed his eyes and began whispering words in what had basically become a lost language. Lost, but not unrecognizable to Anyka: Ancient Fae.

After a moment, dark energy crackled around the

fabric like black flames. Then the fire washed down Nazyr's hands all the way to his elbows. He held the fabric straight out, his words growing louder. His eyes opened, the flames reflected in them, but he seemed to see nothing of the real world.

Finally, the flames went out and, with the fabric still in his hands, he slumped back in the chair, panting as though he'd just run for his life.

In a way, Anyka thought, he had.

He sat quietly for a long minute or two, catching his breath. In that brief span, he suddenly looked older than he was to Anyka. Finally, he straightened and nodded at her. "The amulet is ready."

He unfolded the fabric to reveal a long chain of iridescent black metal holding a curious talisman. The amulet was comprised of a spherical glass locket that contained several bits and pieces of things. One of those things glinted behind the glass.

"What's in that?" Anyka wasn't genuinely sure she wanted to know but if that was going around her neck, she had to ask.

"A strand of Lady Cynzia's hair. A small snippet of a feather pen she once owned. A scrap of her prison gown, slightly stained with blood, and a broken shard of one of her onyx earrings. There is also a strand of your hair, a scrap of your coronation gown, and one of your fingernail clippings."

Anyka grimaced. Magic dealers were such odd types. "How did you come by such personal items of mine?"

He shrugged. "I merely collected them from around

the castle, my lady. In preparation for this very thing, I assure you."

Assured was the last thing she felt. She resolved to employ more cleaners when she returned home. "Why am I any part of it?"

"You must be for the spell to be successful. The idea is that this locket will fool any protective magic into thinking that you are Lady Cynzia. Although..." He held out the necklace. "You must wear this without cease for the setting of one sun and the rising of one moon so that the magic within can meld with you and do its work properly."

It wasn't the prettiest piece of jewelry she'd ever owned. She took it, weighing it in her hands. Then she slipped it around her neck and tucked it beneath her bodice. It seemed very much like something no one else needed to see.

She looked at him again. "Then by tomorrow I should be able to search for and find Lady Cynzia's grimoire?"

He bobbed his head in confirmation. "Yes. Of course, it won't be that easy. We have no idea which library the book is in. Or if it really is in one of the libraries here at Willow Hall. For all we know, it was moved to storage a century ago. Or it sits on a shelf in some room, completely ignored for what it is. It might be anywhere in this place."

"Good thing I have all of you to help me then." She got up. "I will see you at dinner. You will sit at my table."

It wasn't a question, but he nodded. He still looked tired. "Of course, my lady. Thank you."

She strode toward the door, which Trog opened for her.

"Good day, Nazyr." She left without waiting for an answer and went back to her suite.

Once inside, she pulled the amulet free and stood by the window to look at it in better light. The contents inside the glass locket were fairly discernible, which did nothing to endear the thing to her. She didn't like it at all. If it didn't work, she was going to feel as if Nazyr had pulled some kind of prank on her.

The door to her quarters opened and a voice called out. "Your majesty, are you in?"

"Yes, Wyett. I'm here." She hid the amulet away and went to meet him in the sitting room. "Did you make any progress?"

"Not toward finding the grimoire, no. But I did find out something interesting about Queen Sparrow."

Anyka took another step closer to him. "Oh? What might that be?"

Wyett didn't look happy. "She took out every book in the History Library pertaining to the Malveaux curse."

# Chapter Thirty

Nearly two hours later, Ro and Gabriel had gone through every book they'd brought back. Several of them more than once. All they'd been able to come up with was that Lady Cynzia had been sent to Tenebrae to serve a life sentence. Not a word or a hint about who had been responsible for doing it.

Ro pushed the last book away. "I can't read any more. My eyes are going to cross. And I've found nothing that tells me if Cynzia really is still alive and if she'd want revenge on Grym or Radiant."

"Neither have I." He closed his book. "We've done all we can. Regardless of whether Lady Cynzia lives, this diary of hers definitely could be some kind of setup. For all we know, that diary might be bespelled in such a way as to hurt *anyone* who attempts to use it. Some kind of magical ambush meant to be one last retaliatory strike. If it's aimed at anyone, my guess would be the Grym."

"You think?"

"I do. Posey said she only knew about the poem because her great-great-grandmother was half Grym. Lady Cynzia isn't as well known amongst the Radiant, but she's a legendary figure in Grym history. *Much* better known, for sure. It makes sense to me that it was a Grym who sentenced her to Tenebrae. If a Radiant had done it, they would have talked about it. It would be known."

"Good point." Ro groaned. "You realize what this means?"

"I'm not sure I do."

"We have to warn Queen Anyka."

Gabriel's brows rose. "Do we?"

"Of course we do. If there's some kind of plot afoot to harm her or one of her people and we don't say anything, we're essentially complicit."

"I don't know if I'd go that far."

"Gabriel."

He let out a long sigh. "No, you're right. You do realize there's almost no chance she'll believe you. If anything, she'll think you're trying to set her up."

"I'm sure you're right about that. But I don't see that I have a choice. Unless you have another idea?"

"I don't. I'm sorry. We might want to consult Professor Larksford," he said, referring to her First Professor of Protocol.

Ro groaned again. "You know how I feel about protocol."

"I do, but there might be a certain way a thing like this should be done."

"Again, you're probably right." She acquiesced. "Okay, let's get him here. Who else should be part of this?"

"I'd say there are quite a few of the professors that should be here. Uldamar, definitely. Also Prince James. Your aunt and Posey, I'd imagine. Anyone you want to keep abreast of the situation. Word is going to spread very quickly once this gets out. There won't be much hope of containing it."

"Well, that sucks." Ro frowned. "I really don't want there to be a free-for-all over this diary. The last thing we need is some well-meaning citizen getting their hands on it and getting hurt. Or, worse, taking a crack at any of the spells inside and turning us all into mice."

Gabriel visibly fought to control his expression, but a brief smile flickered across his face anyway. "I don't think that's something you need to worry about. It's more likely one of Lady Cynzia's spells would have us all bleeding out of our eyes or searching for a tower to jump off of."

Ro shot him a look. "Thanks, that's definitely better."

He laughed out loud this time. "My apologies."

"Telling her *is* the right thing to do." Ro knew it was, but she also knew she was about to create a small firestorm of trouble. Maybe not that small, actually.

"You sound like you're trying to convince yourself."

"I kind of am. I know it's not going to be well received. I know she's going to doubt me and think I'm up to something or creating trouble for her in order to make myself look good or starting some kind of political theater. But that's not who I am."

"Unfortunately, she doesn't know you well enough to understand that."

"I wish I could get her to trust me before this all goes down, but there's no way to make that happen."

"The best you could do is talk to her one on one."

"By which you mean the two of us plus our security.

It's never going to be just the two of us. You and that gargantuan bodyguard of hers will be there."

"He's a troll."

Ro laughed. "You can say that again."

Gabriel's eyes narrowed. "He really is a troll. The Malveauxians have long had a treaty with the trolls."

"Oh. You mean like he's an actual troll. Good to know. Do we have treaties with anyone? I feel like that's something someone should have mentioned."

"I believe we did, but Summerton has been without a ruler so long, those treaties were probably considered null and void some time ago."

Ro made a mental note. "Something else for me to work on then. All right, let's gather everyone together that we can and have this meeting. The sooner we can get it over with, the better."

"When are you going to speak to Anyka?"

"As soon as I can and as soon as there's a good time. Hopefully, I'll see her at dinner, and I can ask for time to meet with her then."

He got up from the table. "I'll gather as many as I can myself but I'm going to send a few footmen out as well to let the professors know the queen requests their presence."

"Please do. And get Althea Cloudtree, too. I'm sort of considering her as her husband's proxy while he's away. Keeping her in the loop means she can bring him up to date when he returns."

"I'll make sure she's here."

Ro stood. "Thank you. Maybe I should run down and look through the libraries, see who I can find."

"Respectfully, please don't. Not without me. I know you want to help, but I can do it faster and easier if I don't have to worry about you. Especially now that I know there could be a real threat within this palace."

She sighed but smiled. "Sorry. Of course I'll stay here. I still think I'm just a regular person sometimes, able to do anything I want."

He nodded as he came closer. "I can't imagine how hard that adjustment is. If you'd rather I send someone else to gather—"

"No, go on. I'll be fine."

He stayed where he was. Just a few inches away from her. "There will be a guard at the door."

"I know." She looked up at him, amazed at how his handsomeness never seemed ordinary to her. No matter how many times she saw his face, she was always taken with how beautiful it was. "You can kiss me now."

He smiled. And did just that. "I'll be back as soon as I can."

"I'll be here."

With that, he left.

An hour later, during which Ro spent some quality time with Benny, the last of those invited made their way into the sitting room with Gabriel behind them. He'd even had to take a boat out onto the lake to get one of the professors and her husband, who had been boating.

Ro admired his dedication to her but realized that she needed more than just Gabriel and Posey as her secretary. She needed...well, she wasn't sure what the position would be called, but a sort of Girl Friday. A lady's maid, maybe? She'd have to ask Gabriel about that later.

She stood in front of the fireplace so she could see everyone. They were pretty well packed in, but she didn't plan on keeping them long. "It's come to my attention that there might be a threat to Queen Anyka. Possibly to myself, as well, but—"

A few of them gasped.

Ro held her hands out. "Let me explain before anyone gets upset." She'd already explained to Uldamar, Violet, Posey, and JT, because they'd been the first ones Gabriel had rounded up. She launched into that same explanation, but with more details about Lady Cynzia's diary, to the rest of the group before her.

She had Posey recite the poem again as well as pass out a few copies that she'd written down. Ro hoped someone here might find a clue no one else had.

She also hoped they would keep it quiet.

"I trust you understand the significance of what's before us and why it must be kept confidential." She had very little hope of this information remaining secret, but that didn't mean she wasn't going to try. "I do not want a word of this to spread among the citizens."

She stared very seriously at those assembled before her, making eye contact as she looked through the group. "If I see one citizen in the libraries searching for something or overhear a conversation about hunting for this book or get any kind of whiff that word has gotten out, I will be furious."

She went silent for a long moment, just looking at

them. "You haven't had the opportunity to see me angry, but I'm sure my son can attest that it is not something you'd want to experience for yourself."

JT nodded and glanced around. "She's right. Don't make her mad."

A few smiled, but they seemed to understand.

Ro needed them all on the same page, however. She went a bit farther. "I will consider breach of this information akin to treason. In case any of you were wondering just how serious this is."

Lots of nods greeted her this time. That was better. "Does anyone have any questions?"

Prilla Bowsinger, First Professor of Manners, raised her hand.

"Professor Bowsinger?"

"Have you spoken with the Willow Hall staff about this? Certainly Trence would know if there was such a thing hidden here."

"I haven't. I have been very cautious about who to trust with this information. Trence is a lovely man, very eager to help, but I don't know him. I don't know any of the staff here. I've been told they are a mix of Radiant and Grym and that they take a vow to serve both Radiant and Grym equally, as they should, and consider themselves neutral when it comes to allegiance to a particular kingdom.

"All the same, I've not said anything to them. That might change in the coming days, however." Ro frowned. "We might have to ask for their help. But I will make that decision."

When no other hands went up, Ro asked a question of

her own. "Professor Larksford, what's the protocol for something like me meeting with Queen Anyka to discuss what we've learned so that I can warn her?"

"It can be as simple as you asking for a few moments of her time to as complicated as a formal request in writing that she join you at her earliest convenience."

"So it's all right for me to ask her in person at dinner? Because that's what I'd like to do. This needs to be discussed as soon as possible, in my opinion."

He nodded. "That would be permissible. Especially as this trip is technically considered time off for both monarchs and therefore a more relaxed atmosphere."

"Good enough. Thank you," Ro said. "I guess all that's left is for us to get to dinner and for me to hope that Queen Anyka agrees to talk with me." She glanced at the clock behind her. "We have an hour until the chimes ring. Use that time wisely. If anyone is able to interpret the poem more precisely, let me know discreetly at dinner. Thank you for your attention. You're free to go."

As the crowd dispersed, Gabriel came up to her, but said nothing. Just stood close.

She was tired, more mentally than physically. And she really wanted to take the circlet off for a while. It wasn't that heavy, but it was like wearing a headband all day. There were pressure points. "I think I'm going to lay down for a few minutes before dinner."

He nodded. "Very good. I'll be here if you need me."

"Thanks."

JT, who was nearby, looked over. "Mom, if you need a nap, take one."

Aunt Violet said goodbye to Posey, then joined them. "Did someone say nap? That sounds like a wonderful idea." She sighed. "Things sure have gotten complicated. Don't tell her I said anything, but Posey feels bad for bringing up the diary in the first place."

"She shouldn't," Ro said. "In fact, I'm grateful she did. Without her, who knows what might have happened."

Although none of them knew how this was really going to work out. All Ro could do was pray for the best. Even if that's not what seemed likely to happen.

## Chapter Thirty-One

"The nerve of that woman," Anyka muttered as the hairdresser fixed her locks for dinner. The older woman had done Anyka's makeup first, and Anyka was already questioning whether her eyes looked as good as they could. "How dare she involve herself in this search? Lady Cynzia's grimoire belongs to me. It galls me that one so newly ascended would think she has the right. She's not even Grym."

Wyett, who stood nearby, his expression remained rather impassive. "If that was her intention. To involve herself in the search, I mean."

Her brow bone needed a little more highlighting. "What other reason would she have for getting those books out?"

"It might be that she was trying to familiarize herself with Malveauxian history so that she might better understand the Grym queen."

Anyka slanted her gaze at him and thought about what he'd said. "I am loathe to admit it, but that does seem like something that woman would do. She strikes me as being very *accommodating*."

"It's possible," Wyett went on. "That Queen Sparrow knows nothing of Lady Cynzia. It's my understanding that many Radiant fae have heard very little about the former Minister of Magic."

Anyka reached forward to pick up a fluffy eyeshadow brush. She dabbed it in the pan of colors still on the counter and touched it to her brow bones for more sparkle. "That wouldn't surprise me. The Radiant are woefully uneducated about the Grym."

Wyett's mouth bent, almost like he was about to smile, before straightening out again. "As the Grym are about the Radiant."

Anyka glanced at him but made no comment in return. He was right, of course, but Radiant history had never seemed important to her, so she'd never encouraged the Minister of Education to include much of it in the standard curriculum.

She tossed the eyeshadow brush back onto the counter. "Regardless of her reasoning for taking those books out, I find it highly suspicious and very curious."

Wyett nodded. "There is much to be said for timing."

"But you don't think she's up to anything, do you. I can hear it in your voice."

"It's not my place to give my opinion, my lady."

She pursed her lips. "It is when I'm asking you. Why do you think she took those books out?"

He hesitated. "I don't know for sure. None of us can unless we ask her, of course, but everything I've heard about Queen Sparrow, all those I've spoken with who've had personal interactions with her, say that she is very nice, seems genuinely concerned with the well-being of her people, and talks often about how she wants peace between the two kingdoms." He paused again. "She just doesn't sound to me like a woman intent on creating trouble. Quite the opposite, actually."

"Or she sounds like the kind of woman who's very good at setting herself up as a woman no one would ever think would want to overthrow Malveaux. And that could be exactly what she's up to."

"Yes," Wyett said quietly. "Perhaps that's her game after all. If so, she is far more skilled at political intrigue than most would believe."

"Your sarcasm is not welcome."

"Forgive me, your majesty. But I do not believe Queen Sparrow means you harm."

"That will be cold comfort if she slips a knife in my back."

New light filled Wyett's eyes. "If that happens, I will kill her myself."

Anyka smiled. It was good to know her valet was so willing. She tucked that away for future reference. "That is far more comforting." She glanced in the mirror as the hairdresser did the final touches. "Enough. Go now."

The woman curtseyed and left.

Anyka sat back, admiring her reflection. "Princess Beatryce is quite taken with Willow Hall. Even more than I expected her to be."

Wyett nodded. "She's been seen chatting with quite a few young men."

Anyka arched her brows. "Has she?"

"Yes, my lady."

"Has she been seen doing anything *more* than chatting?"

"Not to my knowledge, but that wasn't a line of questioning I pursued."

Anyka frowned. "It's one thing to have a little dalliance, but Princess Beatryce isn't even betrothed. Such a thing could mar her reputation." She shook her head. "One more issue for me to worry about. And speaking to her will do nothing."

Wyett tipped his head to one side. "Telling someone not to do something often results in that thing becoming even more desirable."

Anyka huffed out a sigh. "That is very true. Especially with Beatryce. I cannot have her getting involved in some affair that—wait. These young men she was chatting with. Were they Grym or Radiant?"

"I'm not certain, my lady."

Anyka dug her nails into the arms of the chair. "Either way, this behavior cannot go beyond chatting. But I know Beatryce and she will eat up the attention. She craves interaction." Anyka growled at the ceiling. "I shouldn't have brought her here. It was a stupid decision. I should have known better."

"My lady, you did nothing wrong. No one can be blamed for Princess Beatryce's interest in the opposite sex. She's had beggar-little to choose from."

"I know," Anyka sighed out the words. This was a matter that had been on her heart for some time. "And it's partially my fault. I've kept a lot of eligible suitors away from her because all they wanted was the power that comes with her hand. Beatryce deserves someone who will treat her well and love her for more than just the crown she'll someday give him. Not an easy thing to come by in a royal marriage, I assure you."

"You want for her what every mother wants for their child. No one would fault you for that."

Anyka took a breath, the image of Sebastyan coming to mind. Under normal circumstances, she never would have been allowed to marry him. But he'd saved her life. And she'd been in mourning over her parents. No one had said a word to her.

But no princess who was heir to the throne would have ever been otherwise allowed to wed someone of such a middling position. "I need to find her a husband, Wyett. Until I can do that, she needs a worthy distraction. Are there any men here that might be suitable? I feel as though I already know the answer to that even as I ask it."

His eyes narrowed. "Will you be looking among the Radiant?"

"For a suitor?" Anyka scoffed. "Of course not. Can you imagine the uprising if Beatryce was betrothed to a Radiant? That man would sit on the throne next to her someday. A Radiant on the Grym throne? You know better, Wyett. The people would revolt."

"Perhaps I don't know better, my lady. And forgive my boldness, but I don't think the people would be as upset as you believe. Not if he was a good man who clearly loved Princess Beatryce. And not if the way were paved for such a union."

She stared at him. "You mean...broker peace with Summerton?"

He shrugged. "Would that be so awful? Reestablishing trade would make you beloved—"

"Are you saying I am not currently beloved?" Her gaze pinned him.

"I was about to say beloved twice over by your citizens." He lifted his chin ever so slightly. "Obviously, you are already beloved."

She went back to studying her reflection. She knew that wasn't entirely true. There were many citizens who didn't love her. And some who outright hated her. They knew better than to make their opinions known, but she'd be a fool to think otherwise.

No ruler, not even the great Queen Sparrow, would ever have the full admiration of her entire kingdom.

Such was the nature of ruling. Loved by some, hated by some. She'd learned to ignore the worst of it over the years.

She glanced at her nails, which were still in good shape and needed no touchups. "As far as someone who might distract Beatryce... I don't know every Grym who made the trip here. Those I invited were allowed to bring a guest, if they so desired. Some brought their entire families."

She hadn't put a limit on it, because she hadn't known how many Radiant would be coming and she didn't want to be terribly outnumbered. "Perhaps one of the ministers has a son about the right age? One who might hold Beatryce's interest? Even one of the higher-ranking royal guards wouldn't be out of the question."

Wyett nodded. "I'll look into it."

"He doesn't have to be marriage material, obviously, but he must be respectable and a supporter of the crown. All I need is someone to amuse her while she's here. Someone who can buy me time to find her a suitable mate."

"I'm sure that's possible."

"I hope so." If anyone could do it, Wyett could. She glanced at the time. "I must dress for dinner. You'll accompany me when it's time to go." Trog was great protection, but Trog and Wyett would make her untouchable and with the news that Sparrow might know about Lady Cynzia's grimoire, Anyka was taking no chances. "Send my lady's maid in, will you?"

He bowed. "Yes, my lady. I'll wait for you in the sitting room." Then he left.

Anyka got up and walked to the dressing room. She had to wear a gown that would hide the amulet she was wearing. Maybe something with a high neck.

She chose one of her favorite gowns. There was nothing summery about it, but she didn't care. It was the most beautiful shade of deep blue suede that had been scraped and softened to the feel of silk.

And while it had a high neck, it left her arms and shoulders bare. At home, she'd always worn it with a close-fitting knit jacket of black marula, but here she could do a light cape and be fine. She could probably even go without.

Jenny, her lady's maid came in. "You called for me, ma'am?"

"Yes." Anka pulled out the dress in question. "This gown. Black slippers and my onyx beads."

The strands of faceted onyx would distract from the shape of the amulet under her gown.

The young woman went to work helping Anyka get into the dress and then fastening the tiny buttons in the back. Once Anyka was in the dress, Jenny brought her shoes and jewelry and helped her into those as well.

When that was all done, Anyka went to the full-length mirror and had a look. She turned from side to side. "Something's missing."

The suede gown was beautiful, but even with the onyx jewelry it was a little plain.

"Some ornaments for your hair, my lady?" Jenny produced a spray of black feathers dusted with crystals and dangling bits of onyx.

"Yes, put that in." Anyka was wearing a narrow circlet of silver and the ornament helped without covering that nod to her royal status. She sighed at what she saw in the mirror. "It's still not enough."

"There's a new black cape that might work," Jenny suggested.

"New?" Anyka frowned. "Where did it come from? Show me."

"I believe a few items ordered by your valet arrived too late to be packed with the rest of your things, so they were brought separately." Jenny pulled a tissue-wrapped package from one of the shelves. She unwrapped it and shook it out.

The cape was sheer-spun black marula wool but it had been covered in tiny iridescent crystals, making it glisten like dew in the moonlight.

Anyka smiled. "That is gorgeous. Put it on me."

The maid fastened it with little clips that attached it to the neck of Anyka's gown in the back. That allowed the cape to flow out behind her without covering any skin, although if she got cold, she could easily pull it around her.

She turned before the mirror, pleased with what she saw. "That will do very nicely. You're dismissed."

Jenny curtseyed and left.

Anyka smiled at her reflection.

Once again, Wyett had come through. No doubt he'd find a companion for Beatryce. And possibly even kill Queen Sparrow if Anyka needed him to.

Things were looking up.

# Chapter Thirty-Two

Ro was nearly ready to leave for dinner when she snagged her jacket on the door handle of her bedroom and tore one of the seams. "You have got to be kidding me."

Luena, who'd shown up not long after the professors had all left, looked over from where she was setting out Ro's outfit for the following day. "Oh, that's not good. But thankfully, it's easy to fix."

"It is?"

Luena nodded. "I just need the jacket and about ten minutes and I'll have it as good as new. Let me just run and get my sewing kit."

"Thank you."

"Of course, your majesty." Luena smiled. "That's what I'm here for."

As Luena left, Ro took the jacket off and laid it over the center island in the dressing room. Underneath, she had on a slim black tank top, something that had come with her from the mortal world. It was actually a shaping garment, but she liked the snug fit and the smooth look it gave her under clothes. And the fact that it didn't look like a shaping garment.

She went out to the sitting room where Aunt Violet,

Posey, Vincent, JT, Raphaela, and Gabriel were waiting on her.

"I just tore my jacket, but Luena said she can fix it. However, you all don't need to wait on me. Uldamar and Althea will be at that big table all by themselves. You all go on and Gabriel and I will come when my jacket's repaired."

JT got up. "You sure, Mom? I don't mind waiting."

"No, go on. And if you don't want to sit down immediately, wander through the tables and say hello to some of the citizens. I'm sure they'd love that. You, too, Aunt Violet."

Violet smiled and shook her head. "No one wants to meet me."

Posey snorted. "Yes, they do, and you know it. Just this morning a man came up to you when we were in the library. Asked you if you'd like to join his book group."

"Posey." Aunt Violet gave her friend a stern look.

Posey was undeterred. "Well, he did. And you said you'd think about it."

Ro laughed but she actually thought Violet should find a nice man. No reason for her to be alone if she didn't want to be.

JT waggled his brows. "Auntie Vi, when were you going to tell us about this new *friend* of yours?"

"You just settle down, James Thoreau. He's not my friend. He's not anything."

Ro shrugged. "He could be, if you play your cards right."

"Maybe." Aunt Violet stood up. "I'm going down to

dinner. Get up, Posey, because you're going with me. Can't have you sharing any more of my secrets." She winked at Ro. "See you down there."

"See you there."

Luena came in, basket in hand. "I'll have it done in a jiffy, your majesty."

"Thank you, Luena."

JT followed after Violet. "I'll head down, too. Maybe I can catch a glimpse of Auntie Vi's new boyfriend."

From the hall, Violet said, "I heard that, young man."

Laughing, JT closed the door as soon as Raphaela was out.

Which left Gabriel and Ro mostly alone. She sat next to him on the couch. "Long, interesting day, huh?"

He nodded. "I'll say." He chuckled softly.

"What's funny?"

"For years, I would wake up every morning and wish with every fiber of my being that something interesting would happen."

She smiled. "I guess being in charge of palace security is pretty boring when there's not actually anyone in the palace."

He leaned his head back. "You have no idea. Imagine... a museum with no attractions."

"Exhibits. But, yes, that would be awful."

"My life's not boring anymore."

She had to laugh. "Sorry about that."

He rolled his head so he could see her. "Don't be. I can't say I love everything that's happening but have never enjoyed my job more. I never thought I'd end up working for someone like you. Or that Summerton would have such an amazing woman as queen."

She tipped her head back and gazed into his eyes. "I never thought I'd be queen, obviously, but I certainly never imagined I'd have the most dangerous man in the kingdom guarding me. It's quite an honor, really."

"Who said that about me?"

She shook her head, lips pursed. "I can't reveal my sources. Why do they call you that?"

He shook his head, eyes glinting in amusement. "I can't tell you." Then his expression became more serious. "Although there is something I have to tell you. And you might not like it."

She braced herself. "What now?"

"Raphaela likes JT and from what she's told me, he likes her right back."

Ro felt a little smirk cross her face. "It doesn't surprise me that my son and I have similar tastes when it comes to companionship. Do you think that's going to be an issue?"

"It would be hypocritical of me to say it was. Not with the things that have happened between us."

She nodded. "I agree. He's an adult. So is she. They can make their own choices."

"All true. But I get the impression from Raph that JT is reluctant because he thinks you won't approve."

"Really?" That surprised Ro but then, JT might not know what was allowed and not allowed in his new role as prince. "All I want for him is to be happy. I know he'll be expected to take the throne someday, but that shouldn't be to the exclusion of his happiness."

Gabriel sat up, his gaze shifting to the table in the middle of the room. "The most she could be to him is a mistress. As you might imagine, I don't love that idea."

"Neither do I. I need to speak to Larksford. Or someone. This idea that royalty can't marry for love is ridiculous. It's time that changes."

Luena came back in. "I have your jacket, my lady." She held it out so that Ro could slip into it.

Ro got up and did just that, letting Luena help her. Ro glanced down to where the tear had been. "Wow, you really did make it look like new. I can't see where it was repaired."

Luena smiled. "Happy to help, my lady."

"Thank you. Now you get down to dinner, too."

"Yes, ma'am." She took off, sewing basket in hand.

Gabriel stood up and adjusted his shirt and jacket, which he'd put on for dinner. "Are you ready to go?"

"I am."

They left the suite together, Gabriel getting the door for her. As they walked toward the portal elevator, he spoke softly. "Nervous about talking to Queen Anyka?"

Ro shook her head. "Not nervous, really. A little concerned she won't want to meet me to talk, and I'll have to give her some hints about how urgent and serious this is. I mean, if I have to, I'll tell her everything right there. I don't want to do it that way, but I'm prepared to."

"Wise. Hard to tell what a woman like that will or won't do."

There was a couple approaching the portal at the same time Ro and Gabriel were. They stepped aside to let Ro go ahead of them. She got into the portal and waved them in. "Come on, there's room."

The man glanced at Gabriel before answering. "Thank you, your majesty, that's very kind. But we can wait."

"Thank you," Gabriel said. Then he shut the doors.

"Hey," Ro said. "That wasn't very nice."

Gabriel faced her, eyes dark. "No, but it *was* procedure. You cannot invite others you don't know into a small, enclosed space like this. What if they were assassins? It would be the perfect opportunity to harm you." He sighed and lowered his voice. "I know you meant well, but—"

"Assassins? Really?" Ro crossed her arms.

"This isn't a game. It's your life we're talking about."

She dropped her arms and her smirk. "You're right. I'm sorry. I just can't look at everyone like they're out to get me or I'll never want to leave my room."

He nodded. "I'm sorry, as well. I know this is hard on you and a lot to get used to, but you must try."

"I know." She felt a little chastised, but he was right. "Sorry."

"You don't need to apologize. Let's just get you down to dinner and forget about this." He dialed the gems for the first floor.

She didn't like having cross words with him. She understood he must be feeling the extra tension of what was going on. Just because there might be danger here in the form of Lady Cynzia's diary and that danger was probably aimed at the Grym who were in attendance didn't mean it might not affect all of them, Radiant and Grym alike.

And Ro had put herself in the crosshairs, since she was actively involved in the hunt.

They stepped out of the portal, and Gabriel took his usual place next to and slightly behind her. They were stopped a few feet from the entrance to the dining hall by Trence.

"My apologies, your highness, but might I have a moment of your time?"

"Of course," Ro said. "What can I do for you?"

Trence smiled. "I just wanted to let you and the First Professor know that a contingent of royal guards has just arrived from Summerton. Their horses have been stabled and they've been garrisoned in the guards keep."

Gabriel nodded. "Welcome news."

Ro nodded. "Yes, very good. Thank you."

Trence reached into his jacket and pulled out a folded piece of paper that had been sealed with wax. "One of them carried a note for you."

He handed it over. She looked at the mark that had been pressed into the wax. It bore the letter C with a little tree inside it. She smiled as she glanced toward Gabriel. "From Spencer, I think."

Trence bowed. "Have a good evening, my lady."

"Thank you." Ro snapped the seal and opened the paper. The note inside was short and to the point. *Research done. Enlightening. Return by morning.*

She looked at Gabriel. "Obviously, he didn't want to reveal much in his note, but it sounds promising."

"It does."

Ro folded the paper back up, her gaze shifting into the

dining room. The two royal tables were easy to see at the head of the hall. She looked at her table. JT and Raphaela were laughing with Aunt Vi and Posey. Uldamar and Althea were deep in conversation with a few other professors they must have invited.

Next to them, at Anyka's table, there didn't seem to be as much jocularity. In fact the man seated just two chairs from Anyka looked downright unhappy. Ro stared at the man. There was something about him that...

Recognition punched her in the gut. She sucked in a breath and turned around, putting her back to the room.

"What's wrong?" Gabriel asked.

She took a few steps in the direction of the foyer. Anything to get herself out of the line of sight of the dining hall. She opened her mouth to get more air into her lungs, but the feeling that she couldn't breathe remained. Gabriel followed. She grabbed hold of his arm. "I need to sit down. I need to be away from here."

He nodded and led her to a door off the enormous foyer. He opened it and guided her into a small drawing room. She sat on the couch he took her to. He sat beside her. "What's going on? What's wrong? Are you sick? Hurt?"

She shook her head. "There's a man at Anyka's table. A man I haven't seen in a very long time. I—I'm sure it's him. It must be. I just— Why is he—" A sob choked off the rest of her words.

"Who is he?" Gabriel asked. "Did he threaten you? How do you know him?"

She took a few more shuddering breaths, her hand over

her mouth. She would not cry or fall apart or break down. She couldn't. She was queen. She had too many responsibilities.

"Ro, you have to tell me who he is."

She nodded and put her hands in her lap. "He's Rhys Saunders Shaw. He's JT's biological father."

# Chapter Thirty-Three

"You're sure?" Gabriel asked.

Ro nodded as she pulled herself together. "It's been a long time and he doesn't look exactly the same as he did in the mortal world, but that is definitely him. Probably not his real name, but I will never forget the man who left me high and dry with a baby on the way. That is *definitely* JT's biological father."

Just saying the words helped Ro calm down. For some reason, admitting out loud who the man at Anyka's table was made it easier to deal with. Like having the truth out in the open made it this black and white thing that she could see more clearly.

She didn't know what to do about Rhys being here. Not even a little bit. But at least she could manage her own emotions. What was done was done. He was there. In that dining hall. In close proximity to the son he didn't even know he had.

What would JT think? How was she going to tell him? She couldn't tell him at the table. But did that mean he'd have to go through the entire meal with his father at the next table but never realizing it?

"This is nuts." Ro sniffed. "How am I supposed to deal with this? I can't go in there. But I have to."

She exhaled and tipped her head back.

"You don't have to," Gabriel said.

She straightened her head. "Yes, I do. Not only am I expected to be there, but my family will wonder what happened to me if I don't show up. And I'm supposed to talk to Queen Anyka about meeting with me later. How am I going to stand by her table to speak to her with that man there? What if he recognizes me? What if he says something?" She swallowed, trying to dislodge the knot in her throat. "This is a nightmare."

Gabriel looked a little stumped himself. "It's no secret that Prince James has Grym blood in his veins. Obviously, his father was Grym. Anyone who looks at him can tell that."

Ro nodded. "Right. But that man is sitting *at* Anyka's table. He might actually be someone important. That could be so much worse than if he was just a nobody from Malveaux." She groaned. "Why did he have to come to my university? There are universities all over the world!"

Gabriel's eyes narrowed with concern. "Were you...of age when you had this relationship with him?"

"Yes, I was twenty-three. I was a consenting adult." She sighed. "I guess the best thing to do would be to tell JT. I don't want him figuring it out because of something Rhys, or whatever his name really is, says. Will you get JT and bring him here, please?"

Gabriel nodded and got up, then hesitated by the door. "I don't like leaving you alone. And this door doesn't lock."

"No one knows I'm in here. I'll be fine." And a few minutes alone would be good for her.

"All right. I'll be quick." He slipped out.

She put her head back and closed her eyes. She'd honestly hoped never to see Rhys again. She'd been fairly relieved when JT had said he wasn't interested in locating his father. But that decision had been taken out of their hands.

She hoped JT wasn't too upset by all of this. She had a thousand different emotions running through her and none of them were happy ones.

A soft knock and the door opened. Gabriel let JT in as he spoke to Ro. "Raphaela and I will be outside the door, should you need us, my lady."

"Thank you."

"Also, Uldamar told me who he is."

Ro chewed on the inside of her cheek. "Do I want to know? Don't answer that. Give us a few minutes."

"Of course."

JT gave her a curious look as Gabriel shut the door again. "What's going on, Mom?"

She patted the cushion beside her. "You probably want to sit down for this."

He sat. "Okay. What's up?"

"There's no easy way to say this so I'm just going to tell you. Your biological father is here. I don't know if he'll recognize me or not, but I didn't want you to find out by overhearing something and putting two and two together."

JT sat back. "That was not what I was expecting you to say."

"I'm sure."

"He doesn't know about me, right?"

"Right. But again, I'm sure he'll figure it out when he sees that you're Grym and does the math."

JT exhaled deeply. "I don't want a relationship with him. I've been thinking about it since you asked me in the carriage and there's no reason for one. He left you and didn't care enough to ever get in touch with you again. That's all I need to know about him."

Her son's loyalty to her had always touched her heart. "Unfortunately, he might think differently. You're a prince now. Heir to Summerton's throne. There are a lot of reasons for him to want to know you."

JT shook his head. "I don't care. I'll be civil. But we're not about to go outside and have a game of catch."

Ro smiled. "I respect and support your decision. I don't really want to have anything to do with him, either. He put me in a very dark place for a while. But at the same time, I have you because of him. And you're the best thing that's ever happened to me."

JT grinned. "Mom, you're a *literal* queen. You rule over an entire kingdom and we now live in a castle. Not to mention, we're vacationing in a palace that's bigger than the one we call home."

"All true, and you are *still* the best thing that's ever happened to me."

He took her hand. "We'll get through this."

"I know we will. I suppose I should get Gabriel in here and find out who this man really is. Although, if you're not interested in that…"

"No, I need to know who he is. Might help me understand what he's going to expect."

"Okay." She got up and opened the door. "Why don't you both come in?"

Gabriel nodded. "As you wish." He and Raphaela entered. She stayed by the door, but Gabriel came closer to where JT was sitting.

Ro returned to her seat. "What did Uldamar tell you? Who is he?"

Gabriel didn't look happy. "His name is Nazyr Marwood and he's Queen Anyka's Minister of Magic."

Ro's mouth came open. "So he's Uldamar's counterpart."

Gabriel nodded. "He hasn't been around as long as Uldamar, but yes. He serves in essentially the same role."

"Hold up," JT said. "Are you saying my father is a wizard?"

"Yes, basically," Gabriel said.

"Then why can't I do magic?"

Gabriel took a breath before answering. "That's probably a better question for Uldamar, but my guess is, it just hasn't manifested in you yet." He looked at Raphaela.

She nodded. "I know you didn't ask me but that's what I'd say, too, your lordship. You're young and you're still shaking off the mortal world. Detoxing it from your system. I'm sure it's only a matter of time before your gifts begin to show themselves."

"Maybe," he said. "But I might talk to Uldamar about it all the same."

"I think that would be smart," Ro said. She looked at Gabriel. "Would we be right in assuming that Nazyr's magic tends toward the darker side?"

"I can't say for sure, but considering that he works for Anyka, I'd say that's a reasonable assumption."

"Wait a moment," Ro said. "You know Marwood is one of the surnames given to Lady Cynzia. Any chance he could be related?"

"No idea," Gabriel said. "But I'd like to see what Uldamar thinks about that, too."

"So would I," Ro said. She patted JT's knee. "Not sure what that means for you, but at least you know what might be coming."

"Now I am definitely talking to Uldamar," JT said. "About all of this. Are you actually going in to dinner?"

"Yes," Ro said. "I need to talk to Queen Anyka about getting together later so I can fill her in on the possible danger."

Gabriel looked like he wanted to say something.

"What are you thinking?" she asked him.

"In light of Professor Cloudtree's note, maybe that talk with her could wait until he returns."

Ro thought about that. "I wish he'd been more specific about what he's discovered." She shook her head. "As much as I'd like to wait for his information, I'd feel better letting Anyka know what we've discovered. Then, if anything happens, it won't be because she wasn't warned." Ro stood. "I need to tell her. And I have to go in to dinner."

JT got up, too. "Can we keep this whole thing quiet, though? About Nazyr being my father? I know it might get out. But..." He shook his head and looked at Ro. "I'd rather it not. Even though I realize that's probably just wishful thinking."

Raphaela put her hand on her heart. "You have my word."

"Mine, too," Gabriel said.

Raphaela nodded. "My lips are sealed.

"Thanks." Then JT offered his arm to Ro. "Want an escort, Mom?"

"I'd love one."

With Gabriel walking ahead of them and Raphaela walking behind, Ro and JT went back to the dining hall. He took her to her seat, pulled out her chair for her, then went to his own. She sat and smiled at those around her table, nodding and making small talk.

She'd say something to Anyka once dessert was served. By then, Ro figured her blood pressure would be back to normal and she'd have the comfort of a full belly. And perhaps a glass or two of wine.

Althea Cloudtree was seated on the other side of Gabriel. Ro leaned forward to talk to her. "We've just received word that Spencer should be back by morning."

Althea smiled. "That's marvelous. Thank you for letting me know, your majesty."

Dinner proceeded as though time had sped up and before Ro knew it, a beautiful dish of chocolate mousse flecked with gold leaf and accented with gleaming golden-pink berries had been set before her.

She glanced over at Anyka's table. Nazyr wasn't looking at her. Maybe he didn't recognize Ro now that she was in her true fae form. She had lost a little weight, too. Although the last time he'd seen her, she'd been quite a bit skinnier. Who wasn't in their twenties? So maybe her extra weight was providing her with the perfect disguise.

A little hope fluttered in her chest. She put her hand on Gabriel's arm. "I'm going to speak to Queen Anyka."

"You want me to come with you?"

"No, I want you to stay here and protect my dessert from JT."

He smiled. "As you wish."

She got up and walked over to the other royal table. Almost immediately, the dagger in her boot warmed up. Not enough to be uncomfortable, but enough that she was aware of its presence. "Good evening, Queen Anyka."

Anyka glanced up, wiped her mouth with her napkin, then stood. "Good evening, Queen Sparrow. To what pleasure do I owe this unexpected visit?"

Nothing in Anyka's expression made Ro believe her visit was genuinely a pleasure. "My friends and I have discovered something that might be dangerous. Mostly to anyone who's Grym, although we think there's a chance it could be meant for you. I know that sounds farfetched but if I didn't tell you and something happened, I wouldn't be able to live with myself."

Anyka stared at Ro. Then one brow arched slowly. "You've discovered something. Right here in Willow Hall?"

"Yes, that's right. I was hoping you'd have a few minutes later to meet with me so that I can tell you the whole story."

Anyka's lips pursed. "As intriguing as that sounds, why

should I believe this isn't some kind of setup? Maybe this is the danger I need to be wary of?"

Ro sighed. The woman was a little exhausting. "I've done nothing to indicate I mean you any kind of harm, have I?"

"No," Anyka said.

"And you know why that is? Because I don't mean you any harm. My hope is peace between our kingdoms. Good things for both of us and all of our people. I said as much in my coronation speech. I've said it to anyone who will listen. I even mentioned it in the note I sent to you. I'm sorry if your life has led you to be immediately suspicious of those around you, I really am. That's no way to live. But you can take me at my word. I mean what I say. All I want to do is talk. And keep you safe."

Ro wanted to keep them both safe, but Anyka sure wasn't making it easy.

# Chapter Thirty-Four

No one had said anything like that to Anyka since her parents had been alive. Not with such genuine feeling. Something in Queen Sparrow's voice touched some deeply hidden part of Anyka's soul. Anyka nodded. "I could spare a few moments after dinner. Where would you like to meet?"

Queen Sparrow smiled. "Wonderful. Right after dinner would be great. There's a drawing room off the big foyer right here. We can walk over together if you don't mind waiting for me to finish my dessert."

Anyka nodded. "That's fine. After dessert then."

"Great." Queen Sparrow went back to her seat.

Anyka sat down, but slanted her gaze toward the woman to see if she gave anything away in talking to those at her table. But there was nothing odd that Anyka could see. No sly glances or nods as if to indicate Sparrow had pulled something off. Just a look of relief on her face. Like she hadn't really believed Anyka would agree to talk to her.

Queen Sparrow was terrible at politics and even worse at maintaining a cool public persona. Anyka believed that anyone in power should be able to hide their real emotions and true intentions.

Queen Sparrow was as readable as a book.

Anyka looked around her own table. Everyone seemed content and occupied. Beatryce was talking to the Minister of Art, who was a lively man capable of holding a conversation with anyone. Not married, either. But too old for Beatryce. Or at least Anyka imagined that's what Beatryce would think.

Anyka wasn't so sure the man might not be a contender. Something to think about. He came from a good family of minor nobility. She looked at the other side of the table. Nazyr was staring at the Summerton table.

She watched him for a moment, then finally asked, "What are you looking at? Do you see something interesting?"

He shook his head and paid attention to his dessert, which he hadn't touched yet. "You said the queen was a crossover from the mortal world?"

Anyka nodded. "That's right. She found *Merediem* there and pulled it free of its stone. Why?"

He dug his spoon into the mousse. "She reminds me of someone. That is all."

He was lying, but she couldn't be bothered with that while in the midst of all these people. She'd speak to him about it later. She picked up her spoon. Lystra was eating at a different table this evening. Anyka thought a little distance might be good tonight.

Ishmyel was nearly done with his dessert. "What was that conversation with Queen Sparrow about? I couldn't hear a thing over the other conversations."

Anyka took a small portion of the mousse, just to see if

she liked it. "Don't you know it's not polite to eavesdrop on other people? Especially the queen?"

"I do know that but forgive me if I don't quite trust Queen Sparrow as much as you do."

Anyka almost laughed. She didn't trust the woman, either. She tried the mousse. It was sweet, but also dark and a little bitter. Delicious. "Trog wasn't far away. He'd have snapped her in two before she landed a blow."

"I know. I just can't help but worry," Ishmyel said. "There's never a time I stop being your uncle."

She smiled at him. At times, he was enjoyable to be around. He'd been especially nice on this trip, making her think she'd been wrong to keep him at arm's length. "Queen Sparrow just wants to talk to me after we're done with dessert. Claims she's found something in Willow Hall that might be dangerous to those of us who are Grym. Most particularly me."

He grimaced. "That's a rather wild excuse to get you alone."

"I won't be alone. I'll have Wyett and Trog with me." She took a bigger bite of her dessert. "And I don't believe it's an excuse. She genuinely thinks she's found something dangerous. I'm sure it's nothing. I'll humor her. It won't take but a few minutes and it'll buy me some goodwill down the line."

"Do you want me to go with you?"

She shook her head. She knew he was curious, but she could handle this herself. "What I want you to do is keep an eye on Beatryce. Subtly."

He looked confused. "Why?"

"Because I think she might be enjoying herself a little too much with some of the young men here."

"Ah." His dish empty, he set his spoon down. "I can do that."

"Good. I would appreciate it very much. I'm concerned that she'll get in over her head and get into trouble."

"Not on my watch," Ishmyel said.

"That's what I was counting on." She had one more spoonful of the mousse, then tucked the berries into her purse for Galwyn and pushed the dish away. "I'll see you later this evening, then. Back at the suite."

He nodded. "Are you doing anything after your meeting?"

She started to say no, then realized it would probably be wiser for her to be seen out and about. Wouldn't do to be hidden away in her suite, only coming out to search for the grimoire. Much better if people got used to seeing her. Then when she *was* searching, her appearance wouldn't be such a rarity. "I'm not sure. Is there music again tonight?"

"There's music every night, my dear."

"Then perhaps I'll attend that."

"That's wonderful. Enjoy yourself. And be safe."

"I will." She got up, glancing at Wyett, then Trog, silently ordering them to join her. She went to Queen Sparrow's table, reminding herself to keep a smile on her face and an open mind.

Queen Sparrow looked up. "All ready?"

"I am." Anyka quickly smiled with the sort of expression she hoped implied she was looking forward to their chat.

"Wonderful. So am I. That mousse was really good." Queen Sparrow pushed her chair back and her guard jumped to his feet to help.

Gabriel Nightborne. Anyka almost frowned. He was always at her side. Lystra had her work cut out for her.

The two queens walked side by side out of the dining hall, trailed by their security. Apparently, it was something to see, because the sound in the dining room fell away considerably.

Queen Sparrow smiled and waved as they left. Like they were in a parade. Anyka just barely managed not to roll her eyes, forcing herself to wave, too.

As soon as they were out, she dropped her hand to her side.

"The drawing room is just right around the corner," Queen Sparrow said.

Anyka nodded. The sooner this was over with, the better.

As they approached, Gabriel went ahead of them to open the door.

Anyka let Sparrow enter the room first. She made eye contact with Wyett and Trog again, tipping her head toward the room to let them know she wanted them inside with her.

Both of them understood. Trog and Wyett stood against the wall on the same side of the room where Anyka sat.

Gabriel shut the door, then walked around the couch to stand behind Queen Sparrow.

Anyka frowned at Wyett.

He quickly shifted his position to stand behind her.

"So." Anyka adjusted the skirt of her gown. She was pleased that she'd changed, as Queen Sparrow had not. "What is this dangerous thing you've found? What is that mortal expression... I am all ears?" She laughed, the absurdity of the moment getting to her. "I suppose that's even more true when you're fae, hmm?"

Queen Sparrow chuckled. "That's a good one. It definitely works better for us, doesn't it?"

"Us," Anyka repeated. She didn't consider Sparrow the same as her at all. "That must seem like a strange thing to you still. Being fae, I mean. You haven't been in the fae realm long, have you?"

"No. And I know I have a lot to learn. I'm trying, but just being in this world teaches me something new and interesting every day. Which is actually a pretty good segue into why I asked to speak to you."

Anyka folded her hands in her lap. "I cannot wait to find out what it is."

"Have you ever heard of a woman by the name of Lady Cynzia? I'm sure you have."

Anyka stiffened. She stared at Sparrow, trying to figure out what kind of game the woman was playing.

Queen Sparrow went on as if she had no agenda and Anyka realized that, once again, she'd underestimated the woman. Queen Sparrow was far more calculating than Anyka realized.

"I know," Queen Sparrow said. "That she's a significant historical figure to the Grym. I confess, I'd never heard of her until just the other day."

Anyka nodded. "She is a rather...divisive figure. Why are you bringing her up?"

"Because it's come to our attention that her diary might very well be hidden somewhere here in Willow Hall. But more than that, we believe the diary could be spelled so that whoever finds it will be injured in some way. Or worse. From everything I've read about Lady Cynzia, I believe there's no telling what it might do."

"If such a thing even exists, which I doubt. I'm sure the existence of such a book is just a myth." Anyka's blood chilled. Sparrow knew about the grimoire. She might not know exactly how valuable it was, but she knew of its existence. That was *not* good. She touched the tip of her right ear. Was there any chance Sparrow had already found it?

Anyka doubted that but needed to know more. "What did you mean by 'everything you've read'?" She couldn't believe Sparrow would actually admit to taking those books out of the library.

Queen Sparrow nodded. "What I meant is that I've been poring over books from the History Library, trying to make sense of it all. I didn't want to bring this to you without some kind of proof, but I don't have much. Just a handful of accounts of her life and activities that have led us to think she's going to want revenge on the Grym for her time in Tenebrae. There was even one author who claimed she might still be alive."

"That," Anyka said. "Is most definitely not true." Nazyr would have said as much if he believed that to be the case.

"Well, that's something, I suppose." Queen Sparrow sighed. "Anyway, the bottom line is I didn't want you or any of your people to stumble across the book and end up suffering because of it. If it does exist."

Anyka really didn't understand the woman across from her. She sounded so sincere. Was it possible she really meant the things she said? Did she really have no desire to rule both kingdoms? "That is kind of you to be so concerned. But you must have other things you'd rather be doing than worrying about me."

Queen Sparrow smiled. "Like I told you, I want peace between us. Working toward that is my goal. If something were to happen to you, that wouldn't get me any closer to peace, would it?"

Anyka lifted her chin slightly. "I suppose not."

So Sparrow *was* up to something. But all that something was...was peace.

# Chapter Thirty-Five

Anyka had had enough. She stood up. "I appreciate your information. I must admit, I'm not entirely sure what to do with it, but I'll be on the lookout for any strange books that might suddenly appear before me. Although, as I said, I do not believe such a book even exists."

Queen Sparrow got to her feet as well, her constant smile oddly gone. "I get that you think I'm a joke. You've made that pretty clear."

Behind her, Gabriel Nightborne cleared his throat as if trying to distract the woman he worked for.

Anyka just raised her brows. "I don't believe I've done or said anything that would imply those are my feelings toward you."

"Except you have." Sparrow glared at Anyka. "I have no doubt that your lack of respect for me comes from a multitude of places. Let's see if I can name a few, shall we?" She started ticking them off on her fingers. "I'm Radiant. I'm a crossover. I've only been fae for five minutes. I wasn't raised as a royal. I have no royal blood. I also have no experience in this kind of thing. That's six. How did I do?"

Anyka wasn't so cavalier as to answer that question.

Instead, she was smart enough to understand that she'd upset the woman. And while that didn't truly bother Anyka, she didn't want outright animosity between herself and Queen Sparrow. "My apologies if I've done or said something to make you feel this way."

"*If?*" Sparrow put her hands on her hips. "Do you want peace between our two kingdoms or don't you? It's not a tough question. At least I don't think it is. To me, peace is the easy answer, because it's always the answer."

Anyka chose her words carefully. "Peace seems like the easy answer until it's put into practice. Then it reveals itself to be much more complicated. This is one of the things that experience has taught me."

"I see." Sparrow nodded with conviction. "Who was that peace with?"

"What?"

"That complicated peace that you just mentioned. Who was it with?"

Anyka narrowed her eyes slightly. "Summerton. As you ought to know. That peace ended the day my parents were murdered."

"I do know about that. A truly awful, terrible thing. For which you have my deepest sympathies. It was as awful and terrible as the King of Summerton's wife and two children being murdered just two weeks prior."

Anyka knew what Sparrow was trying to do. Anyka wasn't going to let her get away with it. "So you think my parents being murdered was fair? That their lives balanced out the lives taken in Summerton? I would have died, too, had I drunk the poisoned wine meant to celebrate my birthday. Then it would have been three for three."

"No murder is justified. But your parents never would have died if King Reedly's grief hadn't turned to madness. It's no excuse. But it is an explanation. His family was also poisoned. You probably know that already, though. Like how you also probably know that the poison used was something only found in Malveaux? Just like how the poison that killed your parents came from Summerton fire lilies."

Anyka crossed her arms. She'd been prepared to say as much but Sparrow had said it first. "What is your point?"

"That there is no changing the past. What's done is done. Let's leave the past behind us and move on. You didn't poison King Reedly's family."

"No, I did not." Anyka shook her head. That had been her mother's doing, though she'd only meant to kill the queen.

"Just like I didn't poison your parents. We are different people. There is no reason we can't create a different future for our kingdoms."

"There is one reason," Anyka said.

"What's that?"

"Trust. You said yourself you've been fae for five minutes. I have always been fae. I have been queen since I was sixteen and the crown was thrust upon me. I have decades of experience on the throne. And you want me to treat you as an equal?" Anyka shook her head. "That has to be earned."

"And how exactly am I supposed to do that?"

Anyka shrugged. "That's not my concern, is it?" She strode toward the door.

Wyett managed to get to it before her and opened it. She walked through, waited one beat for Trog and Wyett to exit as well, then kept on going. "That was a waste of time," she muttered.

"At least you know she knows about the grimoire," Wyett said softly from his place behind her.

"She might know about it, but she hasn't a clue what its real value is. Or what it's capable of doing. She doesn't even know if it's really here." Anyka shook her head. "Like I said, waste of time."

Although Anyka had learned that Queen Sparrow had a backbone. That was interesting. Apparently, all it took was a little pressure on the right areas and Sparrow's mettle would appear. That was valuable. Anyka liked knowing where an opponent's levers were and how to push them.

"What about her offer of peace, my lady?"

Anyka sighed and wondered if she was too lenient with Wyett. He overstepped frequently, but at the moment, he seemed to consider himself a peer. "That is for me to consider, but you heard my answer. I don't trust her."

"She seems—"

"Enough. You are my valet, not my council."

"Forgive me, my lady."

He was quiet all the way back to the suite, not once uttering a sound. Not even a, "Yes, my lady." He seemed upset.

Anyka didn't care. For all that she enjoyed Wyett's

capabilities, he was still a servant and he needed to know his place. The guard at the door opened it for her. She went in, then turned before Wyett could enter. "You're dismissed for the evening."

He nodded. "Thank you, my lady."

"I'll expect some sort of report on the matter we discussed earlier." If he thought he was getting out of finding Beatryce a suitable companion, he was wrong.

He nodded again but said nothing.

She walked away. He'd have to come in because his bedroom was in the royal suite, a decision Anyka had begun to regret making. She might have very well led him to believe his status was higher than it was.

Trog followed her inside, remaining by the door.

Anyka went through to her bedroom. She didn't feel like going back down just to listen to music. What were the chances that someone would try to talk to her? She had no interest in pretending to listen to citizens. Although perhaps the musical performance would be enough to keep them quiet.

Oddly, she felt a slight longing for Ishmyel's company. He could be very good at keeping annoying people away from her when he wanted to. Maybe she should send a footman to fetch him. Or Wyett.

But she'd already dismissed him. Not that she couldn't recall him. She was queen. She could do whatever she pleased.

So what did she want to do? Besides find Lady Cynzia's grimoire, which she was more determined to do than ever.

She sat on the bed and thought.

What she wanted to do was sit next to her husband in front of a crackling fire while they enjoyed a glass of winter wine. But that would never happen again. Just like she would never be happy again. How could she be when she'd lost so much?

She sighed. The constant grief that surrounded her was the heaviest mantle she wore. What could she do that might give her a moment of contentment?

Listening to the music tonight might be all right. If she could get Ishmyel to sit with her and keep people away. Maybe they could find Beatryce and persuade her to come as well. Anyka smiled. That would be nice. A family outing.

She got up and rang the bell to summon a footman.

Not only would the music hopefully be entertaining, but by going out, Anyka might catch a glimpse of Queen Sparrow.

She was curious to see how the woman would approach her the next time they met, now that Anyka had been so truthful with her.

She imagined Sparrow would shed the cheerful act and her real self would emerge. That would be interesting to see, wouldn't it?

A knock at the door made Anyka realize that since she'd dismissed Wyett, she'd have to answer it herself. What a bother servants were. She walked out to the sitting room. "Come in."

The footman did as he was bidden, bowing as he entered.

"Fetch my uncle for me."

"Yes, my lady."

As he left, Anyka wondered if she should change. Because if the music was amateurish or boring, she just might go in search of Lady Cynzia's grimoire. Even if the amulet wasn't ready to work yet.

## Chapter Thirty-Six

Ro stared at the closed door in disbelief. Anyka was something else. "What a rude piece of work she is."

"Her true self," Gabriel said.

"I don't know," Ro said. "That's a woman with a lot of baggage. And some deep hurts. Feels to me like she's got some very thick walls up."

"Maybe, but that's also a woman who will cause you deep hurt."

Ro looked at him. "King Reedly lost his wife and children and went mad. She lost both her parents and was forced to rule a kingdom. She may not have ever really mourned their loss." Anyka might not be a nice person, but Ro felt for her. Maybe it was the mother in her, but to Ro, Anyka seemed very much like a hurt little girl who'd never been given the chance to grieve properly. Something in her was broken.

Ro wasn't going to be the one to fix it, but someone ought to try.

Gabriel just frowned.

"I know you don't like her, but I still think telling her about the diary was the right thing to do. Even if she didn't believe me."

"I think she believed you. In fact, I think she already knew about the diary."

Ro blinked. "You do? I didn't pick that up."

He nodded. "The way she looked after you told her about it seemed to imply that to me. And then she touched her ear tip. That's a self-comforting gesture and I've seen a lot of fae do it. She needed to reassure herself that everything was going to be okay. Even though you'd found out about the diary."

"Maybe you should be the First Professor of Inter-Kingdom Relations."

He smiled. "You did just fine. You held your own and you called her out on her behavior. Only another royal could get away with that. And only one who was her equal or higher."

"Was I wrong?" Ro grimaced. "I have a pretty long fuse, but her response just burned it all up. I admit, I got mad. I probably said things I shouldn't have."

"No, not at all. You were completely correct. She's been rude and dismissive toward you. Utterly uncalled for and not remotely royal conduct. Not that she's the paragon of such things."

Ro sighed. "Well, I hope to be better than that."

"It's okay to stand up for yourself."

She nodded. "You're right. It is. I guess we should get back, huh? Figure out what we're doing tonight. There's ballroom dancing in the main ballroom, chamber music in the concert hall, and a tenors group singing folk classics in the blue drawing room."

His eyes narrowed. "Are you trying to suggest we should go to one of those?"

"Your enthusiasm is boundless, you know that?" She laughed as they headed for the door. "Hey, at least Anyka didn't say anything about Nazyr, so maybe he didn't tell her that he knew me."

Gabriel opened it for her. "If he's smart, he won't."

"Why not?"

He left the door closed. "Think about how Anyka would react if she discovered that her Minister of Magic, the person she'd probably turn Lady Cynzia's diary over to in order to work the spells inside it, had a blood connection to you in the form of a child?"

Ro blinked. That could be a problem.

Gabriel's brows lifted. "You see what Anyka's like. Do you think she'd trust Nazyr after that? At the very least, she'd want him to use that connection to work his way into your life. She'd force him to work on you and find out everything he could about you."

Ro made a face. "I guess if I was Nazyr, I wouldn't say anything, either."

Gabriel nodded and opened the door. "Doesn't mean he won't try to contact you himself. Especially if he figures out who JT is. But I bet you he won't say a word about it to her." He hastily added, "My lady," as a pair of pages walked by.

He took up his usual position slightly behind her. She stopped and looked at him. "Just walk beside me. I can't talk to you when you're back there."

"It's not protocol."

"I don't care. I'm the queen and I want you to walk with me."

A brief smile played on his mouth as he moved to stand next to her. "As you wish, my lady."

They started walking again. They didn't have far to go. The portal was only on the other side of the foyer. They got in, alone, and went up to the second floor.

"Listen," she said as they got out. "I am more determined than ever to find that book. The moment Spencer returns, I want him brought to the suite so he can tell us what he's found."

"That might be very early."

"I don't care. Finding that book has just become our main focus. For one thing, with the way Anyka is, she can't be allowed to have it. She'll use it against Summerton. I realize that now."

"And possibly you. If not all of us."

Ro nodded as they strolled down the hall. "I don't doubt that, either. But I was thinking, too, that if I can find the book and use it to lift Malveaux's curse, then that ought to prove to her that I mean Malveaux no harm."

"Lifting the curse certainly seems like it would, but then again, you never know how Anyka will interpret a move like that."

Ro frowned. "Making her kingdom better could be a bad thing?"

He shrugged. "Consider who we're talking about."

"Yeah, okay. But the people will know I mean well."

"Will they?" Gabriel clasped his hands behind his back and looked thoughtful. "How will they find out you're the one who lifted the curse? You think *she'll* tell them if it's a good thing? Or do you think she'll take the credit? Unless it goes horribly wrong, no one in Malveaux will know you were in any way connected."

Ro made a little noise with her tongue. "I hadn't thought about that. Maybe…Uldamar can send some kind of magic message to let them all know."

"Maybe."

They were in front of the suite now. As always, a royal Summerton guard was on duty. Gabriel opened her door for her. "Your majesty, I need to go back down and brief the new guards that have arrived. I won't be gone long. When I get back, I'd be happy to accompany you to whatever event you choose this evening."

Ro nodded. "Thank you. Tell the guards I appreciate them coming on such short notice."

"I will, my lady," Gabriel said. He gave her a nod as she went in.

"Mom."

She closed the door and turned to see JT walking into the big sitting room looking very excited. "What's up?"

"I talked to Uldamar about my magic. I told him the whole Nazyr thing. I hope that was okay."

Ro nodded. "That was fine. I think Uldamar's pretty trustworthy. What did he have to say?"

"He can perform a magical detox on me. Get rid of all the stagnant human matter so that I can be fully fae. He said it's the same thing that would happen to me in the next few years, but magically accelerated."

"And it's safe?"

JT nodded. "Yes."

"And after that, your magic will show up?"

"If it's going to, that will help it along. Uldamar said there's no real guarantees, but he also said that Nazyr's fairly powerful, although Uldamar didn't know if Nazyr was actually related to Lady Cynzia or not. He said he'd look into it. Anyway, I should end up with something."

Ro still wasn't convinced. "What about the part where Nazyr's magic is a little on the dark side? If he is related to Lady Cynzia, that might not be such a great thing for you."

JT nodded. "I don't love that part, either, but Uldamar said dark magic doesn't have to be used for dark things. He's promised to help me. So has Raphaela."

Ro smiled for reasons that had nothing to do with magic. "You like her, don't you?"

"I mean, she's cool. Yeah. I like her."

Ro tipped her head. "Do you like her as more than just a friend?"

JT started to say something, then stopped. "I don't know. Maybe."

"I've never known you to be unsure about matters of the heart."

He sighed. "Okay, yeah, I like her. She's beautiful, she looks like a fae warrior princess, she wears head to toe leather every day, and she knows more ways to kill a person than I even realized was possible. She's like one of the female characters from *World of Warcraft* come to life.

Plus, she's got a killer sense of humor. How else am I supposed to feel?"

Ro smiled but said nothing.

He groaned. "Look, I already know nothing can happen. She told me herself. Me being a prince and all."

"If your being a prince wasn't a barrier, would you pursue her?"

His eyes lit up a little. "I'd at least try. She's clearly out of my league, if we're not putting my title into the mix, but yeah, I would definitely go after Raphaela." Then his eyes narrowed. "Why?"

"Because I don't think rank or status should have anything to do with who a royal weds. Radiant fae, regardless of who they are or what position they hold, should be able to marry for love. And I'm going to talk to Professor Larksford about having that particular bit of protocol removed or changed or whatever needs to be done so that love is what matters."

JT nodded. "That's good, Mom. I would hate to have to marry someone because it was for the good of the kingdom. You might end up with an all-right relationship, but then again, you might end up miserable."

"I agree."

"Do you also agree with letting Uldamar work his magic on my magic?"

"You're an adult. If you're comfortable with it and you want to do it, then go for it."

"Thanks. I know I'm an adult, but there are some things a kid still wants his mother's approval for. Even if he is thirty."

She laughed. "I love you, JT."

"I love you, too, Mom. Aunt Violet went over to Posey's room. They're going to the stable arena to watch the warhorse display."

Ro's brows lifted. "I didn't even know that was a thing. Thanks for telling me." That sounded interesting. And probably much more like something Gabriel would actually want to go to.

Although the folk music held some appeal to her. Folk songs often told stories about real people, something Ro was interested in.

She went into the bedroom to change. Benny was sitting in the middle of the bed, cleaning himself.

"How was your day, Benny boy?"

His only response was to shift legs and clean his other foot.

"That exciting, huh?" She went into the dressing room and changed into a much simpler outfit of dark green pants with soft black boots, and a flowy tunic top in a pattern of large green dragonflies and tiny purple beetles on a black background. She added a lightweight cape of soft purple wool along with some different jewelry, swapping out her trillianite and diamond circlet for an uncomplicated one of silver set with amethysts and green garnets.

She made sure she had all of her daggers with her, then went back to the bedroom. She draped the cape over a chair and sat on the bed by Benny. She petted his head and ran her nails down his back. He was purring in no time. "I hope you're doing all right. Of course, I know you'll be hogging the pillows tonight, won't you?"

He flopped over and kneaded at the air.

Ro grinned. "Silly thing." She kissed the belly he'd just exposed, then sat back and thought about everything that had just happened.

She had no idea how she was going to find that diary. She just knew she had to do it before Anyka did.

## Chapter Thirty-Seven

Gabriel arrived at Ro's door about an hour later. "Your majesty." He bowed. "All is in order with the newly arrived guards."

"Great," Ro said. She'd had food brought up for Wiggy, who was still out running around somewhere with her guard escort, and had made sure Benny had plenty of kibble in his bowl. Now she was ready to do something that might take her mind off of Anyka and Lady Cynzia for a bit.

She stepped out of the suite and closed the door behind her. "I know exactly what I want to do."

They started down the hall together.

"Very good. What is it?"

"I want to see the warhorse exhibition in the stable arena." She'd found out the folk music presentation would be repeated.

"Excellent." Gabriel looked her over and his steps slowed. "Although perhaps I should change, too. Something a little more relaxed."

She nodded. "Go for it. I can wait here."

He shook his head. "My guest suite has a sitting room. You're welcome to stay there while I change in the bedroom, but I am not leaving you in the hall."

"No, of course not." She smiled. "Back we go. I'm curious to see the guest suites anyway."

They turned around and headed back. Gabriel let them into his room.

"This is nice," Ro said. It was kind of a mini version of the royal suite, which she was glad to see. That meant Posey's room was just as nice. She settled into a chair to wait.

"I won't be long," Gabriel said.

"Whatever time you need." That only turned out to be about eight minutes.

He returned in the outfit she was most used to seeing him in. Under a leather vest he wore a loose shirt. That was tucked into fitted pants that were tucked into soft boots. He had a sword at his side and daggers at his waist and in both boots.

"Better?" she asked.

He nodded as he fastened one cuff. "Better."

A soft knock at his door turned both of their heads.

"Who's that?" Ro whispered.

Gabriel shrugged. "No idea."

Ro got up, a weird feeling settling over her. Like maybe she shouldn't be seen in Gabriel's room.

"I'll see to it," Gabriel said. "I'm sure it's nothing. Probably just one of the guards wondering about his schedule."

Ro stayed standing.

Gabriel opened the door, but she was on the other side of it so she couldn't see who it was.

"Hello, Gabriel."

A woman.

Gabriel scowled. "Lystra. What are you doing here?"

"I just wanted to talk to you. It's been a long time since we've seen each other."

"For good reason," Gabriel said.

Ro padded quietly across the room and went to stand behind the bedroom door where she could hear without being seen.

Lystra sighed loudly. "I know things have been contentious between us at times. But we're older now. Can't we move beyond that? I just want to talk to you for a few minutes. There are some things I really need to say to you."

"Two minutes. Not a second more."

Gabriel had obviously noticed Ro had moved. Ro watched through the slit between the door and its hinges as he let Lystra in.

She was in a form-hugging black gown that showed every line of her body. The woman was thin, but unlike Anyka, much more curved than angular. On top of that, Lystra was beautiful.

Ro frowned.

Lystra took a look around. "Very nice suite."

"Being a First Professor and the queen's personal guard has some perks."

Lystra smiled. "I bet it does. Getting any other *royal* perks?"

Gabriel just stared at her. "What did you need to say to me?"

She moved closer to him. "We were really good together, once upon a time."

"Were we?"

"We made Raphaela, didn't we?"

"Yes." Gabriel relaxed a little.

"The two of you could have anything you wanted if you came back to Malveaux. Queen Anyka would reward you for returning. In ways you can't imagine."

Gabriel snorted. "I'm pretty sure I can imagine them just fine. If that's what you're here for, on some recruiting visit, you can save your breath."

Lystra dropped one shoulder and the strap of her dress slipped off. "If you came back, you could have me."

Gabriel opened his mouth to reply, but Lystra kept talking. And coming closer. "You know, you wouldn't even have to come back. Not physically." She put her arms around his neck and gazed up at him. "If your loyalties were with Malveaux but you kept your job, you'd be in a perfect position to—"

Gabriel pushed Lystra away. "You dare come here to try to sway me against my kingdom and my queen? Is that why Queen Anyka brought you? To use you as bait?" He laughed. "You're a fool, Lystra. And you're as clueless about me now as you were while we were married. Get out. I don't want to see you again. Not here at Willow Hall. Not anywhere. I'll be warning Raphaela of your intentions, too."

"No," Lystra cried. "I want to talk to her."

Gabriel took her by the arm and guided her toward the door. "I doubt she'll want to talk to you."

He nudged her out, then stepped into the hall after her. Ro couldn't see either of them, but a moment later,

Gabriel came back in and closed the door. His face was slightly red, and he looked like he wanted to break something.

Ro stepped out from behind the bedroom door. "You okay?"

"I am…furious. That she would even think…" He closed his eyes and seemed to be willing himself to calm down.

"It's okay," Ro said. "I'm sure Anyka made her do that."

"I have no doubt," Gabriel said. "I'm sure that's exactly why Anyka brought her." He shook his head and walked to the windows. "Unbelievable."

"Actually," Ro started. "I think it was pretty on brand for Anyka."

He frowned and looked over at her. "On brand?"

"Typical of something she would do. Up her alley. Down her street. Her expected behavior."

"I get it," he said. He let out a sigh and leaned against the window frame.

Ro came over to join him.

He glanced at her. "I'm glad you were here to witness that."

She put her hand on his arm. "Thank you for your loyalty."

He smiled. "As if I could be anything else."

She nodded. "One of the many things I love about you." Then she pointed at him. "Don't let that go to your head."

He laughed. "I shall endeavor to do my best."

"What do you say we go see these warhorses?"

"I would love to." He stepped away from the windows. "I understand they have refreshments. Popcorn, mostly. I know you had that in the mortal world, but fae popcorn is better."

"How so?"

They went to the door and he opened it, letting her go ahead of him.

"We drizzle ours with a mixture of honey, ground buca root, butter, and salt."

"Buca root? That's like cinnamon, I think? I'm definitely going to have to try that. Sounds a little messy, though."

"Most of the best things in life are."

She smiled as they walked down the hall. "That is surprisingly true."

She waited until they were in the portal to speak again. "We have to find that diary before Anyka does. You know that, right?"

He nodded. "You want to do some more looking tonight? It should be pretty quiet after the events. Most people will turn in."

"Yes. I do. I know Spencer might be bringing us some significant new information tomorrow, but I don't think I'll be able to sleep if I don't at least have one more look around."

"We'll make it happen."

The stable arena sat behind Willow Hall in an area Ro hadn't been to yet. It was large, probably able to hold a thousand people. Maybe more. The center looked like sand, but the surrounding tiered seating was beautifully crafted of wood and metal. Colorful banners were hung at regular intervals around the space.

Horses were positioned at various points at the edge of the center area and being led out to the middle, where they were shown off by the handlers.

Ro and Gabriel stood on a walkway on the first level, looking through to the arena. The faint scents of horse and something sweeter reached them.

"Where should we sit?" Ro asked.

"Probably in your assigned seat."

Ro looked at him. "I have an assigned seat?"

"There are two royal boxes, so yes, you do."

She smiled. "That works."

Gabriel took a quick look at the upper levels, found the box, and figured out where they needed to go. It required climbing two sets of stairs, but Ro didn't mind. She'd done a lot of walking here, but otherwise didn't feel like she'd been as active as she was accustomed to.

The royal box was spacious and could have accommodated a dozen people. There was already a Summerton guard stationed at the door. As soon as she and Gabriel were seated, a page approached them.

He couldn't have been more than ten or eleven. With great precision, he bowed low.

"Hello there," Ro said. She smiled. It had been a long time since JT was that little. What a sweet age that had been. "What's your name, young man?"

"Good evening, your majesty. My name is Kieran. I'm the page for this royal box. Would you like some refreshments?"

Ro wanted to ruffle his hair. She refrained. "I understand you have popcorn, Kieran."

He nodded. "Yes, your majesty. And chocolate bonbons and blackberry lemonade. We have beer, wine, and water, as well."

"I think blackberry lemonade sounds delicious." She glanced at Gabriel, who nodded. "Two of those. We'll take some popcorn and chocolate bonbons, as well."

"Very good, your majesty." He bowed again and went to fetch their refreshments.

"Well, he's the most adorable thing I've seen in a long time."

Gabriel smiled. "I love Raphaela and I am blessed to have her as my daughter, but I sometimes think it would have been nice to have a son as well. Although Raph's probably about as close to a son as you can get without actually having one."

Ro nodded. "I get it. I would have loved to have had a daughter. I can't say JT was anything like having a girl child, because he wasn't. He was *all* boy. And I certainly wouldn't trade him for the world. But a second child, a daughter, would have been wonderful. Someone to dress up in cute dresses and hair I could braid or put in pigtails. It would have been nice."

Gabriel nodded in understanding.

She exhaled and flattened her palms against her thighs. "All right. Tell me what I need to know about these horses."

Gabriel knew a lot, which didn't surprise Ro. He had a warhorse himself. Some of the horses on display, however, dwarfed his. He explained those were troll breeds, which was where the Grym warhorse was believed to have originated.

Kieran returned with their refreshments on a tray, moving very carefully so he didn't spill anything. He served Ro first, then Gabriel.

Gabriel tossed the boy a coin. "Well done, son."

Kieran caught it and tucked it into his jacket pocket without looking at it, something Ro thought took remarkable restraint. "Thank you, sir. Er, your lordship."

"Just 'sir' is fine," Gabriel corrected him with a smile.

Ro dug into her popcorn, eager to taste it. It was sweet and buttery, salty and crunchy, with the perfect bite of cinnamon. "This is like kettle corn on steroids."

Gabriel's eyes narrowed. "I understood none of that."

She grinned. "It's really, really good."

He helped himself to a piece from his own bag. "I told you."

"You did." She ate a few more pieces, then took a sip of her drink. "Why aren't you a lord? You're a First Professor."

"It's not a position that comes with a title, and as I have no titled land, I have no inherited title. That's generally how it happens. Coming from Malveaux, that was never in the cards for me."

"I see." But her mind was working away in the background, wondering if there wasn't a way to solve that problem.

When the last horse was paraded through the arena, Ro knew more about warhorses than she'd ever thought possible. It had been a very enjoyable evening, however, and exactly what she'd needed.

Gabriel escorted her to the royal suite and said goodbye at the door. In one hour, after people had dispersed from the various activities, they were going back out.

Back to the libraries.

Back to do some hunting.

# Chapter Thirty-Eight

The music had been enjoyable, the musicians far more talented than Anyka had expected, and although Beatryce hadn't joined Anyka and Ishmyel, the night had been very pleasant all the same. It helped that Anyka's plan of having Ishmyel join her to keep people away had worked beautifully.

He'd kept quite a few citizens from talking to her and even turned away one particularly talkative minister.

Now, she and her uncle had returned to the royal suite and were having a nightcap of blackberry brandy, something that was readily available at Willow Hall. Galwyn was currently perched on the mantel over the fireplace, keeping an eye on them while he devoured a strip of dried venison. The berries she'd brought him from dinner were long gone.

On the walk back to the suite, Anyka had filled Ishmyel in on Queen Sparrow's news about Lady Cynzia's diary.

But that was at the back of Anyka's mind. She was about as relaxed as she'd been since arriving at the Summer Palace. "Just so you know, it's high time Beatryce was betrothed. I've set Wyett the task of finding someone suitable to keep her company until such a man can be found. It won't be easy."

Ishmyel nodded. "There are other kingdoms. One of them must have an eligible son. What of the forest elves?"

Anyka snickered. "Beatryce? Married to a forest elf? They would accuse us of deliberate sabotage."

Ishmyel chuckled softly. "They might indeed." He sighed. "I would be happy to tell you of anyone I can think of."

"Good. I would appreciate it." She took another sip of brandy, then raised her glass to the light to better see the dark purple liquid filling it. "Perhaps I *should* speak to Queen Sparrow about a treaty. Access to this brandy alone would be worth it."

Ishmyel laughed. "It is not hard to drink, is it?"

"No, indeed." She took another sip, savoring the sweet fire it sent down her throat. After a moment, she broached a new subject. "Nazyr lied to me today."

Ishmyel's brows went up. "You're sure of that? About what?"

She nodded. "I am. And I don't know for sure, but it concerns Queen Sparrow."

Ishmyel put his brandy down and leaned forward. "You haven't spoken to him about this?"

"No. Not yet." She sighed. "I know I should. But at the same time, I need him on my side until that grimoire is in my hands. I'm reluctant to upset him before that happens."

"I can understand that. But at the same time, what if whatever he's hiding is of greater significance?"

"You think there could be something more important

than Lady Cynzia's diary? What do you think that would be?"

He shrugged. "I don't know. But I do know that Nazyr spends a lot of time in the mortal world. Always has. The fact that he lied to you concerning the new Summerton queen, someone who spent her entire life in the mortal world, does not seem like a coincidence to me."

Anyka hadn't thought about it like that. "Perhaps I should question him. Gently."

"If you want me to leave, I can go to my quarters."

"No. Stay. Seeing that he's outnumbered could help him be more truthful. But let's not attack him straight away. Let's play it carefully."

Ishmyel nodded. "Invite him for a nightcap?"

"Yes," Anyka said. Ishmyel understood. He'd been involved in royal politics since before she was born. Maybe she should get him to teach Beatryce a bit. It was worth mentioning.

"I'll send a footman for him."

Anyka nodded. "Yes. Do."

He got up, went over to the bell rope, and pulled it.

Nazyr arrived twenty minutes after a footman went to fetch him. Not exactly the prompt response Anyka liked. He bowed. "Forgive me, your majesty. I was in the bath."

He did look a little damp. Perhaps that was the truth. She nodded and used her charm to soothe any feathers of his she might have ruffled. "I am sorry to interrupt your evening, Minister Nazyr. I only thought you might like to share a nightcap with my uncle and myself."

"I am honored." He bowed again. "Thank you for inviting me."

Ishmyel refilled Anyka's glass with blackberry brandy, then poured one for Nazyr before topping up his own. "How was your day, Minister Nazyr?"

Nazyr nodded. "It was busy." He smiled. "Not as busy as yours was, my lady, I'm sure."

"You did finish the amulet, though." She lifted her glass. "Here's to the amulet working and finding that grimoire tomorrow morning."

Her uncle and Nazyr both raised their glasses as well.

They all drank. Anyka made sure to take a very small sip. She'd already had one glass and didn't need to be outfoxed by Nazyr because she'd had too much to drink. "So, Minister Nazyr. What do you think of Summerton's new queen?"

He shrugged. "I find her unremarkable."

"Come now," Anyka said. "With the way you were looking at her, I would say you think more about her than that she's unremarkable."

"I was merely curious about what sort of magic she might have. Aren't you?"

She didn't believe that for a moment. "I've given it a passing thought, but not much more than that. After so many years in the mortal world, I imagine whatever magic she has might be too suppressed to ever show itself." Anyka didn't believe that, either.

Nazyr shook his head. "I don't think that will be true. Remember, she pulled *Merediem* free. There was enough powerful magic involved in that transaction to jumpstart her own. No matter how dormant it might have been."

That wasn't something Anyka had heard before. "Does it work that way?"

"Absolutely. There are spells designed to do that very thing." He picked up his brandy again. "But most crossovers just let their magic surface naturally, which generally happens after a few years in the fae realm."

"And her son?"

Nazyr had just taken a sip. At her question, he coughed suddenly, almost as if he were choking. He quickly set his glass down and wiped the back of his hand across his mouth. "Pardon me, my lady. I'm not used to such strong drink."

More lies, she thought. Nazyr was hiding something. She just didn't know what it was. But trying to get it out of him was ruining her mood. "You're sure that by tomorrow morning, the amulet will lead me to the grimoire?"

"I don't know if the amulet will lead you to it, or if the amulet will cause the grimoire to show itself to you. I can't predict how that will come to pass. I just know that by tomorrow morning, the amulet's magic will be active and ready to do its job." Nazyr drained the last of his brandy.

"How do you propose I find this grimoire then?"

Ishmyel nodded. "I'd like to know as well. There are many libraries in this palace and all of them are large. Some might even be considered vast. Even with magical help, finding one single book, a book that has been purposefully hidden, is not going to be easy."

"No," Nazyr said. "It won't be. But I'll be with you. I'll

cast the spell that will hopefully bring the book to light. To you, anyway. I have a feeling it might glow with the brilliance of a thousand stars, but no one will be able to see it except for you."

Anyka smiled. "That will certainly help. If true."

"I know my magic," Nazyr said. There was just a hint of softness to his words. The brandy was affecting him. "It will work."

"We will see tomorrow." Then, once Anyka had the grimoire in her hands, she would press Nazyr again for what he was hiding about Queen Sparrow.

And this time, Anyka would get the truth from him.

No matter what.

Done with him, she tossed back the last of her brandy. "You're dismissed, Nazyr. I will see you here before breakfast and we will start the search."

He got up and bowed. "Yes, your majesty. Thank you for your hospitality."

He left quickly, obviously eager to return to his own quarters.

When the door closed, Anyka looked at Ishmyel. "You don't think there's any chance he's going to look for the grimoire himself tonight, do you?"

Ishmyel's eyes narrowed. "With that man, anything is possible. You could always put a guard near his door. Someone to keep an eye on him."

She nodded. "That is an excellent idea."

He smiled. "I have another one, if you care to hear it."

The brandy had left her wonderfully warm and in a

generous mood. "I would love to. Excellent ideas are my favorite kind."

"Well," he started. "I don't know if this one is excellent or not. But it is an idea. About Beatryce and who you might betroth her to."

That got Anyka's attention. "Tell me. I am eager to hear it."

"He's Grym," Ishmyel said. "And he's royalty."

Anyka's brows bent. "And I don't know about him? Who is this man?"

"You know about him. I just don't think you've considered him." Ishmyel cleared his throat softly and looked like he might be bracing himself for Anyka's response. "Prince James Meadowcroft."

Anyka sat without saying anything for a few long moments. "You're right. I haven't considered him."

"If that's an unacceptable suggestion, my apologies."

She shook her head. "I don't know how I feel about it. I can see the merits of it. And there are quite a few." She sighed. "I don't think Queen Sparrow would go for it."

Ishmyel lifted one shoulder. "She says she wants peace. What better way to achieve that than through a treaty by marriage?"

"You make a good point. But it's something I'm going to have to think long and hard about. And that kind of thinking is better done sober. I'm going to bed." She got up and held her arm out to Galwyn, who hopped onto it and sidestepped his way up to her shoulder.

Ishmyel laughed. "I'm going to turn in as well. Maybe

by the light of morning, we'll both realize it's not a proposition worth entertaining."

"Maybe. Good night, Uncle."

"Good night, my queen. Sleep well."

She had no doubt she would. But the thought of Beatryce marrying the new Summerton prince was going to stick with her for some time.

# Chapter Thirty-Nine

Ro had changed out of her colorful tunic and into a plain, long-sleeve black T-shirt from the mortal realm. Over that, she wore a basic black cape. She had all three of her daggers as well. It was as close to secret library ninja wear as she could get.

Gabriel came to her door having changed out his shirt for a black one, too.

Apparently, they'd both had the same idea about going into stealth mode.

For the sake of the guard at her door, Gabriel bowed and said, "Are you ready to see the stars, my lady? I understand this is the best time of night to take them in."

She nodded. "I can't wait. I just hope it's not too cold on the water."

"You should be fine with that cape."

They walked in the direction of the boats, the same as they'd done the night before. But this time, they took a different stairway down to the first floor. One that Gabriel had found. He explained it was used primarily by staff.

He went first, checking at the bottom to make sure there was no one around who would see Ro coming out the door. "All clear."

She slipped out. They were on the other side of the

Hall of Libraries. "Do you really think all this sneaking around is necessary?"

"What if Queen Anyka decides she wants to talk about the diary some more, sends her valet to you with a message and the guard at your door tells him you're not there because you've gone to the library?"

Ro nodded. "Okay, fair point. But why would Anyka want to see me when every sane person has already gone to bed?"

"I believe you just answered your own question." He shrugged and opened the door to the Horror Library. "But perhaps I was too cautious."

She patted his chest as she went in. "You were just doing your job. And since Anyka isn't one of the sane people, I take back what I said. Better safe than sorry, right?"

His brow furrowed. "I would rather be able to fight than be sorry."

"It's just an expression." She took a moment and looked around.

The Horror Library at night was creepier than it was during the day. Despite the chandeliers lighting the space and the bioluminescence of the falls illuminating the stained-glass windows, shadows were everywhere. The glow of magically lit chandeliers only seemed to bring them to life.

Ro noted that in this library, the horror theme had been fully embraced. Here, the lights in the chandeliers flickered like candle flames and the fixtures dripped with strands of fake cobwebs for atmosphere.

At least she hoped they were fake.

Further adding to the creepiness were the gargoyles perched throughout the space. On bookshelves. Over the door. Where moldings met. Some of the random objects in the room included taxidermied birds and preserved insects, crystal balls on stands, and displays of various weapons.

The stained glass depicted more of the same, along with spiders, tombstones, coffins, blood-red roses, and bats. There was even a woman weeping by a coffin.

Ro shuddered. "They really went full Hitchcock on the theme."

"What is 'full Hitchcock'?"

Ro shook her head. "I'll explain later." She really had to figure out how to watch movies in a realm that had no electricity. There had to be some kind of setup. A solar battery? Magic? She needed to tell Posey to put movies on her growing to-do list. "But stay close, okay? This place gives me the willies."

"Are the willies like the shivers?"

"Probably. It's just a little spooky. Which I understand it's supposed to be. But I was never one for scary stuff and this is *not* a genre I read."

She moved toward the center of the room where a large cauldron was on display. A placard said it was a replica of an actual caldron used by practitioners of the black arts. Ro made a face at it. "If ever there was a library that might house Cynzia's diary, this feels like a contender."

Gabriel stood close. Closer than usual. Close enough

that his sword brushed her leg. His dedication to following her orders amused her. He looked around. "I agree. And it's one of the smaller libraries, so it should be an easy place to search, too."

She pulled out the piece of paper she'd tucked in the pocket of her cape. It was her copy of the poem. "All right. Let's see if any of this makes more sense now that we're here."

As they stood there, she read it out loud. "Lamp lights flicker, pages fall, darkness heeds the witch's call. One for the queen, fallen in a heap; one for the king, taking a leap; one for the heir and the people weep.

"So cheery," she muttered. "Close the book, put out the light, hide the words in plain sight. Blue in mourning, red in sleep, shadows stretch and move and creep, keeping quiet their secret so deep."

She looked around. "This library definitely has the shadow part down."

"You know," Gabriel said. "In two places in that poem, it mentions or refers to darkness. Darkness heeds the witch's call and put out the light."

"Three," Ro said. "If you interpret lamp lights flicker as them going out."

He nodded. "There might be too much light in this library for us to find the diary."

Ro didn't like where this was headed. "This is already like standing in the middle of a haunted mansion. Now you want to turn the lights out?"

He grinned. "Scared, your highness?"

"I'm not scared," she said. She totally was. "But this

isn't exactly my happy place. Not to mention, I'm pretty well armed. I might accidentally stab anything that startles me."

He held his hands up. "I would prefer to remain unperforated, so try to remember I'm here with you, all right?"

As if she could forget. "I'll do my best. How are you going to turn those chandeliers off? They're magic."

"They are, but they should be the kind of magic that's easily controlled, like what's at Castle Clarion. My personal magic is of a very different nature, but let's see what I can do." He looked up at the chandeliers. "Lights off."

They flickered again as if caught in a sudden gust, then went out.

"That worked better than I expected." Ro swallowed and reached for Gabriel's hand. It was very dark. But as she stood there, her eyes adjusted to the glow coming through the windows from the falls.

"Oh," she said softly. "That's kind of cool. Are you seeing what I'm seeing?"

"The colors from the stained glass? Yes."

She looked at him. He was awash in a kaleidoscope of color. She must look the same. She focused on those colors. "The poem mentions red and blue. But those colors are all over the place."

"Do you see anything on any of the bookshelves that might look different now that the lights are off?"

"You mean like something that has its own light?" Ro went book by book through the shelves nearest them. "Not yet."

"All right, I think we should get closer. Inspect the books one by one if we have to."

She sighed. "You mean separately, don't you."

"It would be faster. And I can probably command the lights to come back on."

"Except I think you're right about the poem indicating darkness is important." She shuddered. "Let's do this. I'd like to say as quickly as possible, but I also know rushing through this isn't going to help us find anything."

"I won't be that far away."

"I know. You take that side, I'll take this one."

He nodded.

They split up and went to search. Ro started on the left side and worked her way down the shelves. It was slow going. Once she thought she'd found something, but when she pulled the book off the shelf, she realized it was just the foiling on the cover that had glinted at her.

Thankfully, the longer she was in the library, the better adjusted her eyes became. By the time she reached the middle of the shelves, she didn't miss the chandeliers at all. Well, not as much.

She glanced over at Gabriel a few times. He was working just as intently as she was. And not finding anything, either.

It took them nearly two hours to go through the entire library. At the end, they met back in the middle.

"Nothing," she said. "You?"

"Nothing." He glanced down at her boots. "Did your dagger heat up at any point?"

"No, but that would have been a great indicator if it

had." She looked back at the rows and rows of books she'd just searched. "I wonder if I should have held it and moved it across every shelf of books."

"I don't think it needs to be that close to work. Then again..." He shrugged.

Ro sighed. "So much for our mission. I guess we can cross this library off."

"Maybe. Maybe not," Gabriel said.

"Wherever Cynzia hid that thing, she did a great job." Roe stared up at the stained-glass windows, willing the answer to come to her. But she was captivated by the image of a young woman weeping beside a coffin, red roses scattered on the ground around her, bats flying overhead and a black cat lingering in the background. The pictures done in glass were very detailed. It made her wonder if what she was looking at was a scene from a book.

She looked at Gabriel as she pointed to the window. "Is that scene just something the glass artist made up or is it from a book?"

He shook his head. "If it's from a book, it's not one I know. But I guarantee the librarian could tell you."

"Tomorrow." She yawned. "We tried and now I'm ready for bed. I can't look anymore. Besides, Spencer will be here in the morning and should have the information we need to finally find this thing."

"Back to the suite, then."

She nodded. "Hopefully, the guard on duty doesn't think our boat capsized and we've drowned in Celestial Lake."

Gabriel smiled as they walked out of the library. "He wouldn't think that. He'd know the merpeople would save us."

Ro almost stumbled over nothing. "There are merpeople in that lake?"

Gabriel's brows lifted innocently. "Didn't I mention that?"

# Chapter Forty

Glass shattered and Ro woke with a start, heart pounding, breath coming in deep gulps. What had just happened? Had she actually heard that sound? Or not? No. There was no glass. Everything was dark. She'd had a dream.

She was still stuck between it and reality and fighting to figure out which was which. The dream was so real. She'd been back in the Horror Library. She'd been terrified at first.

She wasn't there now, though. She knew that. Repeated it to herself. Her heart rate slowed just as her terror in the dream had subsided. She'd realized she wasn't in the library exactly so much as she was looking down on it. She'd somehow become the woman in the stained-glass picture. The one weeping by the coffin.

She'd smelled the freshly turned earth and the dying roses. Felt rain on her skin and the dampness seeping through the knees of her gown. Heard the flutter of wings, the cat's distant cry. Immense sadness had drowned all other emotions. It still lingered within her, actually. The dream's last hold on her.

She'd cried in her sleep, so much that her face remained damp with the tears. Her heart had broken for reasons the dream hadn't clarified, but then, there were no rules for how dreams worked.

Realizing that, Ro, in the form of the stained-glass woman, had lifted her head to look out over the library.

The poem about Lady Cynzia had been turned into a song and it was playing in the background, the words being sung like a funeral dirge. She sang along with it, remembering the words as if they'd been with her all her life.

She gazed at the library below her. At the splashes of color from the stained glass painting the spines of the books. The shadows moving and dancing like fingers pointing. And that's when she'd understood how to find Lady Cynzia's diary.

At least, she'd figured it out in the dream and the glass had shattered all around her. Did that mean she'd figured it out for real? She wasn't sure, but lately, her understanding of dreams had increased dramatically. If her magic really revolved around dreams, she had every reason to think what had been revealed to her was true.

Benny was fast asleep and tucked against her side at the edge of the bed, making it impossible to get out from under the covers. "Benny, I need to get up."

She moved him as carefully as she could, but he woke up anyway, squirming out of her grasp to escape to the other side of the bed.

She swung her legs out and tried to get her bearings in the dark room. She had no idea what time it was but there didn't seem to be any light coming around the drapes. Maybe these were meant to block light like in the rooms on the waterfall side? Someone had mentioned that to her.

She got up and padded over to the windows, splitting the drapes to peek out. No light. Whatever time it was, dawn was still some distance away.

It didn't matter. She couldn't go back to bed. Not with what the dream had shown her. She had to go back to the library now. "Lights on," she said, lighting the bedside oil lamp, which was surprisingly bright, and got dressed.

She put on the same clothes she'd had on the night before, same boots, made sure she had her daggers, too. Benny sat on the bed watching her, looking bothered that she'd disrupted his precious seventeen hours of sleep.

"I know you're judging me," she said to him. "But this is important."

He lay down, breathing out a little cat sigh.

She wasn't about to fuss with jewelry or makeup or hair or any of that. Until she caught a glimpse of herself in the mirror.

She brushed her hair, then clipped the top half back with a barrette. The silver streak in her hair seemed more noticeable than ever. She moisturized her face and put on lip balm. It wasn't makeup, but at least she'd look dewy.

She started out, then paused by the bedside. She did a quick check to be sure she had everything she needed. Wasn't much. She was dressed and she had her daggers. The only thing she was missing was Gabriel.

"Lights off." She extinguished the oil lamp, which made it nearly impossible to see. She carefully found her way out of the bedroom, through the sitting rooms, and into the hall.

The guard looked startled to see her. "Your highness."

"I need Minister Nightborne. Do you know if he's in his quarters?" He should be. She couldn't imagine where else he'd be.

"Yes, your majesty. He's just returned, actually."

Just? Where had he gone? Had he been looking for the diary on his own? "Thank you."

She went across the hall and knocked softly on his door, not wanting to wake anyone else.

Gabriel answered in a long, white nightshirt and bare feet. As soon as he saw her, his gaze darkened. He looked past her into the hall. "Your majesty, what's wrong? Are you in trouble?" He looked her over. "Are you hurt?"

"No, none of that but I need to talk to you."

He stepped out of the way to let her in. "I must admit, you're the last person I expected to see."

"Well, I didn't expect to be at your door at whatever ridiculous hour it is, but here I am." She took a breath, trying to ignore the fact that he was in his nightclothes, hair down and slightly wild, and looking, as usual, better than anyone had a right to. It was very distracting. "The guard by my door said you'd just returned. Where were you? Not that it's any of my business, really."

"Professor Cloudtree has returned."

Ro sucked in a breath. "What did he have to say about Lady Cynzia?"

"Not much. He was exhausted. And due to the hour, I escorted him to his quarters. All he wanted to do was sleep. I know you asked me to come get you, but he was in no shape to talk. I hope you don't mind."

"No, he can have a few hours of sleep. What time is it?"

They both looked at the mantle clock at the same time. It was quarter to six in the morning.

"Nearly six," she whispered to herself, remembering the crucial thread of her dream. "We need to hurry."

Gabriel shook his head. "I'm sorry. I should have made Professor Cloudtree tell me what he knew. Obviously, I was wrong. My apologies. We can go to his quarters now and—"

"No, it's fine. But that is sort of why I'm here."

"Professor Cloudtree? Or Lady Cynzia?"

"Lady Cynzia. I had a dream about how to find her diary."

She appreciated that he didn't question that her dream had validity. He simply said, "Horror Library?"

She nodded. "That's where I was in my dream. We need to go now."

With record speed, Gabriel changed into what he'd had on the previous evening, just as Ro had done. Together, they made their way to the portal and downstairs, the sense of urgency between them hastening their steps.

The chandeliers were still unlit when they went back in. Ro hoped that meant no one had been in there. Specifically, not Anyka.

"Lights?" Gabriel asked.

"No." She walked closer to the stained-glass windows. "When does the sun rise?"

"Here in the mountains, early. Should be any minute

now."

"Good." Ro put her back to the windows and stood watching, the memory of her dream meshing with her current reality until it became a kind of ethereal déjà vu. She'd done this before. Except she hadn't.

The darkness began to fade.

Gabriel came to stand beside her. "What are we looking at?"

Ro pointed. "The colors. There. On the second shelf down from the ceiling. Somewhere around there. See where it's red?"

He looked at the spot, then at the window above them, then back at the spot. "Red from the glow coming through the red glass of the rose petals."

"Yes, that's right. Now watch."

The room got brighter as the sun broke the horizon line and sent its rays over the window. The red splotches turned blue where the light came through the coffin, which wasn't black glass at all like Ro had first thought, but dark blue. "Red in sleep, blue in mourning," she said. "But Lady Cynzia loved riddles. It wasn't just mourning as in grief. It also meant as in the break of day. Just like sleep meant night."

Gabriel let out a soft sound of amazement.

"Stay here," she said. "Guide me to that exact spot. As the sun moves, so will it, but I think we need the original location. I'm going up on the rolling ladder to find that diary."

"I have my eyes fixed."

"Good. I'm going to use my dagger, too. Hopefully, it'll

heat up." Ro raced across the room and pulled one of the rolling ladders to the spot. She looked at Gabriel, who'd stayed by the windows.

"A little more to the right," he said.

She moved the ladder again, got his approval, and darted up the rungs. When she was about halfway, she pulled her magical dagger and used it like a metal detector, holding it over the books.

"Higher," Gabriel called out.

She went another rung up. She reached as high as she could. She went left, then right, then back down again. She repeated the whole thing, finding one spot where the dagger got slightly warm. She'd expected it to get hot.

With a sigh, she pulled out the book that had caused her dagger to warm. It was one she knew well enough to know it wasn't Lady Cynzia's diary.

"Did you find it?" Gabriel came toward her a few steps.

Still gripping the magical dagger in one hand, she shook her head and held the book out so he could see it. "No."

"How do you know? Maybe it's just disguised as...*Pet Sematary*."

She opened the book and took a look inside, just to be sure. "No. This is definitely the book by Stephen King."

"Never heard of him."

She shoved the book back onto the shelf. "Well, he's creepy but he's not Lady Cynzia." Ro felt defeated and deflated. "The diary might have been here, maybe even next to this book, which is why it alerted my dagger, but it's not here now." She sighed. "Someone else beat us to it."

# Chapter Forty-one

Anyka couldn't recall a time in her life when she'd genuinely felt giddy. It wasn't an emotion she'd thought herself capable of.

Until now.

Pure, unbridled elation coursed through her. Giddiness, at its essence. There was no other way to describe what she was feeling as she looked at the book in her lap. Lady Cynzia's grimoire was a beautiful sight to behold. Even better to clutch it in her hands. To know that it was hers. All that power. All of it Anyka's to do with as she pleased.

Unable to sleep, Anyka had finally left her bed at around two in the morning. Pacing the suite hadn't helped tire her out, so she'd eventually decided to dress and go downstairs. To the libraries.

Why not? She was awake, she had on the amulet, and it needed to be tested anyway.

With Trog in tow, she'd started at one end of the Hall of Libraries and worked her way through each one.

In the first library, the Romance Library, nothing had happened. And since she didn't know what, if anything, *was* supposed to happen, her first thought was that the amulet might not be working. Then again, she didn't think

Lady Cynzia would have hidden her grimoire among such tales of fantasy and fluff. Would have been an unlikely spot. But that in itself made it possible.

It was so hard to understand what the woman might have been thinking.

But nothing had happened with the amulet in the second library, either, and that one had been stocked with non-fiction. Anyka had believed that library held possibilities, since Lady Cynzia's grimoire would be page after page of true black magic. A very particular kind of non-fiction.

But alas, not a single thing had occurred with the amulet or otherwise to make Anyka think she was in the right room.

Finally, she'd stepped into the Horror Library. It was so dark that, at first, she wondered if she was in the wrong room. For some reason, the chandeliers in this library had gone out. But then her eyes had started to adjust, thanks to the luminescence coming through the windows from the falls.

For a moment, it seemed like the amulet was reflecting that light. Then she realized the amulet was glowing of its own accord.

That had stopped her in her tracks and caused the breath to catch in her throat.

The glow was soft, initially. *Very* soft. The light from it was so dim she wouldn't have even noticed it if the chandeliers had been lit.

To Anyka, that glow could mean only one thing. The grimoire was somewhere in this space.

She walked the circumference of the library, holding

the amulet out before her and watching it carefully. Midway around, the gleam had intensified.

With Trog holding one of the rolling ladders for her, Anyka had ascended, still watching the amulet.

The glow got brighter and brighter and then dimmer.

She went back down a rung, and passed the amulet carefully along the row of books until the glow was almost too much to look at.

She removed the book that was directly behind it. Within a simple worn binding, the title and author nearly unreadable, had been another book.

One that there was no mistaking.

Even if it hadn't been bound in supple black leather, trimmed in snakeskin, and stitched with sinew, Anyka would have known what she held in her hands. Even without the blood-red ruby and chips of onyx set into the clasp, Anyka wouldn't have questioned what she was holding. The book vibrated with power.

She'd come down, had Trog put the ladder exactly where he'd found it, and hurried back to her room.

Now, hours later, she'd yet to open the book. Instead, she'd sat here on her balcony all that time, with the book in her lap, preparing herself. It wasn't that she was scared. That wasn't accurate. It was just that she thoroughly understood what she'd come into possession of.

This book would change her life. It would change the lives of many. Ruin many more. It might upend life in Malveaux. Life in Summerton, too. If she chose to use it for such things.

She knew how much weight those choices would put

on her, just like she understood that the magic contained within the grimoire would not be worked without a price.

In some cases, a very steep one.

Such knowledge was a lot to take in. And she was worried that if she opened the book, the power would sink its claws into her and there would be no turning back. That was what kept her from opening it now.

That was what was rumored to have happened to Lady Cynzia. She hadn't been born the black-hearted witch history liked to paint her as. Thinking that was foolish. No one started out that way. Instead, it was something she'd become. Because of the magic. Because she'd wielded dark power that had demanded sacrifice. And Lady Cynzia had lost herself to it.

Would the same thing happen to Anyka?

There really was only one answer to that question. Of course it would. Black magic consumed the user. They were taught that in school as little children. Warned about it. She'd watched her own mother slip further and further away as she delved into the ancient arts.

Now Anyka herself was on the precipice of testing that warning.

As much as she'd wanted the book, now that she had it, her mind had become a battlefield of indecision. Could she lose Beatryce over this? Would the power change Anyka that much?

She honestly didn't know, but the thought pained her. As impulsive as her daughter could be, she was still Anyka's only child. In Beatryce, Sebastyan lived on.

Anyka sighed as just thinking his name caused pain to nip at her heart.

Oh, how she missed him. He'd have told her to hide the book away in the royal vaults and pretend it never existed. She knew that. He'd hated the use of dark magic. Said he always had, but that her parents' deaths were all the proof he needed that no one should have that kind of power.

Maybe...he wasn't so wrong about that.

She sighed and stared out at the brightening sky, but already the cloud cover was creeping across the Malveauxian side of Willow Hall.

The gloom soured her mood.

Whatever she did, she'd at least have to tell Nazyr that his amulet had worked. She narrowed her gaze, her eyes focused on nothing while her mind was hard at work.

What if she gave the book to Nazyr and made him do her bidding? He already dabbled in questionable magic. What was a little more?

It wasn't a perfect solution. Giving up control didn't sit well with her. And it would mean she'd have to watch Nazyr as sharply as she could to make sure he didn't abuse the book's power or use it for his own gain. In fact, there was no way to truly prevent that.

It seemed to Anyka that it would only be a matter of time before the darkness overtook him. At that point, she'd have no choice but to be rid of him. The actions of past rulers made perfect sense to her.

Just like Lady Cynzia had been sent to Tenebrae, Nazyr would have to follow in her footsteps. Or be disposed of by other means.

Anyka glanced toward Trog, who stood at the balcony door. Trolls were especially good at *other means*.

Perhaps giving Nazyr the book was the answer after all.

Then something batty Queen Sparrow had said came back to Anyka. Something about Lady Cynzia possibly still being alive.

Anyka sat up. Was that possible? Because wouldn't the best solution be to return the book to its rightful owner and let her work the magic?

But if Lady Cynzia was alive, why had she hidden her grimoire away in the first place? Why hadn't she kept the book with her?

Anyka thought she might know the answer to that. It was the same reason she was so reluctant to open the book.

The power was too much.

She jumped up and carried the book back inside. She took it to her bedroom, where she tucked the grimoire back into its false cover, then hid it away in the top drawer of her dresser. Galwyn watched her from his perch. The book would be safe. No one knew she had it, so it wasn't as if anyone would be looking for it.

She put Galwyn on her shoulder, then went to Wyett's room and knocked on the door.

He opened it, already dressed and ready for the day. "My lady."

There was only one way Anyka knew to uncover the truth about Lady Cynzia. "Fetch me a tracker."

Wyett's brows lifted ever so slightly at her mention of such a person. "As you wish."

"Price is no object." Good trackers were expensive. But the more they were paid, the fewer questions they got to ask. "I need one with no qualms, few scruples, and an exemplary record."

"I understand. I will get the very best."

"Good. In the meantime, have coffee sent up. And some fish and berries for Galwyn. Once Beatryce and my uncle are ready, we'll all go down for breakfast."

"I'll take care of that, my lady."

Anyka was tired, but the coffee would help. She took a seat in the sitting room to wait, closing her eyes for just a moment. Galwyn hopped off to sit on the back of the chair.

The tracker would be key. He would find Lady Cynzia. If she were actually still alive. Until then, Anyka would just have to bide her time.

# Chapter Forty-two

Disappointment washed over Ro. They'd been so close. And now...nothing. The book was gone.

"We should go," Gabriel said. "Get out of here and get back to the suite."

She nodded without any enthusiasm. She'd failed. What else was there to do?

But he didn't move right away. She looked up at him. "What is it?"

He took a breath. "I...might be able to get the book back. No promises. But I'd like to try."

She narrowed her eyes. "From Anyka? Because that has to be who has it. Even if she claimed it never existed. I shouldn't have told her about it. This is my fault."

"No, it's not. I'm sure she knew about the diary already. And, yes, I believe she's in possession of the book now."

"And you think you can get it back? How?"

His eyes held an odd light. "Do you trust me?"

She nodded. "Explicitly." She meant that with all of her heart.

"Then, and I say this meaning you no disrespect, don't ask me any questions. Answering them won't be good for either one of us. Just do as I say, and if it's at all possible, I will make this right. It'll be better for you not to know certain things."

"It's hard not to ask questions when you say things like that." Nearly impossible, actually. She had so many questions. What was he up to? What was it better for her not to know about? How was he going to get the book back? Especially if it was in Anyka's royal suite, which seemed likely.

"I know. Please, just let me do this."

She nodded and sighed. "All right."

"We need to get you back to your quarters."

"Okay."

They slipped out of the library. There were a few guards around, but only Summerton and Willow Hall guards. None from Malveaux. Ro thought that was a good thing.

Gabriel hustled her down the hall, into the portal elevator and closed the doors. "For this to work, you can't say a thing about going to look for the book this morning or about finding where it was or about it being gone. Nothing about your dream or figuring out the poem, either. None of that happened, all right?"

"All right. But what's the *this* that needs me to play dumb for it to work?"

He dialed the second floor. "No questions. But you'll see. I swear it."

"Right. Sorry."

As they went back into the royal suite, Gabriel nodded at the guard stationed there. "Good weather out there today. Nice morning for a walk."

Ro understood that was their cover story. They'd gone for a walk. Dressed like ninjas. She doubted the guard would care or say anything.

Inside, no one was up yet. At least not awake enough to be out of their rooms. Gabriel led Ro through the suite all the way to her bedroom, where he shut the door after she came in.

Benny was sleeping on her pillow.

Ro looked at Gabriel. "Now what?"

"Now I'm going to need your Silversmith dagger."

She understood that part. He was going to use it just like she had, to locate the book. She pulled it from her boot and handed it to him.

He stuck it through his belt. "I won't be coming back here to get you, but I will send for you when I'm ready. Be prepared. I'll be summoning the professors as well."

"Send for me to come where?" She couldn't imagine what he was planning.

"If I can make this happen, back to the Horror Library. It'll all be clear soon. Stay here until I send for you. If anyone asks, you're waiting on word that Professor Cloudtree is ready to meet."

"Okay." None of that really made sense but she was sure it would. At least she hoped so. Just like she hoped whatever Gabriel was about to do wasn't going to put him in a bad situation. "Are you going out the secret passage?"

"No, the same way I came in."

"Is whatever you're about to do dangerous?"

"It..." He sighed and shook his head. "Maybe. Maybe not."

That didn't help. Ro frowned. "Please be careful. Whatever you're about to do, I know it's for me and for the kingdom, but I need you, Gabriel. Come back to me."

"I will. I promise." He hesitated, then kissed her goodbye and left.

She didn't like being in the dark about what was going on, but she trusted Gabriel, so she had no choice. She prayed he didn't get into a situation he couldn't get himself out of. Anything that involved Anyka seemed to have all kinds of potential for trouble.

Ro rang for a footman, then opened the door and spoke to the guard. "When the footman arrives, tell him we'd like coffee and tea sent up."

The guard nodded. "Yes, your majesty."

"Thank you." She went back to the bedroom and got herself ready for the day. She was tired and had no idea what was yet to come, so she chose an easy outfit of pants with a long, split-hem tunic over top with matching slippers. It was all a soft, gentle blue trimmed with gold embroidery and delicate pearls.

She kept her jewelry simple. Gold earrings, gold bracelet, and a gold and diamond circlet. She added the portal ring Gabriel had given her, too. It wasn't necessary here, but she rarely went without it.

She did her own makeup, following what Helana had taught her, but she was hopeless with her hair. She rang again, this time for a footman to fetch Helana.

By the time Helana had arrived to do Ro's hair, so had the coffee. The aroma of that had brought JT and Violet out of their rooms.

Raphaela and Vincent came to the suite not long after that, as did Uldamar. Ro's hair was done in a variation of her now standard braids, and as she said goodbye to Helana, she joined her family and the old wizard in the sitting room.

He tipped his head to her. "Good morning, your majesty."

"Good morning, Uldamar."

"Forgive my unannounced arrival, but I was sent a message that I should be here."

She nodded. She wasn't going to question anything that happened. Just go with it. "I'm glad you are. I'm waiting on news that Professor Cloudtree is ready to speak to me." That seemed safe to say. "When that comes, we can all go down together. Help yourself to some coffee until then, if you'd like."

"Very good."

Half an hour later, which made it nearly an hour since Gabriel had left, there was a knock on the door. A footman bowed when JT opened it. "Your lordship. Professor Nightborne has requested your royal highnesses join him in the Horror Library."

"We'll be right down," JT said. He closed the door and turned. "You heard that, Mom? What do you think he wants?"

"I did hear and I suppose we'll find out when we get there." Ro was doing her best to hold back her nerves, but if Gabriel wanted them in the library, that had to mean things had gone well. "Are you all ready?"

"Just a minute," Aunt Violet said. "I need a different

pair of shoes."

Once Aunt Vi had changed her shoes, they were off. Vincent led, Raphaela took up the rear, and they all piled into the portal elevator.

"This has to be about the diary, right?" JT asked.

"I guess so," Ro answered. She wasn't sure what else to say. She didn't want to lie, either. But this was going to be as much of a surprise to her as it was to them.

When they arrived at the Horror Library, they weren't the first to get there. Quite a group of professors awaited them. All of those who'd been included in the first discussion about the diary. They bowed and curtseyed as they greeted her. Some looked as if they could have used another hour before facing the day, but they were here all the same.

A man she didn't recognize stood with them, wearing a robe marked with the crest of Willow Hall.

"Good morning."

"Good morning, your highness. I'm Peter Scarnsworth, librarian of the Horror Library. It's my pleasure to welcome you."

"I appreciate that. Thank you."

Gabriel was standing by the windows with Spencer Cloudtree, who looked tired, understandably. Beside him was his wife, who looked pleased to have him back. Ro smiled at him. "Professor Cloudtree. I'm so glad you've returned to us."

"I'm happy to be back. And happier still that I bring news." He cleared his throat. "Possibly the answers you've been seeking."

That sent a little murmur through the assembled group.

He continued. "If you could just stand here with me, I will explain."

Gabriel stepped aside, making room between himself and Spencer. Ro stood in the gap, putting her back to the windows just like they were.

"Now, if you'll look up," Spencer said.

As everyone shifted their gazes to where he directed, Gabriel slid Ro's magical dagger back into her hand. She tucked it into her belt next to the others. Bending to put it in her boot might draw attention and she understood that wasn't the goal.

Spencer was explaining what Ro had already figured out in her dream. "The poem works on more than one level. And one of those levels, I believe, gives us the necessary clues to find Lady Cynzia's diary. If I'm right, it will be in your hands, your majesty, very shortly."

She smiled. "Wouldn't that be marvelous."

"It would be. And it will be," Spencer said. "Although we can't see the colors in their correct placement because it isn't the correct time of day or night, I believe that somewhere in those top three shelves, within a range of about ten to fifteen books side to side, you will find Lady Cynzia's diary. At least that's what my calculations have shown me."

"Amazing, Professor Cloudtree." It really was, because she already knew he was right. He'd worked it out. The man had skills. Unfortunately, the book wouldn't be there.

Gabriel stepped forward. "Let's get a ladder wheeled

over. Your majesty, may I suggest that you have a look? It seems most fitting that you be the one to locate it."

"Agreed," Uldamar said.

Gabriel was nodding at her, giving her a look indicating she should say yes. "You can use the dagger Sam Silversmith gave you to help pinpoint the diary." He looked at the crowd around them. "I think we can all agree that if ever there was a time to use a dagger designed to detect dangerous magic, this would be it."

They all laughed and nodded and agreed.

"All right," Ro said. "I'll go up the ladder." Again. She supposed she ought to play dumb as to where the book should be.

Peter Scarnsworth held the ladder in place. "I'll keep it secure, your majesty."

"Thank you." She went up a few rungs, then glanced back at Spencer.

"Higher, my lady."

She allowed him to direct her, then, when she knew she was close, she pulled out the dagger and used it just as she had before.

Except this time, it got *very* hot.

She gasped softly and moved the dagger away. It cooled off quickly but her surprise remained. She glanced down. All eyes were upon her and they were filled with a mix of expectation and apprehension.

She exhaled and gave them all a nod. "There's something here."

# Chapter Forty-three

Minister Nazyr arrived at Anyka's door not long after she sent Wyett to get him. He bowed. "Good morning, your highness." His smile was easy. Like he knew why he'd been called for. He had no idea they would not be searching for the book after all. "You summoned me and here I am. I was wondering if you're ready to have a look for—"

"Come in," she interrupted him. She knew what he was going to say and the less it was spoken about, the better, as far as she was concerned.

She waited until he was inside, and the door closed before she spoke again. "I've already had a look."

He seemed surprised by that. "And the amulet?"

She smiled. She'd been sitting with Beatryce and Ishmyel, having coffee. It had taken a great deal of willpower, but she hadn't said a word to them about finding the grimoire. "It worked beautifully."

Nazyr's mouth fell open. "You mean you found it?"

Ishmyel set his coffee down and blinked at her. "Did you? You've said nothing."

Beatryce, who'd gotten in very late and still seemed groggy, focused on her mother. She was holding her coffee cup with two hands. "What's this now?"

"Lady Cynzia's grimoire. I found it very early this morning." She wiggled her fingers at Trog. "I was in one of the libraries and the amulet just started to glow. I followed it until the glow got brighter and there it was."

Of course, it hadn't been quite that simple, but that was the gist of it. Anyka was rather pleased with herself for what she'd accomplished. "I kept silent about it because I wanted you all here before I told you."

Nazyr looked pretty pleased with himself, too. "I am most happy that the amulet and my magic worked as expected."

He ought to be, she thought, or he'd be having a very different morning. "So am I."

He looked at her expectantly. "Are you going to show it to us?"

"Yes, now that I have you all together." She gave Trog a look. "No one comes in."

Trog grunted in understanding.

"I'll be right back." She held her finger out at Galwyn. "Stay, my pet."

Then she returned to her bedroom, smiling the whole way. She couldn't wait to see their faces when she showed them the grimoire. She wasn't going to allow Beatryce to touch it but if Nazyr or Ishmyel wanted to hold it, that would be fine. Not open it, though. Hold it only.

Until she knew what she was going to do with the book, it shouldn't be opened at all. Not because she believed anything Queen Sparrow had said about it being some kind of trap, but with Lady Cynzia, one never knew.

Whoever opened it would need to be prepared for any

additional spells of defense. Or anything, really. There was no telling what might be contained in that book, just waiting for the right moment to escape.

She opened her dresser drawer and looked inside, moving the underthings and nightgowns. She frowned. She'd put the book in the top drawer, hadn't she?

She'd been tired. Maybe it was in the second drawer. She opened it, too, and it was just as empty.

She yanked out the top drawer and upended it, dumping out a fortune in silk. Her heart pounded in her chest, louder than her thoughts.

The book was in none of the drawers. The book was *gone*.

How was that possible? Bile bubbled up in her throat as her stomach roiled. She pulled the rest of the drawers out and dumped them as well. Nothing.

Sick to her stomach, she staggered back out to the sitting room. "It's gone."

She pointed at Trog. "He knows I had it. He saw it."

Trog nodded. "Trog see."

Nazyr didn't look nearly as concerned as Anyka thought he should, immediately sending her down another spiral in which he was the perpetrator of the theft. "You're sure you had the actual book and not just a charmed facsimile? Some kind of magical placeholder?"

"No." She spat the word out while holding eye contact. "I had a physical book in my hands."

"And the interior looked as you'd expect, full of spells and incantations and notes about such things?"

That took a little of the bluster out of her. "I didn't open it."

His eyes narrowed and he nodded, still far too calm for her liking. "Interesting. There are two possibilities that I see."

She sat across from him, her anger simmering but not yet boiling over. "And those are?"

"First of all, it's very possible the book was under some kind of enchantment that might have only been broken by opening the book and claiming it. Since that never happened, after a period of time, the enchantment returned the grimoire to its hiding place."

She frowned. "Why would that happen?"

"Why would Lady Cynzia hide the grimoire in the first place? My guess is she didn't want it to fall into unsure hands."

Anyka had no response for that. "What's the second reason?"

"It might be that the grimoire can only be taken so far away from its hiding place. There might be a boundary line the book can't cross. And if it does, it's instantly transported back to the shelf you took it from, safe in the spot where Lady Cynzia left it."

"And why would that be?"

He shrugged. "Perhaps Lady Cynzia was willing to let the grimoire be studied, but not owned by any one individual."

Anyka sat back and crossed her arms. "Any other theories?"

"Besides your guard, who else knew you had the book?"

"No one."

"No one saw you carrying it back, no one overheard you talking about it, no one—"

"*No one.*"

"Did you leave your quarters while in possession of the book?"

"No. I've been here the entire time."

"Did anyone come in? A maid, a footman, anyone?"

"No one who left my sight."

Nazyr swallowed and relaxed slightly. "Then it can't have been stolen."

Anyka exhaled as she thought that through. Maybe he had a point. She inched forward on her seat. "In both of your scenarios, if either of them are right, the grimoire would be back in the library. Back exactly where I found it."

"Yes, my lady."

She stood. "Then that's where we need to go."

Beatryce groaned softly. "I'm not ready to go out yet."

"Then stay," Anyka snapped. "Ishmyel—" But he was already on his feet.

Nazyr got up, too.

The three of them, along with Wyett and Trog, made their way downstairs and to the Hall of Libraries.

Anyka strode through the doors of the Horror Library with purpose and quickly came to a stop at the sight of so many Radiant. Queen Sparrow stood among them. In an instant, a fiery cold realization sluiced down Anyka's spine. She refused to believe what she was seeing. "What's going on here?"

The Summerton queen's old wizard lifted his head, a ridiculous smile on his face. "Queen Sparrow has just discovered Lady Cynzia's diary."

"No," Anyka whispered. She cleared her throat. "No. That is Grym property. That is mine. It belongs to me by all rights."

She spotted a man in Willow Hall robes. "Are you the librarian?"

"I am," he said, smiling. "I'm Peter Sca—"

"Tell her that book is *mine*."

His smile disappeared. "I'm sorry, your majesty. That book is not a registered Willow Hall library book. I have no say over its ownership any more than anyone else. Queen Sparrow found it. Everyone in this room just watched her take it down from that shelf." He pointed behind him where a ladder still rested in the exact same spot Anyka had been in hours before. "Seems to me that makes it hers."

Red edged Anyka's vision. That book had been in her hands. She could still feel the embossing on the leather and the hard edges of the sinews binding it. How had it gotten back on that shelf?

Could Nazyr be right that there was some kind of spell on the book? A spell she hadn't deactivated? That didn't feel right to Anyka.

What felt right was that the book had been stolen from her. She ground her teeth together to keep from screaming. How. Had. This. Happened.

Then a voice spoke up. "A book like that ought to be kept somewhere secure."

Gabriel Nightborne. Malveauxian traitor. Useless Grym.

Queen Sparrow nodded. "I agree."

Nightborne looked at the old wizard. "Perhaps you could spirit it away to the royal vaults at Summerton?"

"I could indeed," the old wizard said.

Queen Sparrow handed him the book. He held it between both hands and spoke a few words. In a flash of sparks and a puff of smoke, the book disappeared.

Anyka began to tremble with rage. Her hands itched for the hilts of her daggers.

Then Ishmyel stepped in front of her. "I know. *I know.* But not here. Not now."

He was right, of course. She leaned past him to point at Nightborne. "I know what you've done, traitor. I know what you are." It came to her in a white-hot rush. "There's only one explanation for this."

Every fae in the room went silent to stare at her.

She wasn't afraid to say the word or make the accusation. She pinned her finger in his direction. "*Unsycht.*"

She laughed at how uncomfortable the Radiant suddenly were. How they grimaced and shifted. Nightborne's expression remained stony, but she didn't care.

She no longer cared about anything but proving that book was hers. Not how she might do it, not who might get hurt in the process, not what it would do to her relationship with Queen Sparrow. All of that had been tossed away when that crossover queen had sent her lapdog after the grimoire.

Anyka held his gaze, daring him to say she was wrong. "That's right. I know who you are. I know what you did. And I'm going to prove it."

She pulled her cape around her and marched out of the room but stopped at the door to glare back at Summerton's foolish queen. "If you think this is over, it's not. In fact, it's only just begun."

# Chapter Forty-four

Ro's heart thumped away in her chest like it was working overtime. And maybe it was. Confrontation was not her favorite thing and as confrontations went, that one had been a doozy. But she'd retained control of the diary. That was what mattered.

She'd probably added to that silver streak in her hair, too, but it was too late to worry about that.

Through sheer willpower, she put a smile on her face and addressed the group in the library with her. "Well, that was a much more exciting morning than I thought we'd have in many ways."

Her professors laughed, maybe a little too much, but they all needed the break in tension and took the opportunity she'd given them.

"I think we should all head to breakfast, don't you?" She nodded at them, and they nodded back. "Please, go on. I'll be along shortly."

Professor Larkspur gave her an appreciative look. "Well done, your majesty."

"Thank you." The library began to empty out and Ro's pulse slowed toward normal.

Peter Scarnsworth looked as if he'd been smacked in

the face, but Aunt Violet and Posey were talking to him and seemed to be calming him down.

Ro joined them to say goodbye to him and thank him for his help, then she, JT, Aunt Violet, Posey, Uldamar, Raphaela, Vincent, and Gabriel left for the dining hall.

Her appetite was nonexistent, but she was sure it would come back when she actually had food in front of her. The book was now the property of Summerton. All thanks to the man at her side.

She spoke to Gabriel alone, keeping her voice low. "What was that word Anyka called you?"

He watched everyone around them. "Nothing. An old Grym wives tale. What they call in the mortal world a bogeyman."

"And she thinks you're one?"

"Apparently. I think she's gone too far down the well."

"Too far down the well?"

He smiled, still watching everything around them. "Lost her ability to think clearly. She wants power more than anything and she sees that book as her means to get it."

"You're right about both of those." She looked over her shoulder at Uldamar and spoke to him. "About an hour after breakfast is done, I'd like to convene a meeting of the professors. I think we need to discuss a new gameplan for moving forward with Malveauxian relations."

He nodded. "A wise decision, my lady. That would make us all feel more comfortable. I'll see to it."

"Thank you." She didn't have great hopes for the possibility of peace between the two kingdoms anymore. How could there be with Anyka so clearly antagonized by Ro having the book?

That hadn't been Ro's intention, but what was done was done. And she was certainly not about to hand Anyka the means by which to overthrow Summerton and depose all those in positions of power.

That book was Ro's insurance policy. Her life insurance policy.

The dining hall was full, although the Malveaux royal table was empty.

Breakfast was fine. It smelled wonderful, but all Ro could manage was coffee, fruit, and a lovely yogurt parfait and even then not all of it. She knew she'd be hungry later, but there would be food.

"You didn't eat much," Gabriel said.

"Hard to be hungry after a morning like that."

"You won."

"Did I?" She shook her head as she stared at her plate. "Feels like I've made things worse than they were before we arrived."

"Maybe. But at least this way you'll be alive to work on them."

She laughed softly. "That is true." She looked at him. "Do you think I can recover from this?"

"If anyone can, it will be you."

She really hoped he was right. She stared off through the windows, wishing she was outside. "There are gardens here, right? I've heard them mentioned."

He nodded.

"I'd like to go for a walk in them. Right now."

"We can do that."

"Good. A little fresh air might help." She glanced down at Uldamar, who was sitting next to Aunt Violet. "Auntie Vi, JT, Uldamar, just so you know, I'm going for a walk in the gardens before the meeting, but I won't be late."

"Enjoy yourself, dear."

"Marvelous," Uldamar said. "Might I have a quick word with you in the hall before you go?"

"Of course." She got up, causing everyone else to rise. She smiled and nodded at them all. "Enjoy your food. I'll see you very soon."

Then she and Gabriel made their way to the hall.

Uldamar joined them, looking in both directions.

"Come on," Gabriel said. "The sitting room is private."

As soon as they were inside with the door closed, Uldamar relaxed. A little. "What do you want me to do with the book, your majesty?"

She narrowed her eyes in confusion. "The book?"

He reached into his robes and pulled out the diary.

She gasped. "I thought that was in the castle vaults."

He smiled. "My apologies, my lady, but that was merely a parlor trick for the sake of Queen Anyka."

"Great trick." Ro exhaled. "And not a bad idea to make her think the book is miles away." She thought for a moment. "Would you be all right holding onto it? I really don't know where to put it. And all I want to do before I make another decision is have a nice walk in the gardens. I need a break from all of this."

Uldamar nodded. "I understand completely. I can safeguard it with some other magic until you tell me where you'd like it kept."

"Perfect. Thank you."

He bowed. "Enjoy your walk."

"I will." As he left, Ro looked at Gabriel. "How quickly can we get outside?"

"From here?" He smiled. "Pretty quickly."

A man of his word, he had her in the gardens not two minutes later, thanks to a narrow passage between two ballrooms reserved for staff.

She tipped her head back and inhaled the air. It was good to be outside. The trees and flowers were beautiful. The paths were casually paved with large slabs of rock. Every so often, the tree branches made a canopy over the path. Birds flitted about, as did some insects.

The feel was wilder and less planned than the gardens at Castle Clarion, but she didn't mind that one bit. There was a lot to see, including some slim, black-barked willow trees near the riverbank that were breathtaking. "I've never seen anything like those."

"They're mountain willows and the reason Willow Hall has its name. They only grow at this elevation and near water. Pretty, aren't they?"

She nodded. "With that black, papery bark and those bright green leaves? Spectacular."

There was a bench in the midst of a small grove of them. A few yards beyond that was the river. Only the part within the Summerton boundary was in the sun. She sat, enjoying the warmth of the day. "Join me?"

"I will. But only because I have royal guards on regular

patrols now that include these gardens." He sat close, his leg just touching hers.

"You think of everything."

"When it comes to your security, that's my job."

She sat silently for a moment, but she couldn't get her mind to be quiet. Not until she had an answer. "What is an *unstitched*?"

"*Unsycht*. As I said, it's like one of your bogeymen. A made-up creature designed to scare children into eating their porridge and going to sleep when they're supposed to."

"Gabriel, it's me you're talking to. What is it really? Why did everyone act like Anyka had said a bad word in the library?"

He stared out at the river, staying quiet for a few beats. "When the curse fell over Malveaux, overcast skies and inclement weather weren't the only things that happened. New kinds of magic began to manifest in the Grym. Darker kinds of magic. Not much was said about it, until one very particular kind was discovered."

She said nothing, just listened.

"Some Grym were being born with the ability to completely disappear. I don't mean just become invisible. They could vanish without a trace of breath, without being detectable, because their shape still took up form in a space, without giving off a hint of warmth or life. They became nothing. *Unsycht* is an old fae word that means absence. A void."

Her brows rose slightly. Now that seemed like an interesting talent to have.

"Rumors began to spread that the *unsycht* could do anything and get away with it. Murder people in broad daylight. Steal at will." He glanced over at her. "Poison food and drink unawares. Anything bad that happened without explanation? *Unsycht* did it."

She nodded. "Bogeymen."

"It didn't take long for a royal decree to be issued declaring the *unsycht* mutations of nature and unfit to live. Being an *unsycht* was made illegal. A crime against the kingdom. Anyone found with the magic would be executed or, if they were lucky, merely sent to Tenebrae to live out the remainder of their days."

Ro grimaced. "That doesn't seem fair."

"It wasn't. But then, that was life in Malveaux. You survived at the whim of whoever sat on the throne. That hasn't changed."

Ro felt a deep hollowness inside her body. An ache for the people who lived under such rule. She thought about Gabriel and his family. How his parents had risked so much to get them out of Malveaux.

She looked at him. Thought about everything that had just happened. Then about things he'd done previously. The way he was so good at disappearing. Or appearing just when she needed him.

He'd told her not to ask questions, but there were some she *had* to know the answers to. "Does the Malveaux royal suite have a secret passage like the Summerton one?"

"It's my understanding they were built with identical layouts."

She had one more question, even as her heart churned with emotion. "Are you... *unsycht*?"

He kept his eyes on the river. "There are some questions better left unanswered."

But that was an answer, Ro thought. She took his hand. An answer that told her everything she needed to know.

Want to be up to date on new books, audiobooks, and other fun stuff from me? Sign-up for my newsletter on my website, www.kristenpainter.com. No spam, just news (sales, freebies, releases, you know all that jazz.)

If you loved the book and want to see the series grow, tell a friends about the book and take time to leave a review!

# ALSO BY KRISTEN PAINTER

PARANORMAL WOMEN'S FICTION

**Midlife Fairy Tale Series:**

The Accidental Queen

The Summer Palace

**First Fangs Club Series:**

Sucks To Be Me

Suck It Up Buttercup

Sucker Punch

The Suck Stops Here

Embrace The Suck

**Code Name: Mockingbird** (A Paranormal Women's Fiction Novella)

COZY MYSTERY:

**Jayne Frost Series:**

Miss Frost Solves A Cold Case: A Nocturne Falls Mystery

Miss Frost Ices The Imp: A Nocturne Falls Mystery

Miss Frost Saves The Sandman: A Nocturne Falls Mystery

Miss Frost Cracks A Caper: A Nocturne Falls Mystery

When Birdie Babysat Spider: A Jayne Frost Short

Miss Frost Braves The Blizzard: A Nocturne Falls Mystery

Miss Frost Chills The Cheater: A Nocturne Falls Mystery

Miss Frost Says I Do: A Nocturne Falls Mystery

Lost in Las Vegas: A Frost And Crowe Mystery

Wrapped up in Christmas: A Frost And Crowe Mystery

**HappilyEverlasting Series:**

Witchful Thinking

PARANORMAL ROMANCE

**Nocturne Falls Series:**

The Vampire's Mail Order Bride

The Werewolf Meets His Match

The Gargoyle Gets His Girl

The Professor Woos The Witch

The Witch's Halloween Hero – short story

The Werewolf's Christmas Wish – short story

The Vampire's Fake Fiancée

The Vampire's Valentine Surprise – short story

The Shifter Romances The Writer

The Vampire's True Love Trials – short story

The Dragon Finds Forever

The Vampire's Accidental Wife

The Reaper Rescues The Genie

The Detective Wins The Witch

The Vampire's Priceless Treasure

The Werewolf Dates The Deputy

The Siren Saves The Billionaire

The Vampire's Sunny Sweetheart

Death Dates The Oracle

**Shadowvale Series:**

The Trouble With Witches

The Vampire's Cursed Kiss

The Forgettable Miss French

Moody And The Beast

Her First Taste Of Fire

Monster In The Mirror

**Sin City Collectors Series**

Queen Of Hearts

Dead Man's Hand

Double or Nothing

**Standalone Paranormal Romance:**

Dark Kiss of the Reaper

Heart of Fire

Recipe for Magic

Miss Bramble and the Leviathan

All Fired Up

URBAN FANTASY

**The House of Comarré series:**

Forbidden Blood

Blood Rights

Flesh and Blood

Bad Blood

Out For Blood

Last Blood

**The Crescent City series:**

House of the Rising Sun

City of Eternal Night

Garden of Dreams and Desires

*Nothing is completed without an amazing team.*

*Many thanks to:*

*Cover design: Cover design and composite cover art by Janet Holmes using images from Shutterstock.com & Depositphotos.com.*
*Interior Formating: Gem Promotions*
*Editor: Raina Toomey*

## About the Author

USA Today Best Selling Author Kristen Painter is a little obsessed with cats, books, chocolate, and shoes. It's a healthy mix. She loves to entertain her readers with interesting twists and unforgettable characters. She currently writes the best-selling paranormal romance series, Nocturne Falls, and award-winning urban fantasy. The former college English teacher can often be found all over social media where she loves to interact with readers.

For more information go to www.kristenpainter.com

For More Paranormal Women's Fiction Visit:
www.paranormalwomensfiction.net

Made in the USA
Columbia, SC
19 March 2024